Gonul Candas' Turkish Table

2nd Edition

Gonul Candas' Turkish Table

2nd Edition

arkadaş

arkadaş CO. LTD.
Mithatpaşa Cad. No: 28 / C Ankara
Tel: +90 312 434 46 24 (pbx) • Fax: +90 312 435 60 57
e-mail: info@arkadas.com.tr
www.arkadas.com.tr

Translation
Michelle Brown
Levent Keskin

Editor
Meltem Özdemir

Editorial Production
Selen Y. Kölay

Cover Design, Layout and Graphics
Mehmet Yaman

Contributors
Türkan Tölegen
Serdar Pehlivan
Ankara Şehir Kulübü (Animar A. Ş.)

Printing
Özkan Matbaacılık ve Gazetecilik Ltd. Şti.

Ankara, December 2007
2nd Edition

ISBN: 978-975-509-472-4

To my family…

A NOTE TO THE READERS

People today love their life and are increasingly more adept in their environment. Even being a modern housewife is a difficult job, requiring knowledge, creativity, skill and patience, while at the same time providing happiness to one's family. Although the role of home-maker is often stereotyped as easy, girls and women who take on this role must be innately capable and skilful.

As society becomes more fast-paced, people are increasingly seeking comfort and simplicity for refuge. One such oasis can be found in the foundation of one's family, where aside from finding tolerance and help, one can enjoy a home-cooked meal.

In order for the family to be successful, its members must assist each other and continue to expand their knowledge and abilities. This book can help do so by introducing new foods that family members can easily prepare. Included in this book are simple recipes for dishes, desserts, cakes and cookies that you may have previously imagined to be very difficult to prepare. Following the directions, you will be able to successfully prepare these dishes, proving your ability at cooking, and this book will become a faithful friend in your kitchen.

While writing this book, I took into consideration both the nutritional principles that I have acquired in my professional career, as well as my experience as a home-maker.

I would like to thank my husband, sons, sister, friends and the esteemed lady and gentlemen readers, Mr. Cumhur Özdemir who is the owner of the Arkadaş Publication Company, and Mrs. Meltem Özdemir who is the editor, for inspiring me to write this book.

Gönül CANDAŞ

CONTENTS

I - Soups

II - Beef, Chicken, Giblets and Fish

III - Fresh Vegetables, Legumes with Meat-Olive Oil

IV - Salads, Pickles

V - Rice, Macaroni and Eggs

VI - Pastries, Buns, Pizzas

VII - Desserts

VIII - Cakes, Cookies

IX - Jams, Marmalades, Liqueurs, Beverages, Ice Creams, Candies

Approximated Values of Some Ingredients by Grams and Ounces for Practical Measurements

INGREDIENT	A CUP	HALF A CUP	ONE-THIRD OF A CUP	TABLES-POON	TEASPOON	HALF A TEASPOON
FLOUR	110 g 3.85 oz	50 g 1.75 oz	35 g 1.25 oz	14 g 0.5 oz	5 g 0.18 oz	3 g 0.1 oz
SUGAR	180 g 6.3 oz	100 g 3.5 oz	50 g 1.75 oz	25 g 0.875 oz	8 g 0.3 oz	4 g 0.15 oz
ICING SUGAR (POWDER SUGAR)	130 g 4.5 oz	75 g 2.6 oz	38 g 1.35 oz	18 g 0.6 oz	5 g 0.18 oz	2 g 0.07 oz
RICE	165 g 5.8 oz	82 g 2.9 oz	55 g 1.9 oz	20 g 0.7 oz	7 g 0.25 oz	3 g 0.1 oz
OIL	180 g 6.5 oz	90 g 3.15 oz	60 g 2.3 oz	10 g 0.35 oz	3 g 0.1 oz	1.4 g 0.05 oz
WATER, MILK	200 g 7 oz	95 g 3.3 oz	65 g 2.3 oz	14 g 0.5 oz	4 g 0.14 oz	1.8 g 0.06 oz
SEMOLINA	150 g 5.25 oz	70 g 2.5 oz	40 g 1.4 oz	10 g 0.35 oz	5 g 0.175 oz	2 g 0.07 oz
ALMOND-HAZELNUT	120 g 4.2 oz	60 g 2.1 oz	35 g 1.23 oz	15 g 0.53 oz	4 g 0.14 oz	2 g 0.07 oz
COCONUT	55 g 1.9 oz	27 g 1 oz	15 g 0.5 oz	8 g 0.3 oz	2.5 g 0.09 oz	1 g 0.035 oz
GRATED CHEESE	95 g 3.3 oz	45 g 1.6 oz	30 g 1.05 oz	15 g 0.525 oz	4.5 g 0.16 oz	3 g 0.1 oz
YOGHURT	210 g 7.4 oz	100 g 3.5 oz	70 g 2.5 oz	35 g 1.25 oz	12 g 0.4 oz	6 g 0.2 oz
SALT	220 g 7.7 oz	105 g 3.7 oz	65 g 2.3 oz	27 g 0.95 oz	7 g 0.25 oz	2.5 g 0.9 oz
YEAST	145 g 5.1 oz	70 g 2.5 oz	45 g 1.6 oz	17 g 0.6 oz	4 g 0.14 oz	2 g 0.07 oz
BULGUR	135 g 4.7 oz	70 g 2.5 oz	47 g 1.7 oz	17 g 0.06 oz	4 g 0.14 oz	2 g 0.07 oz
LENTILS	155 g 5.4 oz	80 g 2.8 oz	55 g 1.9 oz	20 g 0.7 oz	5 g 0.175 oz	2.5 g 0.0875 oz
COCOA	105 g 3.7 oz	50 g 1.8 oz	35 g 1.23 oz	20 g 0.7 oz	6 g 0.21 oz	2 g 0.07 oz

A COUPLE OF TIPS

Starting from the theory that "HEALTH WITH A SMART AND BALANCED NUTRITION CAN BE RE-GAINED AT ANY AGE" I have reduced the amount of fat, although to a level that will not spoil the taste of the dishes, and referred to them as LIQUID OIL, which can come from any non-saturated fat group such as sunflower, soy, corn or olive. This kind of oil helps prevent arteriosclerosis because it reduces the level of cholesterol in the blood.

Animal products in saturated fat groups such as meat, eggs, milk, cheese, butter and tail fat increase the level of cholesterol in the blood. People who have the habit of consuming butter and tail fat may suffer in later periods from blocked veins, which limit the supply of blood to the brain and heart, as a result of arteriosclerosis.

However, fats have a vitally important positive effect on health and nutrition. They contain fatty acids that cannot be produced by the human body. Fats also preserve body temperature and ease digestion while giving flavor to dishes, and are a good and economic source of energy, as 1 gram of fat provides approximately 9 calories. They also delay hunger by extending the digestion process, and contain Vitamins A, D, and E. We should not ignore the benefits of fats and refrain from using them in our dishes because they may cause arteriosclerosis. Instead, we should use them moderately by decreasing the amount of fat we use, putting uncooked fat into our dishes, decreasing the preference for fried dishes, using a deep small pot with plenty of oil (as if boiling) to fry food, and eating less pastries (borek), buns, cookies, desserts and cakes. The average person can have 2 tablespoons of oil in his/her dishes. In addition, it is recommended to keep oil in glass bottles away from direct sunlight and below room temperature.

Eating less salt has a positive effect on the circulatory system. Sprinkling too much salt over dishes and eating food that contains excessive salt and preservatives cause water to leak from the veins to the tissues. This leads to EDEMA, resulting in a swelling of the body (especially the ankles), and the heart and kidneys become tired from being overworked.

I minimized the amount of salt in the recipes or left the amount for you to decide. In addition, depending on the property of the dishes, some meals can be cooked without salt, allowing you to sprinkle salt on before eating, which supposedly makes it easier for the body to dispose of.

NUTRIENTS NAMED AS CARBOHYDRATES

100-125 grams of sugar and flour products should be consumed every day. If we assume that 1 gram of carbohydrate contains 4 calories that makes a total of 400-500 calories. Sugar and flour, which are categorized as CARBOHYDRATES are needed to keep the body mobile, regulate brain functions, contain water and electrodes, and preserve nutrients by replacing them (especially with meat, milk and eggs) to produce energy and keep the acid-base balance of blood and body fluids. Apart from these, the use of fats and proteins from other groups of nutrients can occur with the help of carbohydrates.

Beef, lamb, poultry, seafood, dairy products and other food such as eggs, and dry legumes are classified in the PROTEIN nutrient group.

The recommended daily amount of protein for an adult is 1 gram for every kilogram of his/her body weight. Thus, an adult weighing 65 kilograms should consume 65 grams of protein. Around 35 percent of this need should be supplied from animal products (meat, milk, eggs, poultry and fish), and 65 percent from vegetable proteins (beans, chick-peas, lentils, green peas and broad beans).

The daily protein need of growing children is 2-3 grams for every kilogram of their body weight. 50 percent of this need should be supplied from animal products and 50 percent from vegetables. Animal proteins increase intelligence levels, and protein has an influence on the intelligence level of 0-4 year olds because brain and nerve cells develop during this age.

The protein need of pregnant and breastfeeding women are the same as growing children; half from animal products and half from vegetables.

Milk is a valuable source of nutrients and protein for people of all ages and conditions. The calcium in milk plays an important role in the structure, protection and function of bones, teeth, muscles, nerve and blood cells.

An adult should consume 2 glasses, and growing children, pregnant and breastfeeding women should drink 2-3 glasses of milk or dairy products per day.

Eggs, which are an ideal source of protein, are an important ingredient for the preparation of soups, dishes, desserts and cakes. It is advised that growing children consume 1 egg per day by itself or in food, and adults over 40 years of age consume 1 egg a week because the amount of fat in the egg yolk causes the level of the cholesterol in the blood to increase.

Vegetables and fruits are sources of vitamins and minerals and we can fully benefit from those, which can be eaten raw.

Although they are kept in a refrigerator, fruits and vegetables lose their vitamins over time. For example, green beans that have been kept in a refrigerator for 2 days lose half of their vitamins. To prevent the loss of vitamins while cooking, the pot lid should be closed tightly and not opened frequently. If the pot is left open for the first 2-3 minutes when the vegetables are boiling, fatty acids that cause vegetables to turn black can evaporate. Following this, the pot must be covered with a lid to prevent the vegetables from turning black and to let them turn a yellow color. When boiling vegetables, one should cook them in a little water until it evaporates and remove them while they are still crunchy. If there is any water left in the pot, it should not be thrown away as it can be used for soup or stock. Vegetables such as cabbage and cauliflower should be cooked for only a short time with the lid half open, and should be left a little crunchy.

It is not recommended to cook large amounts of food to reheat later, since food kept in the refrigerator and later reheated loses its nutritional value. Thus perishable foods, particularly fruits and vegetables, should be bought in a limited number and used while still fresh. Fruits and vegetables with high levels of Vitamin C cause cholesterol in the blood to fall. Winter fruits such as oranges, lemons, tangerines and grapefruits should be consumed often. A bunch of parsley leaves, which has as much Vitamin C as ten oranges, should be used in winter and summer dishes and salads with the stalks. Vitamin C is very effective in preventing illnesses such as the flu, cold, and gum disease.

I hope that these suggestions will help you remain healthy and prosperous.

I

SOUPS

EXTRACTING BEEF STOCK (BROTH)

Ingredients

- 1 kg beef bones
- 1 onion
- 1 carrot
- Celery or parsley stock
- 1 teaspoon of black pepper
- 1-2 cloves
- 1-2 laurel leaves
- 1-2 teaspoons of vinegar

Directions

1. Wash the bones and boil them in plenty of water. After they come to a boil, remove the froth that has accumulated at the top of the stock.
2. Quarter the onion, and add into the stock with carrots, celery or parsley stock, black pepper, cloves, and laurel leaves.
3. Boil on medium heat for one and a half hours. After cooling, strain the broth.
4. Once the broth has cooled, skim off fat which has risen to the top.
5. This broth can be used in soups that require beef stock, sauces, cold olive oil dishes and other meals.

VERMICELLI SOUP WITH ONION

Ingredients

- 6 cups of beef stock
- 2 onions
- 2 tablespoons of oil
- 1 tablespoon of flour
- 4 tablespoons of barley vermicelli
- 1 cup of milk
- ½ a bunch of parsley
- Salt, black pepper

Directions

1. Heat oil in a soup pot on low temperature. Add in onions and parsley stalks and sauté.
2. Add flour and stir occasionally. Add beef stock.
3. Once the mixture comes to a boil, add in the vermicelli. Cook on medium heat until the vermicelli is soft.
4. Add in chopped parsley leaves and milk.
5. Add in salt and pepper.

VERMICELLI SOUP WITH LEMON

Ingredients

- 6 cups of beef stock
- 4 tablespoons of barley vermicelli
- 1 tablespoon of oil
- 1 tablespoon of flour
- 1 egg yolk
- Juice of 1 lemon
- Salt and pepper

Directions

1. Lightly fry 1 spoon of oil and half a spoon of flour in a pot.
2. Add in the broth and bring to a boil. Then slowly mix in vermicelli. Lower the heat, and cook until the vermicelli is soft.
3. In a small bowl, beat together the lemon juice and egg yolk. Then mix in half a cup of water and add to the soup.
4. Add in salt and pepper before the soup boils and remove from heat.

VERMICELLI SOUP WITH TOMATO

Ingredients

- 6 cups of beef stock
- 2 tomatoes
- 1 tablespoon of oil
- 1 tablespoon of flour
- 4 tablespoon of barley vermicelli
- Salt, pepper

Directions

1. Fry the flour with the oil in a soup pot for a short time.
2. Add grated tomatoes and after stirring a few times add in the beef stock.
3. Once it comes to a boil stir in the vermicelli.
4. Lower the heat, and cook until the vermicelli is soft.
5. Add in salt and pepper and remove from heat.

RED LENTIL SOUP

Ingredients

- 8 cups of beef stock
- 1 ½ cups of red lentils
- 2 onions
- 2 tablespoons of oil
- 1 tablespoon of flour
- 1 cup of milk
- 1 egg yolk
- Salt, black pepper

Directions

1. Wash lentils; soak them in water for 30 minutes, and strain.
2. Lightly fry small chopped onions in a soup pot with oil. Add the flour and stir occasionally.
3. Add the beef stock and lentils and cook until the lentils are soft.
4. Using a sieve, strain the mixture into another pot, pressing with a spoon.
5. Five minutes before serving, beat the egg yolk and milk together, slowly stir the egg and milk mixture into the soup and remove from heat. Add salt.
6. If desired, serve with lemon.

GREEN LENTIL SOUP WITH VERMICELLI

Ingredients

- 8 cups of beef stock
- 1 cup of green lentils
- 1/3 cup of barley vermicelli
- 2 onions
- 2 tablespoons of oil
- 2 tablespoons of flour
- ½ cup of milk
- 1 ½ teaspoons of salt
- 1/2 teaspoon of black pepper
- 1 teaspoon of dried mint

Directions

1. Wash lentils and soak them overnight in water.
2. Fry small chopped onions in oil until they turn light yellow. Add the flour and stir occasionally.
3. Add the beef stock and drained lentils.
4. Once the lentils are cooked, add the vermicelli. Boil on a low heat for 10 to 15 minutes. Add salt and black pepper.
5. Before serving, stir in the milk and dust with dried mint.

Note: You can change the taste by reducing the lentils by half a cup and replacing with chickpeas and chickpeas stock.

DAWN SOUP

Ingredients

- 8 cups of beef stock
- 4-5 ripe tomatoes or 2 tablespoons of tomato paste
- 2 tablespoons of oil
- 2 tablespoons of flour
- 1 egg yolk
- 1 cup of milk

Directions

1. Fry the flour with oil in a soup pot until the flour turns slightly pink.
2. Add diluted tomato paste or grated tomato and beef stock, and stir.
3. Boil for 10 minutes on a medium heat. If any tomato skins or balls of flour remain, filter the soup through a sieve.
4. 5 minutes before serving, beat egg yolk and milk together and slowly stir into the soup. Add salt and remove from heat.

VEGETABLE SOUP

Ingredients

- 8 cups of meat stock
- 2 onions
- 2 tablespoons of oil
- 1 tablespoon of flour
- 2 tablespoons of rice
- 1 potato
- 1 carrot
- 1 small celery root
- 6-7 spinach leaves with stalks
- 6-7 sprigs of parsley
- 1 egg yolk
- 1 cup of milk
- Salt

Directions

1. Wash the vegetables, and grate the carrot, potato and celery. Chop the spinach and parsley.
2. Sauté the chopped onion in a soup pot with oil. Add flour and stir occasionally.
3. Add prepared vegetables, beef stock and washed rice and then cook well.
4. Sieve the mixture using a spoon. Add salt.
5. In a separate bowl, whisk together egg yolk and milk, and add the mixture into the soup. Remove from heat.

LEEK SOUP

Ingredients

- 8 cups of beef stock
- 1 onion
- 2 tablespoons of oil
- 1 tablespoon of flour
- 3 leeks
- 2 carrots
- 2 tablespoons rice
- 1 egg yolk
- Juice of 1 lemon
- Salt

Directions

1. Wash leeks and carrots, then peel and dice or grate them.
2. Sauté the chopped onion with oil in a soup pot. Add flour and stir occasionally.
3. Add in the beef stock, leeks, carrots, and washed rice.
4. In a separate bowl, beat egg yolk and lemon juice together and add 2-3 tablespoons of water. 5 minutes before serving slowly stir this mixture into the soup. Add salt and remove from heat.

GREEN PEA SOUP

Ingredients

- 8 cups of beef stock
- 1 1/2 cups of dried green peas
- 2 onions
- 2 tablespoons of oil
- 1 tablespoon of flour
- 1 carrot
- 1 cup of milk
- 1 egg yolk
- Salt

Directions

1. Wash the peas and soak them overnight in water.
2. Sauté the chopped onions with oil in a soup pot. Add flour and stir occasionally.
3. Add in drained peas, grated carrots and beef stock. Cook on medium heat until the peas are soft.
4. Sieve the mixture with a spoon. In a separate bowl, whisk together egg yolk and milk and stir into the soup five minutes before serving. Add salt and remove from heat.

FRESH BROAD BEAN SOUP WITH YOGURT

Ingredients

- 8 cups of beef stock
- 200 grams of fresh broad beans
- 1 onion
- 2 tablespoons of oil
- 2 tablespoons of flour
- 2 cups of plain yogurt
- 1 egg
- 3-4 sprigs of dill
- Salt

Directions

1. Wash beans and cut into small pieces.
2. Sauté the chopped onion with oil in a soup pot, and add beans. Stir occasionally.
3. Add 7 cups of beef stock and cook until the beans are soft.
4. In a separate bowl, beat together egg, flour and yogurt. Dilute mixture with 1 cup of beef stock and stir into the bean pot. Bring to a boil on a medium heat while stirring.
5. Add in salt and chopped dill and remove from heat.

POTATO SOUP

Ingredients

- 8 cups of beef stock
- 2 tablespoons of oil
- 2 onions
- 1 tablespoon of flour
- 4 potatoes
- 1 cup of milk
- 1 egg yolk
- Salt

Directions

1. Sauté chopped onions in a soup pot until they turn light yellow. Add flour and stir occasionally.
2. Add in the peeled and grated potatoes and beef stock.
3. Cook potatoes to a pulp, then sieve the mixture with a spoon and add salt.
4. In a separate bowl, whisk together egg yolk and milk and slowly add to the soup. Remove from heat.

Note: *If it is desired, fry bread crumbs with oil and add to the soup as a garnish.*

ONION SOUP

Ingredients

- 8 cups of beef stock
- 2 tablespoons of oil
- 2 tablespoons of flour
- 4 onions
- 1 egg yolk
- 1 cup of milk
- 2 tablespoons of grated yellow cheese
- 1 teaspoon of black peppercorns
- Salt

Directions

1. Chop onions into large pieces. Sauté chopped onion with oil in a soup pot until they turn light pink. Add in flour and stir occasionally.
2. Add beef stock and black pepper and cook until the onions are soft.
3. Sieve with a spoon
4. In a separate bowl, whisk together egg yolk and milk, and stir into the soup. Add salt and remove from heat.
5. After serving, sprinkle soup with grated cheese.
6. If desired, melt the cheese by putting the soup cups under overhead heat in an oven.

LAST MINUTE MEAL

Ingredients

- 8 cups of beef stock
- 1 cup of cracked wheat
- ½ cup of chickpeas
- 2 onions
- 2 tablespoons of oil
- 4-5 chard leaves or a half bunch of parsley leaves
- 2 cups of plain yogurt
- 1 teaspoon red pepper
- Salt

Directions

1. Clean cracked wheat and chickpeas and soak in tepid water overnight. Boil cracked wheat and chickpeas together in beef stock the following day.
2. In a separate pot, sauté chopped onions with oil until they turn light yellow and add to the cracked wheat and chickpeas mixture.
3. In a separate bowl, whisk yogurt with a fork. Dilute by adding half a cup of water in and stir mixture into the soup.
4. Add diced chard or parsley leaves and remove from heat.
5. Once served, pour a mixture of oil and red pepper over the soup.

YAYLA SOUP

Ingredients

- 8 cups of beef stock
- ½ cup rice
- 1 egg
- 1 tablespoon of flour
- 2 cups of plain yogurt
- 2 tablespoons of oil
- 2 teaspoons of dried mint
- 1 teaspoon of dried red pepper
- Salt

Directions

1. Wash rice and bring to a boil in beef stock.
2. Beat together yogurt, egg and flour, and dilute with half a cup of water.
3. Add mixture to the boiling rice and let simmer. Add salt.
4. When serving, sprinkle with dried mint and a mixture of heated oil and red pepper over the soup.

BORC SOUP

Ingredients

- 8 cups of beef stock
- 2 tablespoons of oil
- 2 onions
- 2 cloves of garlic
- 2 potatoes
- 1 carrot
- 1 stalk of small celery
- 1 small beetroot
- 5 cabbage leaves
- 1-2 long green peppers
- ½ bunch of parsley stalks
- 1 tablespoon of tomato paste
- ⅓ tablespoon sugar
- ½ teaspoon of lemon extract
- Salt

Directions

1. Wash and peel vegetables, and cut into small pieces.
2. Sauté chopped onions with oil in a soup pot. Add prepared vegetables and sugar, stirring occasionally.
3. Add tomato paste, bay leaves and beef stock, and cook.
4. In a separate bowl, mix together garlic, salt and lemon extract and add to the soup. Cook for 10-15 minutes. Turn off the heat and remove bay leaves.
5. If desired, the soup can be served with sugar-free cream or whisked yogurt.

WEDDING SOUP

Ingredients

- 8 cups of beef stock
- 1 piece of boiled meat
- 2 tablespoons of flour
- 2 tablespoons of oil
- 2 eggs
- 2 lemons
- 1 teaspoon of dried red pepper
- Salt

Directions

1. Boil the beef stock in a soup pot
2. In a separate bowl beat together egg, lemon juice and flour. Dilute by adding some beef stock.
3. Slowly add mixture into the boiling beef stock. Add salt and remove from heat.
4. Chop the boiled meat into small pieces, fry with oil and add to the soup with dried red pepper.

FISH SOUP

Ingredients

- 8 cups of boiled fish stock
- 2 onions
- 2-3 cloves of garlic
- 1 carrot
- 5-6 sprigs of parsley or stocks of celery
- 2 tablespoons of oil
- 1 tablespoon of flour
- ½ cup of rice
- 1 egg yolk
- Juice of 1 lemon
- 1-2 bay leaves
- Salt
- Black Peppercorns

Directions

1. Preparation of fish stock: Clean the fish, cover in water and bring to a boil. Remove any foam, which concentrates on top. Add quartered onions, black peppercorn, parsley and bay leaves and let simmer. Remove from heat and sieve once stock has cooled. Fish with mayonnaise is made from the fish meat and the fish stock can be used for fish soup.
2. Chop carrot, onion, garlic, and parsley leaves into small pieces. Sauté vegetables with oil in a soup pot. Add flour and stir occasionally.
3. Add fish stock and washed rice and let simmer.
4. In a separate bowl, whisk together egg yolk and lemon juice with a fork and add to the soup five minutes before serving. Add salt and remove from heat.

ERZINCAN SOUP WITH MEAT BALLS

Ingredients

- 8 cups of beef stock
- 200 grams of ground beef
- 2 onions
- 7-8 sprigs of parsley
- 2 tablespoons of flour
- 2 tablespoons of oil
- 1 tablespoon of tomato paste
- 1 cup of vermicelli macaroni
- 2 cups of plain yogurt
- 2 cloves of garlic
- 1 teaspoon of dried mint
- Salt
- Black pepper

Directions

1. Mix together ground beef, salt, black pepper and diced parsley, and knead ingredients into the meat. Shape into hazelnut-sized balls and cover in flour.
2. Sauté chopped onions and parsley stalks with oil in a soup pot. Add tomato paste, stirring occasionally. Then add beef stock and salt and bring to a boil.
3. Add vermicelli macaroni and meatballs, and let simmer.
4. Crush garlic, and mix together with yogurt in a separate bowl. Dilute with half a cup of water, add to the soup and stir. Let cook for 5 minutes, remove from heat, and sprinkle with dried mint.

Note: *If desired, serve with fried breadcrumbs.*

CINGILLI SOUP

Ingredients

FOR DOUGH:

- 1 egg, half a cup of water, salt, flour

FOR STUFFING:

- 3 tablespoon of ground beef, 1 onion, salt, black pepper

FOR SOUP

- 4 cups of beef stock
- ½ a cup of chickpeas
- 2 tablespoons of oil
- ½ a tablespoon of tomato paste
- 1 lemon
- 1 teaspoon of dried mint

Directions

1. Wash the chickpeas and soak overnight. The following day boil chickpeas in a pressure cooker until soft.
2. PREPARATION OF THE DOUGH: Sift flour into a pot and add egg, salt and half a cup of water into the middle of it. Mix until the dough becomes stiff. Cover and leave for 15 minutes.
3. PREPARATION OF THE STUFFING: Mix diced onion, ground beef, salt and black pepper.
4. Uncover the dough, lightly flour it, and roll it out to a thickness of 1mm. Cut the dough into 3 cm squared pieces, and put the stuffing in the middle of each piece. Bring the 4 edges of each piece together and secure by pressing with your fingers.
5. PREPARATION OF THE SOUP: In a soup pot fry tomato paste with oil. Add beef stock, boiled chickpeas, the chickpeas stock and salt, and bring to a boil.
6. Add dough to the soup and reduce heat. Cook approximately 20 minutes, until the dough rises to the top of the soup.
7. Add lemon juice, and sprinkle with dried mint.

YUVARLAMA (From Gaziantep)

Ingredients

- 250 grams of mutton meat cubes
- 250 grams of ground beef
- ⅓ cup of rice
- ½ a cup of chickpeas
- 3 onions (1 for meat balls)
- 2 tablespoons of oil
- 1 egg
- 1 ½ cups of plain yogurt
- Salt
- Black pepper

Directions

1. Wash the chickpeas and soak overnight.
2. Wash the rice, sieve and crush in a mortar to bulgur size.
3. Mix together ground beef, cracked rice, grated onion, salt and black pepper, and knead. Shape meat into balls a little larger than chick peas.
4. Boil 7 cups of water in pressure cooker. Add meat cubes and chickpeas, and close the lid. Once a steady steam makes the pressure cooker whistle, lower the heat and cook for 25 minutes. Remove from heat.
5. Once the soup has cooled, open the lid and add the meatballs. Slowly cook uncovered.
6. In a separate bowl, whisk together the yogurt and egg. Dilute with a few spoonfuls of the soup and then add the mixture into the soup.
7. Sauté diced onions in oil, add red pepper and sprinkle with dried mint. Pour vegetables into the soup.

MUSHROOM SOUP

Ingredients

- 8 cups of beef stock
- 200 grams of mushrooms.
- 1 onion
- 2 tablespoons of oil
- 2 tablespoons of flour
- 1 long green pepper.
- 1 cup of milk
- Salt

Directions

1. Sauté small chopped onions in a soup pot with oil until they turn light yellow. Add flour and stir occasionally.
2. Chop and wash mushrooms, add to the soup with the beef stock, and cook on medium heat. Chop pepper into circles and add to soup with salt.
3. Five minutes before serving add milk.

SALTED TRIPE SOUP

Ingredients

- 1 kilogram of beef tripe
- 1 onion
- 1 teaspoon of black pepper corns
- 2 tablespoons of oil
- 1 tablespoon of flour
- 3-4 cloves of garlic
- ⅔ cup of vinegar
- ½ teaspoon of red pepper
- Salt

Directions

1. Wash the tripe, dredge with salt, wrap the pieces of meat inside each other, and wait a few hours. Then scrape the tripe with a knife and wash.
2. Put tripe in a pressure cooker with 8 cups of water and bring to a boil. Skim off foam, and add quartered onions and 2 black pepper corns. Cover and heat until the pressure cooker whistles. Lower heat to a medium temperature and cook for one hour and then remove from heat. Once cooled, skim off fat and cut the tripe into large pieces.
3. Lightly fry flour with oil in a soup pot. Add chopped tripe and 8 cups of tripe stock and boil for 10 minutes. Remove from heat and add salt.
4. Serve soup with crushed garlic and vinegar.

BEYKOZ TROTTER WITH SAUCE

Ingredients

- 10 pieces of goat or lamb trotter.
- 8 cups of water
- 1 egg yolk
- Juice of 1 lemon
- Salt

Directions

1. Burn off the trotter hair and scrape with a knife, taking off the hair in between the nails. Wash by rubbing with hands.
2. Put meat in a pressure cooker with 8 cups of water and cover. After a steady steam, lower the heat to a medium temperature, cook for 1 hour and remove from heat.
3. Once cooled, uncover, remove trotter bones, and add salt.
4. In a separate bowl, whisk together egg yolk and lemon juice with a fork and dilute with a few tablespoons of water. Add the mixture to the soup and serve.

CAUCASIAN SOUP

Ingredients

- 8 cups of beef stock
- 1 onion
- 2 tablespoons of oil
- 4-5 leaves of a cabbage
- 2 leeks
- 1 carrot
- 1 small red beet
- 1 small stalk of celery
- 1/3 cup of barley vermicelli
- 1 egg yolk
- 1 cup of milk
- Salt

Directions

1. Wash and dice cabbage, leeks, carrot, beet and celery.
2. Sauté chopped onion in a soup pot until it turns light yellow. Add all of the vegetables, stirring occasionally.
3. Add beef stock and boil until the vegetables are cooked halfway through.
4. Slowly add in barley vermicelli. In a separate bowl mix together egg yolk and milk and add into the soup once the vegetables and vermicelli are cooked. Add salt and remove from the heat.

TARHANA SOUP

Ingredients

- 6 cups of beef stock or water
- 4 cups of tarhana
- 2 tablespoons of oil
- 1 tablespoon of ground beef
- 1 tomato or tomato paste
- Salt

INGREDIENTS FOR WINTER TARHANA

- ½ kilogram of plain yogurt
- 4-5 onions
- 3 ripe tomatoes
- 3 peppers for paste, 7-8 long green peppers
- Parsley and dill stalks
- Salt
- Flour

Directions

PREPARATION OF WINTER TARHANA:

1. Wash tomatoes, parsley and dill stalks, peel the onion and chop into large pieces. Put vegetables into a large steel or glass pot, add yogurt and salt, and stir. Add sifted flour, knead well, and cover for 9 to 10 days.
2. Knead each day to keep the dough from getting soggy. During this period, the vegetables in the dough will soften, and the dough will ferment, giving the tarhana its taste.
3. In small quantities, pour the tarhana on a clean cloth. Once it is slightly dried, crumble into smaller pieces, then sift into a fine powder. Dry completely in an area away from sunlight and keep in cloth bags.

PREPARATION OF THE SOUP:

1. Melt the tarhana with a cup of tepid water.
2. In a soup pot, fry the ground beef in oil. Add grated tomato or tomato paste, stirring occasionally. Add 5 cups of beef stock and the melted tarhana.
3. Stir while boiling, add salt, cover and remove from heat.

Note: *While you are preparing the tarhana soup add 1 tbsp of tarhana per person.*

BALKAN SOUP

Ingredients

- 8 cups beef stock or chicken stock (without fat)
- 2 tablespoons of oil
- 2 onions
- 1 tablespoons of flour
- 4 potatoes
- 1 carrot
- 1 small stalk of celery
- 1 piece of cooked chicken meat
- 1 pickle with 1 cup of pickle juice
- 1 egg yolk
- Salt

Directions

1. Wash celery, carrot and potatoes. Peel and dice carrot and potatoes.
2. Sauté chopped onions in a soup pot, add flour and stir occasionally. Add diced vegetables and beef stock and cook.
3. In a separate bowl, mix together egg yolk and pickle juice, then add to the soup. Dice the pickle and chicken meat, add into the soup, and add salt. Remove from heat.

II

BEEF, CHICKEN, GIBLETS AND FISH

ROAST MEAT

Ingredients

- Half a mutton thigh
- 2 tablespoons of oil
- 1 onion
- 2 cloves of garlic
- 2 sprigs of celery
- 1 carrot
- 1 tomato
- 1 teaspoon of black peppercorns
- Salt

Directions

1. Rub salt onto both sides of the meat (this allows the meat to cook better without needing to remove the fat).
2. Fry meat in a large pot with oil.
3. Add chopped onion, garlic, celery, carrot, and black peppercorns. Lower the heat and fry everything together.
4. Add grated tomato and 3-4 cups of water and cook on a medium heat for 2 hours, turning the meat occasionally.
5. After the meat is slightly cooled, slice and put on a serving plate. Sieve vegetable and oil mixture with a spoon in the pot and pour over the meat.
6. Serve with potato puree, carrot and sautéed peas.

MUTTON WITH VEGETABLES (Boiled)

Ingredients

- 1 kg mutton meat with bones.
- 3-4 small onions
- 3-4 potatoes
- 1 small celery stalk
- 1 carrot
- 1-2 egg yolks
- Juice of 1-2 lemons
- 6-7 sprigs of parsley
- Salt
- Black pepper

Directions

1. Boil 4 cups of water in a pressure cooker. Wash the meat, add to the water, and remove any foam.
2. Cover the pressure cooker, and once it comes to a steady steam, cook for 25 minutes and remove from heat.
3. Once cooled, uncover and add peeled, whole onions and potatoes and chopped carrot and celery. Add salt and black pepper.
4. Cover and cook for 10 minutes.
5. In a separate bowl whisk together egg yolks, lemon juice and 2-3 tablespoons of water. Once the stock has cooled, uncover and add the mixture into the meal. Sprinkle diced parsley over the dish.

MUTTON WITH BARLEY VERMICELLI STEWED IN EARTHENWARE POT

Ingredients

KEBAB INGREDIENTS

- Half a kg of cubed mutton meat
- 2 tablespoons of oil
- 2 onions
- 2 Charleston long green peppers
- ½ teaspoon of black pepper
- 1 teaspoon of salt

INGREDIENT OF VERMICELLI

- Half a package of barley vermicelli (250 g)
- 2 tablespoons of oil
- 2 tomatoes
- 1 teaspoon of salt
- ½ cup of yellow cheese (grated or in strips)

Directions

1. Heat oil in a pot, add meat and cook at a high temperature, turning occasionally. Add in largely chopped onions, fry for 2-3 more minutes, and then add 1 ½ cups of water. Cook until the meat is soft. Add salt and black pepper.
2. Boil 6 cups of water in a separate pot. Add in ⅓ tablespoon of salt and the barley vermicelli, and boil for 15 minutes. Sieve the vermicelli and rinse with cold water.
3. In a separate pot, fry grated tomatoes with 2 tablespoons of oil, stirring until the water evaporates. Add in sieved vermicelli and stir.
4. Put the vermicelli and tomato mixture in an oven plate and place the meat on top. Pour the remaining meat sauce over the meat and sprinkle grated cheese on top. Put sliced long green peppers in between the pieces of meat. Cook for 10 minutes in an oven and serve.

KUZU KAPAMA

Ingredients

- 1 kg of mutton with bones.
- 1 tablespoon of oil
- 1 onion
- 7-8 scallions
- 4-5 chard leaves
- 4-5 romaine lettuce leaves
- 1 carrot
- ½ bunch of dill
- Salt
- Black pepper

Directions

1. Put meat into a pressure cooker. Break chard and lettuce leaves into small pieces and chop onion, scallions and carrot into large pieces. Mix vegetables and add them into the pot, sprinkle with salt and black pepper, and pour oil lightly over them.
2. Pour in 1 cup of water from the side of the pot and cover. Cook on medium heat until it steams, then cook for 20-25 minutes and release the pressure.
3. Once cooled, uncover and put on a serving dish. Sprinkle with diced dill.

VEAL AND MUSHROOM WITH SAUCE

Ingredients

- ½ kg of cubed beef meat
- 6 small onions
- 2 carrots
- 200 g of mushrooms
- 4 tablespoons of oil
- 1 egg yolk
- Juice of 1 lemon
- 1 teaspoon of thyme
- 1 bay leaf
- Salt
- Black pepper

Directions

1. Put 5 cups of water, thyme, and bay leaf in a pot and bring to a boil. Add in the meat, remove the foam and simmer for 30-40 minutes.
2. Add 6 peeled, whole onions and diagonally-chopped carrots into the pot. Cook for another 25 minutes and add salt and black pepper. Remove from heat and cover.
3. Wash mushrooms and chop into three or four pieces. Heat 2 tablespoons of oil in a pan; add mushrooms and the juice from half of a lemon, and sauté until the water has evaporated. Add salt and black pepper.

PREPARATION OF SAUCE:

4. Fry 2 tablespoons of oil with 1 tablespoon of flour until it turns light yellow. Add 2 cups of meat stock and cook, stirring occasionally. In a separate bowl, whisk together egg yolk and the juice of half a lemon, dilute with 2-3 tablespoons of water and add into the sauce. Add salt and black pepper.
5. Place the meat, onions and carrots on a large dish with the mushroom sauté, and pour the prepared sauce on top. Serve warm.

FOREST KEBAB

Ingredients

- 1 kg of cubed mutton or beef meat
- 2-3 tablespoons of oil
- 2 onions
- 3 potatoes
- 3 carrots
- 1 cup of fresh peas
- 1 tomato
- 2 teaspoons of thyme
- Salt
- Black pepper

Directions

1. Put meat, chopped onions and oil in a pressure cooker and sauté.
2. Add grated tomato and stir occasionally.
3. Add 2 cups of water and cover. After it steams, cook for 20-25 minutes on a medium heat.
4. Uncover once cooled. Add peeled and chopped carrots, potatoes, peas, salt, black pepper, and thyme. Cook until the vegetables are soft with the pressure released from the pressure cooker.

STEAMED KEBAB

Ingredients

- 1 kg of cubed mutton meat
- 2 tablespoons of oil
- 3 small onions
- 3-4 cloves of garlic
- 1 tomato
- 1 teaspoon of thyme
- 1-2 bay leaves
- Salt
- Black pepper

Directions

1. In a pressure cooker, stir together oil, chopped onions, garlic, grated tomato, thyme, bay leaves, salt, and black pepper.
2. Cover and cook for one hour on a low heat. Remove from heat and uncover once it steams.
3. Serve with rice and salad.

STEAK WITH TOMATO SAUCE

Ingredients

- 1 kg of steak
- 2 tablespoons of oil
- 1 onion
- 1 carrot
- 1 small celery
- 1 potato
- 2 cloves of garlic
- ½ tablespoon of tomato paste
- ½ cup of red wine (if desired)
- 1 bay leaf
- Salt
- Black pepper

Directions

1. Fry the steak in a pot with oil.
2. Sauté diced onion, garlic, carrot, celery, potato and bay leaf in the same oil, stirring occasionally.
3. Lay tomato paste on top of the steak and, if desired, pour wine over the steak.
4. Add in 3-4 cups of water and cook on a medium heat until the meat is soft. Add salt and black pepper.
5. Place the steak onto a serving plate. Sieve the cooked vegetables with a spoon and pour over the steak as a sauce. Serve with rice or French fries.

VEAL SCHNITZEL

Ingredients

- 6 pieces of tenderized steak
- 1-2 onions
- 3 tablespoons of flour
- 2 eggs
- 4 tablespoons of breadcrumbs
- 1 cup of oil
- Salt
- Black pepper

Directions

1. Chop onions and layer in between steaks in a pile. Cover and refrigerate for 4-5 hours or overnight.
2. Once cooled, remove onions, and salt and pepper both sides of the steak.
3. Bread steaks by first dredging them in flour, then covering them in whisked eggs and breadcrumbs. Pack together with hands.
4. Fry steaks until they turn pink.
5. Serve with French fries and salad.

STEAK WITH CHEESE

Ingredients

- 8 steaks
- 1 onion
- 200 g of cheese strips
- 2 tablespoons of butter
- Salt
- Black pepper

Directions

1. Chop onions and layer in between steaks in a pile. Cover and refrigerate for 4-5 hours or overnight.
2. Melt cheese and butter together in a pot by stirring on a very low heat.
3. Once cooled, remove onions from the steak, salt and pepper both sides, and cover lightly in oil.
4. Using a flame free coal heat or on an electric grill, fry both sides of the steaks until cooked, but before they are dry.
5. Pour melted cheese equally over the meat, and serve with rice, French fries and vegetable sauces.

KEBAB WITH YOGURT AND PITA BREAD

Ingredients

- 1 kg of cubed mutton meat
- 2 onions
- 2 tomatoes
- 2 tablespoons of oil
- 2 tablespoons of butter
- 3 pieces of pita bread
- 500 grams of yogurt
- Salt
- Black pepper

Directions

1. Chop onions and mix into the meat. Cover and refrigerate for 4-5 hours or overnight.
2. Heat oil in a pot, add in the meat, (which has been separated from the onion) and grated tomato, and stir occasionally.
3. Add 2 cups of water, and cook on a medium heat until the meat is soft and the water has evaporated. If necessary, add more water until the meat is cooked properly. Add salt and black pepper.
4. Cut the pitas in small pieces and heat them in a pan. Place them on a plate and pour melted butter over them.
5. Pour whisked yogurt over the pitas, and then top with cooked meat.

SHISH KEBAB

Ingredients

- 1 kg cubed mutton or lamb meat
- ⅓ cup olive oil
- 1 onion
- Juice of ½ a lemon
- ½ bunch of parsley
- 2 ripe tomatoes
- 2 large green peppers
- 1 red onion
- Salt
- Black pepper

Directions

1. In a bowl, add together chopped onion, lemon juice, olive oil, and black pepper.
2. Add the meat into the mixture and leave for at least 3-4 hours.
3. Chop tomato and green pepper into meat-size slices.
4. Skewer meat and vegetables to the spit equally and moderately, in a meat-tomato-meat-pepper order.
5. Using flame free coal heat or an electric grill, fry both sides of the meat turning occasionally without drying them. Sprinkle with salt.
6. Serve with chopped red onions (in circular shapes) and parsley leaves.

MANISA KEBAB

Ingredients

FOR KEBAB

- 750 g small chopped beef cubes
- 3 tablespoons of oil
- 2 onions
- 2 green peppers
- 2 tomatoes
- 1 pack of cultured mushrooms (200 g)
- Salt
- Black pepper

FOR CREPE DOUGH

- 3 eggs
- 1 cup and 1 tablespoon of flour
- 2 cups of milk
- 1 teaspoon of salt
- 1 tablespoon of oil

Directions

1. In a pressure cooker, stir together meat, chopped onions, green peppers, and tomatoes, and salt and black pepper.
2. Cover and let steam, then cook on medium heat for 20 minutes. Uncover once cooled. Add washed and quartered mushrooms, stir, and cook another 5-10 minutes until all the water evaporates.
3. PREPARATION OF CREPE: In a bowl, mix eggs, salt, oil, and flour together and slowly stir in milk, giving the dough a thin consistency.
4. Oil a small pan and put on low heat. Using a small ladle, put a spoonful of crepe mixture onto the pan, and thin by tilting the pan. Flip once first side is cooked.
5. Put one tablespoon of kebab on both sides of the cooked crepes. Fold them in half and place on a serving plate, back to back.

ANKARA TAVA

Ingredients

- ½ kg of mutton with bones
- 1 onion
- 1 bay leaf
- ½ cup of chickpeas
- 1 cup of rice
- 2 tablespoons of oil
- 1 tablespoon of pine nuts
- 1 tablespoon of currants
- 1 small tomato
- 2 long green peppers
- ½ a teaspoon of black pepper
- ½ a teaspoon of cinnamon
- 1 teaspoon of salt

Directions

1. Wash the chickpeas and soak them overnight.
2. Boil 2 cups of water in a pressure cooker, add washed meat, bay leaf, quartered onion, sieved chickpeas and salt, and cover.
3. Once the pressure cooker steams, reduce heat and cook for half an hour. Uncover when cooled.
4. Wash the rice and place it in a pot, sprinkle with 1 teaspoon of salt. Cover with tepid water and leave for 15-20 minutes
5. In a separate pot, fry the pine nuts in oil until they turn light pink and place them in a separate bowl. Add 1 ½ cups of the mutton stock to the oil from the pine nuts. Bring to a boil and add sieved rice. Reduce heat and cook until the water evaporates. Remove from heat and let the rice steep for 10-15 minutes.
6. Add chickpeas, fried pine nuts, washed currant, salt, black pepper and cinnamon, and stir.
7. Place the rice on an oven plate, set the meat over the rice (fatty sides facing up), and add sliced tomatoes and quartered green peppers on top. Lightly grill in the oven.

ELBASAN TAVA (Elbistan Fry)

Ingredients

- ½ kg of mutton with bones.
- 2 tablespoons of oil
- 7-8 fresh onions
- 1 cup of yogurt
- 2 tablespoons of flour
- 1 egg
- Salt
- Black pepper

Directions

1. In pressure cooker, fry the meat with oil. Add slivered onion (cut 2-3 cm apart), salt, black pepper, and 1 ½ cups of hot water and cover.
2. Reduce heat once it steams. Cook for 20 minutes, and uncover once cooled.
3. In a separate pot, whisk together yogurt and flour, then boil on medium heat with some mutton stock. Once it cools add in egg and stir. Add salt, black pepper.
4. Set the meat and onions on an oven plate, pour yogurt mixture over meat and cook on low heat for 15 minutes.

BREADED LAMB CHOPS

Ingredients

- 8 pieces of lamb chops
- 2 tomatoes
- 2 long green peppers
- 2 tablespoons of oil
- 2 packets of filo dough
- 1 cup of oil (for frying)
- Salt
- Black pepper

Directions

1. Boil two cups of water in a pot. Add in lamb chops and remove foam. Cook until the meat is tender, then remove and sprinkle with salt and pepper.
2. Grate tomatoes and chop green pepper, and fry in a pot with 2 tablespoons of oil until the mixture thickens.
3. Divide the filo dough into quarters. Put one lamb chop on each piece of filo dough and cover the lamb chops in sauce, wrapping the filo dough over them with the ends showing. Stick the edges of the dough with water.
4. Fry in hot oil until the filo dough turns pink. Cover the lamb chops with a paper towel to absorb excess oil.

LAMB CHOPS WITH BÉCHAMEL SAUCE

Ingredients

- 8 pieces of lamb chops

FOR BÉCHAMEL SAUCE

- 2 tablespoons of oil
- 3 tablespoons of flour
- 1 ½ cups of milk
- 2 eggs
- 1 tablespoon of grated yellow cheese
- 1 cup of oil (for frying)
- Salt
- Black pepper

Directions

1. BÉCHAMEL SAUCE: Fry flour with oil in a pot. Add milk and cook until thick by stirring occasionally, keeping it from scalding. Cool until tepid, and then add eggs, grated cheese and salt.
2. Set the lamb chops in a greased pot. Cover and cook on a medium heat.
3. Remove the cooked chops and place on paper towels to absorb excessive oil. Salt and pepper both sides.
4. Holding the bones, roll the lamb chops in the sauce. Then fry the chops in hot oil until the color is pink.
5. Wrap the bones with gilded paper and serve.

HOME MADE DONER KEBAB

Ingredients

- 6 pieces of thinly sliced steak
- 150 grams of lean ground beef
- ½ cup of oil (for frying)
- Salt, black pepper
- 2 tomatoes
- 2 long green peppers
- 3 pitas
- 2 tablespoons of butter

Directions

1. Layer steaks and ground beef on top of each other, wrap tightly with aluminum foil and place in the freezer until you are ready to prepare them.
2. When preparing doner kebab, chop pitas into small pieces and heat in oven.
3. Remove the meat from the freezer, slice with a sharp knife, fry in hot oil, and then sprinkle with salt and black pepper.
4. Spread the pitas onto the serving plates and place equal proportions of meat onto each one. Pour melted butter on top.
5. Serve with grilled tomatoes and green peppers.

KADINBUDU MEATBALLS

Ingredients

- 750 grams of lean ground beef
- 2 onions
- 3 tablespoons of rice
- 3 eggs (1 for meatball dough, 2 for frying)
- ½ bunch of parsley
- 3-4 tablespoons of bread crumbs
- 1 cup of oil (for frying)
- 1 teaspoon of salt
- 1 teaspoon of black pepper
- 1 teaspoon of cinnamon

Directions

1. Wash the rice and boil with one glass of water until the water is absorbed.
2. In a separate pot, fry diced onions, parsley stalks, and half of the ground beef together until all the juices are absorbed. Then add mixture to the remaining ground beef and mix.
3. Add diced parsley, salt, black pepper, cinnamon and 1 egg to the meat, and knead it together. Add the rice last to prevent it from pulping, and knead a few more times.
4. Divide the mixture in egg sizes and make oval shaped meatballs.
5. First, roll the meatballs in bread crumbs flour and then dip in whisked egg. Pour the remaining egg over the balls and fry them in hot oil.

MEATBALLS

Ingredients

- 500 grams of lean ground beef
- 2-3 cups of bread crumbs (or hand-crumbled stale bread)
- 1-2 onions
- 1 egg
- ½ bunch of parsley
- 1 teaspoon of salt
- 1 teaspoon of black pepper
- 1 teaspoon of cinnamon
- 1 cup of oil (for frying)

Directions

1. Mix ground beef, bread crumbs, grated onions, egg, diced parsley, salt, black pepper and cinnamon together in a bowl, and knead.
2. Let the mixture sit for 15-20 minutes and knead again, shaping the meat into small walnut-shaped balls.
3. Heat oil in a pan, add the meatballs and fry both sides on medium heat, turning occasionally.
4. Serve with fried potato.

Note:

1) *Add 1-2 cloves of garlic when kneading the mixture.*

2) *Cook meatballs with tomato slices, long green peppers or tomato paste and water.*

3) *Bread meatballs by rolling them in flour before frying.*

ROASTED MEATBALLS

Ingredients

- 750 grams of lean ground beef
- 2 onions
- 1-2 cups of bread crumbs
- 3 eggs (2 boiled for the meatballs, 1 egg-for meatball dough and the yolk will be smeared over the dough)
- 2 boiled carrots
- 1 cup of boiled fresh peas
- 1 teaspoon of salt
- 1 teaspoon of black pepper
- 1 teaspoon of cinnamon

Directions

1. In a bowl, mix together ground beef, grated onions, bread crumbs, the egg white of 1 egg, salt, black pepper and cinnamon, and knead. Let mixture sit for 15-20 minutes, and then knead again for a short time.
2. Place the dough on an oven-safe dish, forming it into a circle 6-7 cm from the edge of the plate.
3. Cut the dough in half. Sandwich 2 boiled eggs sliced in half, diced carrots and peas in between the two layers, and close the edges back together by pressing the sides with wet fingers.
4. Spread the leftover yolk of 1 egg over the dough and oil the underneath.
5. To prevent cracking, only use overhead heat in the oven. Once the meatballs cook all the way through to the bottom, remove from heat, place on a serving plate, and slice into pieces.
6. If desired, mix the leftover oil from the oven plate, with 1 tbsp of tomato paste, ⅓ a tablespoon of starch, and 1 cup of water in a separate pot, and bring mixture to a boil. Sieve with a spoon and use as a sauce for the meatballs.

STUFFED MEATBALLS

Ingredients

- 750 grams of lean fine-ground beef
- 2 cups of fine bulgur for meatballs
- 3 onions
- 4 eggs (2 is for dough and others for frying)
- ½ cup of diced walnuts
- 1 tablespoon of pine nuts
- 1 tablespoon of currants
- 2 teaspoons of salt
- 2 teaspoons of black pepper
- 2 teaspoons of dried red pepper
- 1 ½ cups of oil (4 tbsp of it will be used for ingredient)

Directions

1. PREPARATIONS OF STUFFING: Sauté diced onions and pine nuts in a pan until they turn light yellow. Add in half of the ground beef and fry while stirring until the water evaporates. Add in 1 tsp of salt, black pepper, dried red pepper, walnuts and currants, and stir.
2. Put bulgur in a pot with 1 cup of hot water. Cover until the bulgur absorbs the water (about 15-20 minutes). Add in 1 teaspoon of salt, black pepper and dried red pepper, and knead for a while. Add in ground beef and 2 eggs, and knead until the bulgur is blended in. If necessary, add water into the mixture.
3. Shape the mixture into small balls (slightly smaller than egg-size), kneading each piece with your palm, and thinning the center with your fingers.
4. Equally dredge each ball in the breading mixture, and smooth by hand.
5. Steam the balls by setting them on a sieve over boiling water, covering, and boiling for 15-20 minutes on medium heat.
6. Remove from heat and cool until tepid. Then roll balls in whisked egg and fry in hot oil.

Note: *You can serve the meatballs before frying (subtract 2 eggs and 1 cup of frying oil from the ingredients).*

MEATBALLS WITH TOMATO

Ingredients

- 500 grams of ground beef
- 2 cups of bread crumbs
- 1 onion
- 1 egg
- ½ bunch of parsley
- ½ bunch of dill
- 3 tomatoes
- 3 long green peppers
- 3 tablespoons of oil
- ½ teaspoon of salt
- ½ teaspoon of black pepper
- ½ teaspoon of cinnamon
- For fried potatoes: 5-6 potatoes
- 1 cup of oil

Directions

1. In a bowl, mix together ground beef, bread crumbs, grated onion, egg, diced parsley, dill, salt, black pepper and cinnamon, and knead. Let sit for a short while and then knead again.
2. Dived the mixture in two walnut size pieces, and shape mixture into flat meatballs using wet hands.
3. Put three tablespoons of oil into a shallow saucepan. Oil both sides of the meatballs, set them in the pot, and fry on a medium heat while covered. Shake occasionally.
4. Put sliced tomatoes (circle-shaped), chopped green peppers (divided into two pieces) and 2-3 tablespoons of water over the meatballs. Cover and cook on a low heat for 10-15 minutes.
5. Serve with French fries.

BAKED MEATBALLS WITH POTATO PUREE

Ingredients

- 500 grams of ground beef
- 2 cups of bread crumbs
- 1 onion
- 2 eggs (1 for meatballs, 1 for puree)
- 6-7 sprigs of parsley
- 4 tablespoons of oil
- Salt
- Black pepper
- 5-6 potatoes
- ½ cup of milk
- 3-4 long green peppers
- 2-3 tomatoes (For garnish)

Directions

1. Mix ground beef, bread crumbs, grated onion, 1 egg, diced parsley, salt and black pepper, and knead. Let sit for 15-20 minutes and knead again for a short while.
2. Shape the mixture into egg-sized meatballs. Roll the meatballs, and with your palms wetted, make a deep hole in the centre, like a small bowl. Place the meatballs on a plate, pour half a teaspoon of oil in the depression of each meatball, and cook in the oven until the meat is cooked halfway through.
3. Peel and grate boiled potatoes, and mix together with 1 egg, 2 tablespoons of oil, half a cup of milk, salt, and black pepper in a bowl.
4. Put potato mixture in the depressions of the half-cooked meatballs, and cook together until the potato turns pink.
5. Serve with grilled tomato and green pepper.

MEATBALLS WITH EGGPLANT

Ingredients

- 500 grams lean ground beef
- 1 cup of bread crumbs
- 1-2 onions
- ½ bunch of parsley
- 1 teaspoon of salt
- 1 teaspoon of black pepper
- 1 teaspoon of cinnamon
- 5-6 eggplants
- 2 tomatoes
- 3-4 long green peppers
- ½ tablespoon of tomato paste
- 1 cup of oil

Directions

1. Mix together ground beef, grated onions, bread crumbs, diced parsley, salt, black pepper and cinnamon, and knead. Divide the mixture into small pieces and shape into flat meatballs.
2. Cut the ends of the eggplants, peel, cut into thin slices, and soak them in salty water for an hour. Then wash and dry them.
3. Sauté eggplant in oil, then wrap them around the meatballs (two slices of eggplant per meatball), placing ends underneath.
4. Put a slice of tomato and a small piece of green pepper on top of each meatball. Stick a toothpick into each ball to hold everything together, and place in a pot.
5. In a separate bowl, mix together 2 tablespoons of oil, half a tablespoon of tomato paste and 1 cup of water and pour over the meatballs. Cover and cook slowly until ready.

MEATBALLS IN SAUCE (With Carrots and Celery)

Ingredients

- 250 grams of lean ground beef
- 2 tablespoons of rice
- 2 onions
- 1 tablespoon of oil
- 2 carrots
- 1 celery stalk
- 1 egg
- Juice of half a lemon
- ½ bunch of parsley
- Salt
- Black pepper

Directions

1. In a separate bowl, mix together ground beef, one grated onion, diced parsley leaves, egg-white, salt and black pepper and knead the mixture.
2. Add rice to the mixture and knead again. Divide the mixture into small balls (chestnut-size) and roll them between wet hands.
3. Sauté 1 chopped onion, and diced parsley stalks in a pot with 1 tablespoon of oil.
4. Add 6 cups of water to the pot and bring to a boil. Add in diced carrots, celery and meatballs, and boil on a medium heat until the rice and vegetables are cooked.
5. In a separate bowl whisk 1 egg yolk, lemon juice, and 2 tablespoons of water together.
6. Remove the meatballs from heat, add the egg mixture to the pot and stir.

MEATBALLS WITH CRACKED WHEAT

Ingredients

- 500 grams of lean ground beef
- 3-4 tablespoons of fine bulgur
- 1-2 onions
- 1 egg
- 3 tablespoons of oil
- ½ bunch of dill
- 1 tablespoon of tomato paste
- Salt
- Black pepper
- Cinnamon

Directions

1. In a bowl, mix together ground beef, bulgur, egg, grated onion, black pepper, cinnamon and salt and knead.
2. Shape the mixture into small flat balls. Oil a shallow saucepan, place the balls inside, and pour oil on top. Cover and fry on a medium heat, turning the balls by shaking the pan with the lid closed.
3. Dilute tomato paste with 2 cups of water and add to the saucepan. Chop the green peppers into two or three pieces and put over the meatballs. Cook slowly on a low heat.

Note: *If desired, roll the remaining meatballs in whisked egg and fry for a different taste.*

LENTIL BALLS

Ingredients

- 2 cups of red lentils
- 1 ½ cup of fine bulgur
- 3-4 onions
- 1 ½ cups of oil
- 1 tablespoon of tomato-pepper paste mixture
- 5-6 scallions
- ½ bunch of parsley
- ½ dill
- 2 teaspoons of salt
- 1 teaspoon of black pepper
- 1 teaspoon of cinnamon
- 1 teaspoon of red pepper

Directions

1. Wash lentils and boil them in 3-4 cups of water until they are soft and the water has evaporated. Remove from heat, add bulgur and stir. Cover and let sit for half an hour while the bulgur absorbs water and the mixture cools.
2. Wash and dice onions, parsley and dill.
3. Sauté diced onions until they turn light yellow. Add tomato paste and stir. Add mixture to the lentils and bulgur. Add in salt, black pepper, cinnamon, and red pepper, and knead.
4. Lastly add in scallions and dill. Divide mixture into small pieces and press using hands.
5. Place on a serving plate and garnish with salad and pickles.

EKSILI

Ingredients

- 250 grams of lean ground beef
- 1 cup of fine bulgur
- 4 tablespoons of oil
- 1 tablespoon of pepper paste
- 1 onion
- 3-4 scallions
- 1-2 long green peppers
- ½ bunch of parsley leaves
- 4 tablespoons of ground sumac
- 1 tablespoon of flour
- 4 cups of water
- Salt
- Black pepper

Directions

1. In a pot, boil sumac with 4 cups of water.
2. In a separate bowl, mix flour with half a cup of water and add to the sumac pot. Boil for 5 minutes and then let sit.
3. In a saucepot, fry together ground beef, diced onion, scallions, and peppers with oil. Add pepper paste, salt, black pepper and sieved sumac stock.
4. Bring mixture to a boil, add in 1 cup of fine bulgur and cook on a medium heat.
5. Remove from heat before the water has completely evaporated, and stir. Place on a serving plate and garnish with fresh onion and parsley.

ORUK

Ingredients

- 750 grams of ground beef with fat (while meat is being ground add around 1 cup of 2-3 egg sized pieces tail fat)
- 2 cups of fine bulgur
- 1 egg
- 1 onion
- 2 tablespoons of dried mint
- 1 teaspoon of salt
- 1 teaspoon of black pepper

Directions

1. Mix bulgur, egg, grated onion, mint, salt and black pepper and knead while occasionally adding water.
2. Divide mixture into egg-sized pieces and shape into long meatballs. Then place the balls on oiled skewers, pressing with palms.
3. Cook on a flameless coal fire or electric grill until cooked.
4. Serve with salad and pickles.

MEATBALLS WITH POTATO AND CRACKED WHEAT

Ingredients

- 5-6 potatoes
- 1 cup of fine bulgur
- 1 ½ cup of oil
- 7-8 sprigs of fresh onions
- 2-3 long green peppers
- 1 bunch of parsley leaves
- Juice of 1-2 lemons
- 1 teaspoon of dried red pepper
- 1 teaspoon of cinnamon
- 1 teaspoon of salt
- 1 teaspoon of black pepper

Directions

1. Wash, peel and boil the potatoes, then blend or grate them while they are still warm.
2. Put the bulgur in a shallow saucepan, add in 1 cup of hot water, cover and let sit until the water is absorbed.
3. Add grated potatoes, salt, black pepper, dried red pepper, cinnamon, lemon juice and oil to the bulgur pot and knead for a short time.
4. Then add in diced onions, peppers and parsley leaves. Divide into small pieces and press with palms. Serve on a plate and garnish with lettuce or pickles.

Note: *If desired, cook 2 whisked eggs like an omelette, slice into small pieces with a knife, and add to bulgur and potato mixture before kneading, and continue with the recipe.*

CRACKED WHEAT BALLS WITH YOGURT

Ingredients

- 2 cups of fine bulgur
- 2 teaspoons of dried mint
- 1 egg-white
- 3 tablespoons of flour
- 6 onions
- ½ cup of oil
- 2-3 cups of yogurt
- 3 cloves of garlic
- 1 teaspoon of dried red pepper
- 1 teaspoon of salt

Directions

1. Put bulgur in a shallow saucepan, add in 2 cups of hot water, cover and let sit until the water is absorbed.
2. Grate 1 small onion into the bulgur, add egg-white, flour, mint and salt, and mix.
3. Divide mixture into small pieces, and make small balls, pressing with palms.
4. Without breaking the balls, place them in a pot of boiling water on low to medium heat for 15-20 minutes.
5. In a separate pot, fry sliced onions (chopped vertically) in hot oil until crispy, and add dried red pepper.
6. In a separate bowl, mix together yogurt and pulverized garlic.
7. Remove the balls from the water and place them on a serving plate. Pour yogurt and garlic mixture on the meatballs, and top with fried onions.

KARAKIZ BALLS

Ingredients

- 2 cups of fine bulgur
- 2 tablespoons of flour
- 1 tablespoon of starch
- 1 egg-white
- 2 teaspoons of dried mint
- 1 teaspoon of salt

FOR SAUCE

- 1 ½ cups of oil
- 3-4 cloves of garlic
- 1 tablespoon of pepper paste
- 1 tablespoon of cinnamon
- 1 tablespoon of dried red pepper
- ½ bunch of parsley leaves

Directions

1. Put bulgur in a shallow saucepan, add in 2 cups of hot water, cover and wait for the water to be absorbed.
2. Add flour, starch, egg-white, mint and salt into the saucepan and mix together. Knead mixture, adding water as necessary.
3. Shape the mixture into small balls, making indentations into the centers. Boil balls in salty hot water for 10 minutes, then remove and set on a serving plate.
4. In a separate pot, heat oil and add crushed garlic with salt, pepper paste, dried red pepper, and cinnamon. Stir occasionally, and mix with the balls on the serving plate.
5. Sprinkle fresh-diced parsley leaves over the plate and serve.

ONION BALLS

Ingredients

- 4 onions
- 4 tablespoons of flour
- 2 eggs
- 2-3 tablespoons of pepper paste or ketchup
- 1 cup of oil (for frying)
- Salt
- Black pepper

Directions

1. Slice onions vertically (into circle shapes) and put in a large bowl. Add flour, salt, and black pepper and mix.
2. Heat oil in a small pot, add onion mixture by the spoonful and fry until the mixture turns red.
3. Remove and serve with pepper paste or ketchup.

POTATO BALLS

Ingredients

- 6 medium size potatoes
- 3 eggs (1 for balls, 2 for whisking)
- 3 tablespoons of flour
- 1 cup of bread crumbs
- 1 cup of oil
- 1 teaspoon of salt
- 1 teaspoon of black pepper

Directions

1. Wash, peel and boil the potatoes, and grate or puree them while they are still warm. Let sit for half an hour until all the water is evaporated.
2. Add 1 egg, 1 tablespoon of flour, salt and black pepper, and knead. Divide the mixture into egg-sized pieces and shape into long fat balls using palms.
3. Dredge balls with flour, cover with whisked eggs, and then coat with bread crumbs. Fry the balls in hot oil until they turn pink.
4. Remove with a strainer spoon, and place on paper towels to absorb oil.

FRIED LIVER

Ingredients

- 1 cut of mutton liver
- 3 tablespoons of oil
- 4 onions
- 2 long green peppers
- 2 teaspoons of dried red pepper
- 2 teaspoons of sumac
- 2 teaspoons of olive oil
- ½ a lemon
- Salt
- Black pepper

Directions

1. Remove skin and veins from the liver. Chop like cubes.
2. Heat the oil in a pot, and fry the liver until half-cooked.
3. Chop two large onions and green peppers, and add to the frying liver. Fry until the water evaporates while uncovered. Add salt and black pepper.
4. Chop two onions in crescent-shaped slices, rub with salt and wash. Mix onions with diced parsley, dried red pepper, sumac, olive oil, lemon juice and salt. Serve with liver.

GRILLED LIVER

Ingredients

- 1 cut of mutton liver
- 1 onion
- 1 teaspoon of thyme
- 2 tablespoon of oil
- Salt
- Black pepper

Directions

1. Remove the liver skin and slice into pieces.
2. Mix chopped onion, thyme, salt and black pepper together and place mixture between liver slices. Chill in the refrigerator for 2 hours in a covered container.
3. Remove the onions from the liver slices and oil both sides.
4. On a strong coal-lit barbeque or electric grill, fry the liver on both sides. Serve warm and garnish with circle-cut red onions and parsley leaves.

LIVER WRAP

Ingredients

- 1 cut of lamb liver
- The skin of 1 lamb
- ½ a cup of rice
- 4 tablespoons of oil
- 2 onions
- 1 tomato
- 1 tablespoon of pine nuts
- 1 tablespoon of currants
- 1 teaspoon of salt
- 1 teaspoon of black pepper
- 1 teaspoon of cinnamon
- 1 teaspoon of Allspice
- ½ a bunch dill

Directions

1. Wash rice and soak in water for half an hour.
2. Remove the skin off the liver and dice.
3. Heat two tablespoons of oil in a pan, add the liver and fry until the water has evaporated. Remove from heat.
4. Put two tablespoons of oil in a pot, add chopped onions and pine nuts and sauté until they turn light pink. Add in grated tomato.
5. Add sieved rice into the pot and stir occasionally. Add in 1 cup of water and cook on a high heat, then lower heat and continue cooking. Remove from heat and steep for 20 minutes.
6. Add salt, black pepper, cinnamon, allspice, cleaned currants, diced dill and liver to the pot, and stir.
7. Soak lambskin in water for half an hour and cut into pieces. Put an equal amount of ingredients in the center of each lambskin piece and wrap together. Set in a cooking tray with the edges underneath.
8. Grill in the oven until they turn pink.

CALF TONGUE WITH JELLY

Ingredients

- 1 calf tongue
- 1 onion
- 1 teaspoon of black peppercorns
- Parsley and celery leave stalks
- 1-2 bay leaves
- 4 pieces of gelatin
- 4-5 small pickles
- 1 boiled carrot
- 1 boiled egg
- Salt
- Black pepper

Directions

1. Scrape and wash the tongue. Put in a pressure cooker with 2 ½ cups of water and boil. Skim off the foam and add quartered onions, black peppercorns, salt, parsley-celery stalks and bay leaves, and cover. Cook at high pressure until it steams, lower the pressure and cook for 30 minutes.
2. Once cooled, peel and clean the tongue. Chop into small pieces, and mix with chopped pickles and carrots. Add salt and black pepper.
3. Sieve the tongue stock into a bowl, add in washed gelatin and melt. Then add in meat, pickle and carrot mixture.
4. Wet a small gelatin mold, pour in half of the prepared mixture and set egg slices on top. Pour in the rest of the mixture and chill in the refrigerator.
5. Once solidified, remove the meal from the mold, sinking it into tepid water to remove.

Note: Tongue stock should be fat-free.

BRAIN GRATIN

Ingredients

- 2 calf brains
- 1 onion
- 1 teaspoon of black peppercorns
- 1 bay leaf
- 2 tablespoons of oil
- 2 tablespoons of flour
- 2 cups of milk
- 2 eggs
- 3-4 tablespoons of grated or slivered yellow cheese
- Salt
- Black pepper

Directions

1. Peel the skin of the brains under low-pressured tap water.
2. Slowly place meat into a pot with hot water. Add quartered onions, bay leaf, salt, and black peppercorns, lower the heat and boil for 30 minutes. Let cool, then remove brains from stock. Slice vertically, and add salt and black pepper.
3. Fry flour in oil until it turns pink. Add in milk and cook until it thickens, and remove from heat. Once cooled, add in egg, 1 tablespoon of grated cheese and salt, and stir.
4. Oil an oven plate and pour in ⅓ of the mixture. Set brain slices on the plate and pour the rest of the mixture over the meat, then sprinkle with grated cheese.
5. Bake at a high temperature until the top is pink, and serve hot.

FRIED BRAIN

Ingredients

- 2 calf brains
- 1 onion
- 1 teaspoon of black peppercorns
- 3 bay leaves
- 2 eggs
- 3 tablespoons of flour
- 4 tablespoons of bread crumbs
- ½ cup of oil
- Salt
- Black pepper

Directions

1. Peel the skin of the brains under low-pressured tap water.
2. Slowly place meat into a pot with hot water. Add quartered onions, bay leaves, salt, and black peppercorns, lower the heat and boil for 30 minutes.
3. Once cooled, remove brains from the stock and cut in half, horizontally, and then vertically in three or four parts. Sprinkle with salt and black pepper.
4. Dredge the meat slices with four, cover with whisked eggs, and coat with bread crumbs, pressing with hands.
5. Fry in hot oil until they turn pink and place on paper-towels to absorb oil.
6. Serve with salad.

CHICKEN WITH TOMATOES

Ingredients

- 4 pieces of chicken thigh or white meat
- 200 grams of mushroom
- 3 tablespoons of oil
- 2 onions
- 2 tomatoes
- 1-2 long green peppers
- 2-3 cloves of garlic
- 1 bay leaf
- Salt
- Black pepper

Directions

1. Wash chicken and remove the skin. Sprinkle with salt and pepper.
2. In a pot, mix together chopped onions, garlic, long green peppers, grated tomatoes, salt and pepper.
3. Add the chicken pieces in and stir. Pour in oil and half a cup of water to the edge of the pot, and cover. Cook slowly on a medium heat.
4. Wash and cut mushrooms in half (lengthwise) and add them into the chicken pot. Cook for 10 more minutes and remove from heat. Place chicken on a plate, sieving the stock with a spoon.
5. Serve with rice.

CHICKEN WITH VEGETABLES

Ingredients

- 6 pieces of boneless chicken
- 3 tablespoons of oil
- 1 eggplant
- 2 zucchinis
- 2 carrots
- 100 grams of fresh beans
- 1 cup of fresh peas
- 3 onions
- 2 tomatoes, 2 Charleston green peppers
- 3-4 cloves of garlic
- ½ tablespoon of tomato paste
- Salt
- Black pepper

Directions

1. Wash the vegetables. Peel the eggplants and carrots. Chop zucchinis into cubes, remove the tips of the beans and dice, and chop the onions and garlic. Mix everything together in a bowl and add in peas.
2. Wash meat, and set it in a pot. Sprinkle with salt and black pepper, and add in chopped onions and garlic. Pour 1 tablespoon of oil over everything.
3. Add in mixed vegetables, and place tomato slices and chopped green peppers on top.
4. Pour 2 tablespoons of oil and 1 cup of diluted tomato paste on top. Cover and bring to a boil. Lower the heat, and cook until the vegetables are ready but still firm, and serve.

CIRCASSIAN CHICKEN

Ingredients

- 1-1 ½ kg chicken
- 1 onion
- 1 teaspoon of black peppercorns
- 1 bay leaf
- 2-3 cups of walnuts
- 2 slices of stale bread
- 2 teaspoons of dried red pepper
- 2 tablespoons of oil
- 1-2 cloves of garlic
- 7-8 sprigs of parsley leaves
- Salt
- Black pepper

Directions

1. Clean the chicken and rub with a half-squeezed lemon. Cover and let sit for 15-20 minutes.
2. Put 1 quartered onion, 1 teaspoon of black peppercorns, bay leaf and salt inside the chicken.
3. Boil three cups of water in a pot. Put in the chicken and cover. Cook for 40-45 minutes on a low heat.
4. Once cooled, remove the skin, divide the meat into small pieces, put on a serving plate and sprinkle with salt and black pepper.
5. In a bowl, add together ground walnuts, wetted and pressed bread, red pepper, crushed garlic, salt and oil. Press mixture and collect the extracted oil in a separate bowl.
6. Add some chicken stock to the walnut and bread mixture until it has a yogurt consistency.
7. Put this mixture over the chicken meat and smooth with a knife. Pour walnut oil over and garnish with parsley leaves.

CHICKEN GRATIN WITH VEGETABLES AND BÉCHAMEL SAUCE

Ingredients

- 1 kg of chicken
- 1 onion
- 1 teaspoon of black pepper
- 1 bay leaf
- 2 potatoes
- 2 carrots
- 4-5 fresh beans
- ½ cup of fresh peas
- 15-20 very small onions.

FOR BÉCHAMEL SAUCE

- 2 tablespoons of oil
- 2 tablespoons of flour
- 2 eggs
- 1 cup of milk
- 1 cup of chicken stock
- 3-4 tablespoons of grated or slivered yellow cheese
- Salt
- Black pepper

Directions

1. Clean the chicken and rub with half a squeezed lemon. Cover and let sit in a pot for 15-20 minutes.
2. Put 1 quartered onion, 1 teaspoon of black peppercorns, bay leaf and salt inside the chicken.
3. Boil three cups of water in a pot, add in chicken and cover. Cook for 40-45 minutes on a low heat.
4. Remove from heat, and once cooled, remove the skin and bones from the chicken. Cut meat into small pieces and place on a serving plate. Sprinkle with salt and black pepper.
5. Wash vegetables, peel carrots and potatoes and chop into cube shapes. Shell fresh beans and cut them into 1 cm long pieces. Add small onions and peas, and boil in chicken stock until cooked.
6. PREPARATION OF BÉCHAMEL SAUCE: Fry flour with oil in a pot until it turns light yellow. Add 1 cup of milk and 1 cup of chicken stock and cook. Once cooled, add in egg and 1-2 tablespoons of grated yellow cheese, and stir.
7. Pour ⅓ of sauce into an oven tray. Lay the boiled vegetables over the sauce and then place the meat over the vegetables. Pour the rest of the sauce over the meat and sprinkle with grated cheese.
8. Bake on a medium heat in the oven until the color turns pink. Serve sliced or with a spoon.

CHICKEN WITH MUSTARD AND HONEY

Ingredients

- 4 pieces of boneless chicken breast
- 1 onion
- 2 tablespoons of oil
- Salt
- Black pepper
- 1/3 tablespoon of mustard
- 1/3 tablespoon of honey
- 1 tablespoon of butter

Directions

1. Dice onions and mix with salt and black pepper. Put the onions underneath and over the meat in a container and marinate for 2-3 hours in a refrigerator.
2. In a bowl, mix together melted butter, honey and mustard.
3. Remove onions from the meat and cover in oil.
4. On a low-flame barbecue or electric grill fry both sides of the meat and sprinkle with salt.
5. While still warm, coat the meat with the mustard, honey and butter mixture and remove from the heat.
6. Slice into finger-width pieces and serve with salad.

CHICKEN SCHNITZEL

Ingredients

- 2 pieces of boneless chicken breast
- 1-2 onions
- 3 tablespoons of flour
- 2 eggs
- 4 tablespoons of bread crumbs
- 1 cup of oil
- Salt
- Black pepper

Directions

1. Remove the skin from the breast meat, and slice into layers with a knife.
2. Put the meat in between sheets of aluminum foil and thin by beating with hands.
3. Place chopped onions in between meat layers and pile them on top of each other. Let marinate in a covered container while refrigerating.
4. When preparing, remove the onions from the meat. Make small cuts along the meat and sprinkle with salt and pepper.
5. Dredge the meat with flour, then cover in whisked eggs and bread crumbs, and smooth by hand.
6. Fry in hot oil until they turn pink, and serve with rice and salad.

Note:

1) *Boneless white meat can be substituted for breast meat.*

2) *If desired, you can also make schnitzel by slicing the meat into thin pieces and frying.*

CHICKEN WITH MUSHROOM AND CREAM

Ingredients

- 4 pieces of chicken breast
- 1 onion
- 1 teaspoon of black peppercorns
- 4 tablespoon of oil
- 1 ½ cups of milk (if available 3-4 spoons of Créme Chantilly)
- ½ cup of fat free chicken stock
- Salt
- Black pepper
- ½ teaspoon of nutmeg
- 100 g mushroom

Directions

1. In a pot, bring 1 ½ cups of water, 1 tablespoon of oil, a quartered onion, and black peppercorns to boil. Add in skinned chicken breast and cover.
2. Cook the meat at a low heat until only half a cup of water is left in the pot.
3. In a separate pot, lightly fry 2 tablespoons of oil with 1 tablespoon of flour until it turns light yellow. Slowly add milk and boil while stirring. Then slowly pour in half a cup of chicken stock and cook until the sauce thickens. Add salt and black pepper and grate nutmeg. If available add in Créme Chantilly. Stir occasionally to prevent the cream from condensing on top.
4. Wash mushrooms and chop into small pieces. Sauté in a pan with 1 tablespoon of oil and a few drops of lemon juice until the water evaporates.
5. Add sautéed mushrooms into the cream sauce.
6. Set the cooked chicken on a plate. Pour creamy sauce with mushrooms over the meat and garnish with parsley leaves.

BAKED PEKIN DUCK

Ingredients

- 1 Pekin duck
- ½ cup of rum or cognac
- 1 tablespoon of honey
- 8-10 cloves
- Salt
- Black pepper

Directions

1. Clean and wash the duck and dry with paper towels. To assure it is dry, let the duck air-dry for 5-6 more hours, turning occasionally. (The Chinese used to wait 24 hours for the duck to dry, turning occasionally.)
2. Mix half a cup of cognac or rum with the honey, and rub over the entire duck.
3. Sprinkle salt and pepper inside. Make 8-10 cross-shaped cuts in the duck, and place cloves in them.
4. Put the duck in a covered container and fasten tightly. Place container into a heated oven and cook slowly for 2 hours.

PAN-FRIED FISH

Ingredients

- 1 kg of fish
- 1 cup of oil
- 3 tablespoons of flour
- 1 lemon
- 5-6 parsley sprigs
- Salt
- Black pepper

Directions

1. Remove the scales of the fish by rubbing the fish with your hands in a pot with water. Remove the gills and innards and wash thoroughly with water. Sieve fish and sprinkle with salt and pepper.
2. Dredge the fish with flour 20-25 minutes before serving. Shake off excess flour and fry in hot oil until both sides turn pink. When cooked, place on paper-towels to absorb the excess oil.
3. Serve when hot. In a bowl, mix diced parsley leaves and lemon and pour over the fish.

Note: *If using larger fish, slice after they are cleaned. Then sprinkle on salt and pepper and fry in hot oil.*

STEAMED FISH

Ingredients

- 1 kg of fish (mackerel, bonito, anchovy, sardine etc.)
- ½ cup of oil
- 1 tomato
- 1-2 long green peppers
- 6-7 sprigs parsley
- 6-7 springs of dill
- 1-2 bay leaves
- Half a lemon
- Salt
- Black pepper

Directions

1. Remove the scales, gills and innards of the fish and wash thoroughly with water. Sieve fish and sprinkle with salt and pepper.
2. Put fish in a shallow, oiled pot, placing them side by side. Add grated tomato, chopped pepper, parsley, dill mixture, and bay leaves on top.
3. Pour oil over everything, and set thinly-cut lemon slices on top. Pour ⅙ cup of water into the pot from the side. Cover and cook on a low heat for 15-20 minutes.

GRILLED FISH

Ingredients

- 1 kg of fish (bonito, mackerel, gilt-head bream etc.)
- 2 onions
- 6-7 sprigs parsley
- 3 tablespoons of oil
- ⅓ cup of oil
- 1 lemon
- Salt
- Black pepper

Directions

1. Remove scales, gills and innards of fish and wash thoroughly with water. Sprinkle with salt and pepper. For proper cooking, split both sides of the fish with a knife, making ½ a cm deep incisions and cover fish with oil.
2. Dice onions and parsley and mix with salt, black pepper and 1 tablespoon of oil. Stuff fish equally with the mixture.
3. 20-25 minutes before serving, grill fish on a medium heat, using a coal-fired barbeque. Fry both sides properly.
4. Once cooked, place fish on a serving plate and pour olive oil on top. Garnish with lemon slices.

FISH WITH OIL AND ONIONS

Ingredients

- 1 kg of fish (grey mullet, blue fish, bonito, salmon etc.)
- ½ cup of oil
- 2 onions
- 3 potatoes
- 2 carrots
- 1 small celery stalk
- 2 tomatoes or ½ tablespoon of tomato paste
- 4-5 garlic cloves
- 1 lemon
- 1 bay leaf
- 1 bunch of parsley
- Salt
- Black pepper

Directions

1. Clean and wash the fish. Cut fish into pieces, oil and set into a pan. Sprinkle with salt and pepper.
2. Dice onions, and cut potatoes, carrots and celery into circle-shaped pieces, dice garlic and parsley leaves, and add in bay leaf.
3. Sauté vegetables in a pot with oil. Add in tomato paste or grated tomato, salt and pepper.
4. Place sautéed vegetables over the fish and pour in 1-2 cups of water from the side of the pan. Cover and cook on a medium heat until the potatoes are soft. Pour lemon juice over the fish and serve.

FLOUNDER WITH SAUCE

Ingredients

- 1 kg of flounder
- ½ cup of oil
- 1-2 onions
- 2 potatoes
- 2 carrots
- ½ of a small celery stalk
- 2-3 garlic cloves
- ½ tablespoons of flour
- 2 egg yolks
- 1 lemon
- Salt
- Black pepper

Directions

1. Clean the fish and cut into medium pieces. Place fish into an oiled, shallow pot.
2. Chop onions, potatoes, carrots and celery into large pieces and dice the garlic. In a separate pot, sauté the vegetables in oil, and add in bay leaf. Add flour and stir occasionally.
3. Lay sautéed vegetables over the fish and sprinkle with salt and pepper. Add in 2 cups of water to the side of the pot, cover and cook on a medium heat until the potatoes are soft. Add water if desired.
4. Cook until there is about 3 ladle-spoons full of water left in the pot. Mix together egg yolks, lemon juice, and 2-3 tablespoons of water in a bowl, and add to the fish. Cook until ready, occasionally shaking the pot.

FRIED MUSSELS

Ingredients

- 25 shelled, large mussels
- 1 cup of oil
- 1 cup of flour
- 1 egg
- ½ teaspoon of baking soda
- Salt
- Black pepper
- 1 lemon

Directions

1. Cut hair alongside the mussels and wash. Sieve and place on paper towels to absorb any excess water. Then dredge each mussel with flour.
2. In a deep bowl, add together 1 egg yolk, and half a teaspoon of salt, pepper, and baking soda. In a separate bowl, mix the leftover flour with water until it gains a slightly thick consistency.
3. Whisk 1 egg-white and add into the flour/water mixture.
4. In a small pot, heat oil and fry mussels after covering them in the flour mixture. Cook until they turn pink, and then remove with a sieved ladle.
5. Serve mussels hot and garnish with lemon pieces.

MUSSELS WITH OIL AND ONIONS

Ingredients

- 25-30 pieces of large, shelled mussels
- 4 tablespoons of oil
- 1 onion
- 1 potato
- 1 carrot
- 1 celery stalk
- 1 tomato
- 2 garlic cloves
- ½ bunch of parsley leaves
- 1 teaspoon of salt
- ½ teaspoon of sugar
- ½ teaspoon of black pepper
- Half of 1 lemon

Directions

1. Cut the hair alongside the mussels and wash. Place mussels in an oiled pot.
2. Sauté chopped onion, potato, carrot, celery, and garlic with oil. Add in salt, sugar, and pepper. Grate and add in tomato. Stir occasionally and lay over mussels.
3. Add half a cup of water to the side of the pot and cover. Cook on a low heat until the potatoes are soft.
4. Add in lemon juice and parsley leaves and let sit while covered.

STUFFED MUSSELS

Ingredients

- 25 pieces of large black mussels with shells
- 1 cup of rice (⅓ tbsp for each mussel)
- ½ cup of oil
- 3 onions
- ½ tablespoon of pine nuts
- ½ tablespoon of currants
- 6-7 sprigs of parley dill
- 1 teaspoon of dried mint
- 1 teaspoon of salt
- 1 teaspoon of sugar
- ½ a teaspoon of cinnamon
- ½ a teaspoon of allspice
- ½ a teaspoon of black pepper
- Half a lemon

Directions

1. Pour salt over the mussels and let sit for 1-2 hours.
2. Sauté diced onions, parsley, dill stalks and pine nuts in oil. Add in washed rice and stir occasionally.
3. Add in 1 cup of hot water and cover. Cook on low heat until the water evaporates. Remove from heat and let steep for 10-15 minutes.
4. Add dried mint, diced parsley, dill, salt, sugar, pepper, cinnamon, allspice, washed currants and lemon juice and stir. Cover and steep.
5. Wash the salted mussels by scraping them with a knife.
6. Separate the mussels in half, cut the hair inside and wash properly.
7. Stuff the prepared ingredients into the mussels and close securely. Set in a pot, add in a cup of water, cover and cook on a medium heat until the water evaporates.
8. Add ⅓ cup of wine and cook for 5-10 more minutes. Remove from heat, and partially uncover until cooled.
9. Wipe mussels one by one and set onto a plate with lemon slices.

SHRIMP COOKED IN EARTHENWARE POT

Ingredients

- 300 g of shrimp
- 100 g of mushroom
- 3 tablespoons of oil
- 1 small onion
- 2 tomatoes
- 1-2 long green peppers
- 2 tablespoons of grated or slivered yellow cheese
- 1 tablespoon of vinegar
- Salt
- Black pepper

Directions

1. Bring 5 cups of water to a boil, with 1 tablespoon of salt and vinegar. Once boiling, add washed shrimp and boil for 10 minutes. Sieve the shrimps and let cool. Then break the shrimp shells back from the head and remove outer layer.
2. Chop onion and green peppers, and grate the tomatoes. Slice mushrooms lengthwise and add salt and pepper. Mix everything together and add oil.
3. Put half of this mixture in an earthenware pot and set the shrimps on top. Then add the rest of the mixture into the pot and cover. Cook for 20 minutes at a low temperature, and remove from heat.
4. Sprinkle grated cheese on top, cover, and wait for 5 minutes (or put in the oven) for the cheese to melt.
5. Serve while hot.

Note: *If desired, make a salad with the shrimps after boiling them with olive oil, lemon, diced parsley, and salt.*

FISH WITH MAYONNAISE

Ingredients

- 1 kg of sea bass (or grey mullet, catfish etc.)
- 1 onion
- 6-7 sprigs of parsley stalks
- 1-2 bay leaves
- 1 teaspoon of black peppercorns
- Salt

RUSSIAN SALAD
(Preparation: page 175)

- 2 egg yolks
- 1-2 lemons
- 1 ½ cups of olive oil
- 1 teaspoon of mustard powder
- 2 boiled potatoes
- 2 boiled carrots
- ½ cup of boiled peas
- 8-10 small pickle pieces

Directions

1. Clean fish, cut into two pieces and wash. Boil in hot water, removing any foam. Add quartered onions, parsley stalks, bay leaves, black peppercorns and salt. Once the fish is boiled, remove from heat and let cool in its stock.
2. Debone the fish, and set it in a serving plate in large pieces. Sprinkle with salt and pepper.
3. Prepare Russian salad, sparing 4-5 tablespoons of mayonnaise for fish preparation.
4. Mix Russian salad with fish pieces. Shape meal into a fish shape and cover with extra mayonnaise. Decorate with carrot, peas and lemon slices and serve.

III

FRESH VEGETABLES AND LEGUMES WITH MEAT-OLIVE OIL

FRESH OKRA WITH MEAT

Ingredients

- ½ kg of fresh okra
- 250 grams of mutton or beef cubes
- 2 tablespoons of oil
- 2 onions
- 2 garlic cloves
- 1-2 long green peppers
- 2 tomatoes
- 1 lemon
- Salt

Directions

1. Sauté chopped onions and meat in a pot, stirring occasionally.
2. Add grated tomato and continue stirring. Add 2 cups of water and cook until the meat is tender.
3. Wash okra and peel the tops into cones. Add to the meat and onions with chopped peppers and garlic. Add lemon juice and salt, and pour in half a cup of water from the side of the pot.
4. Cover, bring to a boil, and then lower the heat. Remove from heat before the okra becomes too soft.
5. Serve with rice.

MEAT AND VEGETABLE STEW

Ingredients

- 250 grams of mutton or beef cubes
- 300 grams of fresh beans
- 300 grams of eggplant
- 300 grams of zucchini
- 150 grams of okra
- 1 onion
- 2 green peppers
- 2 onions
- 2 garlic cloves
- 2 tomatoes or ½ tablespoon of tomato paste
- 4 tablespoons of oil
- 2 teaspoons of salt

Directions

1. Sauté meat and chopped onions with oil in a pot.
2. Add tomato paste or grated tomato and stir occasionally. Add 2 cups of water and cook until the meat is tender.
3. Wash and chop vegetables, and add to the meat. Add in chopped garlic and stir occasionally.
4. Add half a cup of water to the side of the pot. Cover and bring to a boil.
5. Add salt and lower the heat and cook slowly for 5 minutes. Removing from heat before the vegetables become too soft.

Note: *If desired, use leeks, celery, potatoes, carrots and other winter vegetables to make the stew.*

FRESH BEANS WITH MEAT

Ingredients

- 1 kg of fresh beans
- 250 grams of mutton or beef cubes
- 3 tablespoons of oil
- 2 onions
- 2 garlic cloves
- 1-2 long green peppers
- 2 tomatoes or ½ a tablespoon of tomato paste
- Salt

Directions

1. Sauté chopped onions and meat with oil in a pot, while stirring.
2. Add tomato paste or grated tomato and stir occasionally. Add in 2 cups of water and cook until the meat is tender.
3. Wash and chop fresh beans, and add to the meat and onions along with chopped green peppers and garlic. Stir and add in half a cup of water from the edge of the pot if necessary. Cover and bring to a boil.
4. Lower the heat once it is boiling. Cook until the beans are soft. Add salt, let cook for 2-3 minutes, and then remove from heat.

Note: *Since fresh vegetables release water as they cook, add water slowly, and only if necessary, while cooking.*

EGGPLANT HUNKAR BEGENDI
(The Sultan's Favorite Eggplant Dish)

Ingredients

FOR MASHED EGGPLANTS

- 6 eggplants
- 1 tablespoons of oil
- 1 tablespoon of flour
- 1 cup of milk
- 2 tablespoons of grated yellow or slivered cheese
- 1 bunch of parsley leaves
- Salt
- Black pepper

FOR KEBAB

- 1 kg of mutton or beef cubes
- 2 onions
- 2 tomatoes
- 3 tablespoons of oil
- Salt
- Black pepper

Directions

1. Sauté meat and chopped onions in a pot while stirring. Add in grated tomato and stir occasionally. Add in 2-3 cups of water and remove from heat.
2. Cook slowly until the meat is tender and there is 1-1 ½ ladle-spoons of water left. Add salt and black pepper.
3. Grill eggplants by flipping over occasionally, then remove the skin and dice.
4. Lightly fry flour with oil in a pot until it turns yellow. Add in eggplants, milk, and grated cheese, and cook while stirring. Add salt.
5. Set kebab meat on a serving plate with eggplant sauce and garnish with parsley leaves.

PATLICAN PUR LEZZET

Ingredients

- 6 eggplants
- 300 g of ground beef
- 5 tablespoons of oil
- 2 onions
- 3-4 long green peppers
- 2-3 tomatoes
- ½ bunch of parsley
- ½ bunch of dill
- 2 cups of yogurt
- 2 garlic cloves
- 1 teaspoon of salt
- Black pepper
- Dried red pepper

Directions

1. Grill eggplants, remove the skin from the edge, dice, and place in an oiled tray.
2. Fry ground beef in a pot with diced onions, peppers, and 3 tablespoons of oil. Add in grated tomatoes, stir occasionally and remove from heat. Add in diced parsley, dill, salt and black pepper.
3. Lay this mixture over the eggplants and cover. Cook on a low heat cook for 10 minutes while stirring occasionally (It can be cooked in an oven as well).
4. Serve with yogurt or garlic mixture. Pour oil and red pepper mixture on top.

EGGPLANT KARNIYARIK

Ingredients

- 6 small eggplants
- 250 grams of ground beef
- 2 onions
- 2 garlic cloves
- 2-3 long green peppers
- 3 tomatoes
- 1 cup of oil
- ½ bunch of parsley
- ½ bunch of dill
- Salt
- Black pepper

Directions

1. Cut the ends of the eggplants and peel. Soak for half an hour in salty water, wash and dry.
2. Fry eggplants in oil until they turn pink. Set them on an oven plate and split them in half lengthwise, without cutting through the bottom.
3. Using the same oil from the eggplants, sauté diced onions, garlic, peppers, and grated tomatoes. Stir occasionally and remove from heat once cooked. Add diced parsley, dill, salt and black pepper.
4. Fill the inside of the eggplants with the vegetable mixture and put tomato slices over them.
5. Add 1 cup of water to the side of the oven plate, cover and cook on a medium heat for a short while.

Note: *You can make "Eggplant Oturtma" by cutting the eggplants into 3 cm wide pieces, frying them and cooking them the same way.*

BAKED POTATO OTURTMA

Ingredients

- 1 kg of potato
- 250 g of ground beef
- 5 tablespoons of oil
- 2 onions
- 2 cloves of garlic
- 2 long green peppers
- 3 tomatoes
- ½ bunch of parsley
- ½ bunch of dill
- Salt
- Black pepper

Directions

1. Wash and peel potatoes and chop into large slices. Oil an oven-safe dish and place potatoes inside.
2. In a separate pot sauté chopped onions, garlic, and long green peppers with oil. Add in two grated tomatoes. Stir occasionally and remove from heat. Add in diced parsley, dill, salt and black pepper.
3. Lay sautéed vegetables over the potatoes, and set sliced tomatoes on top. Add in 1 cup of water from the side of the dish. Cook in the oven until the potatoes are cooked. Add water if needed.

FRESH VEGETABLES WITH MINCED GROUND BEEF

Ingredients

- 1 kg of vegetables (fresh beans, zucchini, eggplant, okra, cauliflower, etc.)
- 3 tablespoons of ground beef
- 4 tablespoons of oil
- 2 onions
- 2 cloves of garlic
- 2 long green peppers
- 2 tomatoes
- Salt
- Black pepper

Directions

1. Clean and chop vegetables.
2. Sauté ground beef, chopped onions, garlic, and green peppers in a pot with oil. Add in grated tomatoes and stir occasionally. Add in vegetables, stir and add half a cup of water from the side of the pot.
3. Cover and bring to a boil, then lower the heat. Cook vegetables slowly, allowing them to maintain their firmness.
4. Add salt and lemon, and remove from heat.

DRY BEANS WITH MEAT (Chickpeas, Lentils)

Ingredients

- 2 cups of dry beans
- 300 g of mutton or beef with bones.
- 3 tablespoons of oil
- 3 onions
- 2 cloves of garlic
- 2 long green peppers
- 2 tomatoes or half a tablespoon of tomato paste
- 1 teaspoon of salt
- 1 teaspoon of sugar

Directions

1. Clean beans and soak them overnight in water.
2. The following day, boil them until they are cooked halfway through, saving the bean stock.
3. Sauté meat, 2 chopped onions and garlic in a pot with oil. Add in grated tomatoes and stir. Add in 2 cups of water and let cook.
4. Add in sieved beans, 2 cups of bean stock, sugar, 1 chopped onion and green peppers.
5. Cover and bring to a boil. Then lower the heat and cook slowly. Add salt 5 minutes before removing from heat.

Note: *If you use chickpeas, cook them the same way as the beans. If you use kidney beans, do not use the stock, since it is coloured. If you use lentils, do not boil, but add directly to the meat and vegetables.*

SPINACH OR PURSLANE WITH GROUND BEEF

Ingredients

- 1 kg of spinach or purslane
- 3 tablespoons of ground beef
- 4 tablespoons of oil
- 2 onions
- 2 cloves of garlic
- 2 long green peppers
- 2 tomatoes or half a tablespoon of tomato paste
- 1 ½ tablespoons of rice
- Salt

Directions

1. Wash each sprig of spinach or purslane, chop and soak in a bowl of water. Shake, sieve and wash at least three times, adding 1 tablespoon of salt into the bowl and soaking for half an hour after the first time to get rid of the grit between the leaves.
2. Sauté ground beef, chopped onions, garlic and green peppers in a pot with oil. Add in grated tomatoes and stir occasionally. Add in sieved spinach or purslane and mix. Cover and let cook for a short while.
3. Wash rice, soak in hot water, sieve and add to the vegetables with ⅓ cup of water. Bring to a boil, then lower the heat and cook slowly. Serve with yogurt.

Note: *If desired, save some cleaned spinach leaves to make spinach pastry.*

DRIED BEANS WITH PRESERVED MEAT OR GARLIC SAUSAGE

Ingredients

- 2 cups of dry beans
- 10 slices of preserve of dry meat or garlic flavored sausage
- 3 tablespoons of oil
- 3 onions
- 2 long green peppers
- 2 tomatoes or half a spoon of tomato paste
- Half a teaspoon of salt
- Half a teaspoon of sugar

Directions

1. Clean beans and soak them overnight.
2. The following day, boil them halfway through.
3. Chop two onions into a pot and sauté until they turn yellow. Add in grated tomatoes, sieved beans, 2 cups of beans stock and sugar, and cover.
4. Bring to a boil and then lower the heat. After 10-15 minutes, add in 1 chopped onion and green peppers, stir occasionally, and add salt.
5. Once the beans are cooked, set slices of preserved meat or garlic-flavored sausage on top. Cook for 10 more minutes on a low heat, stir and remove form heat, and let sit while covered.

CELERY WITH MEAT AND SAUCE

Ingredients

- 1 kg of celery
- 250 g of mutton meat with bones
- 3 onions
- 4 tablespoons of oil
- 1-2 long green peppers
- 1 egg yolk
- 1 lemon
- Salt

Directions

1. Sauté 2 chopped onions and meat in a pot with oil.
2. Add two cups of water and cook until the meat is tender.
3. Wash, peel and chop celery, removing the leaves. Chop into slices.
4. Add chopped celery into cooked meat, stirring occasionally. Add in ½ a cup of water to the side of the pot. Chop 1 onion into round slices, and slice long green peppers.
5. Cover and cook on a low heat, without softening the celery.
6. Whisk together egg yolk and lemon juice, and in a pot, add to 2 to 3 tablespoons of water, mixing together by shaking.

POTATO PILAKI WITH OLIVE OIL

Ingredients

- 5-6 potatoes
- 2 carrots
- ½ of a small celery stalk
- 2 onions
- 5-6 cloves of garlic
- 2 tomatoes
- 2 long green peppers
- ½ cup of oil
- ½ bunch of parsley
- 1 teaspoon of sugar
- 1 teaspoon of salt

Directions

1. Dice onions, celery, green pepper, and parsley stalks. Chop carrots into slices that are 1 ½ inches long in diameter. Sauté the vegetables in a pot with oil for a short while.
2. Add peeled and chopped potatoes, sliced ½ cm wide, to the pot. Stir occasionally. Add sugar and salt.
3. Add in grated tomatoes and half a cup of water from the side of the pot and cover. Cook slowly at a low heat, keeping the potatoes from mashing. Remove from the heat.
4. Crack open the lid of the pot and let cool. Place on a serving dish and garnish with parsley leaves.

GREEN BEANS WITH OLIVE OIL

Ingredients

- 1 kg of green beans
- 6 tablespoons of oil
- 2 onions
- 3 cloves of garlic
- 3 tomatoes
- 1 long green pepper
- 1 teaspoon of sugar
- 2 teaspoons of salt

Directions

1. Clean and chop the beans.
2. Add chopped onions, garlic, green pepper and grated tomatoes into the pot. Add in sugar and a spoonful of oil, and mix together.
3. Add ⅓ cup of water to the side of pot and cook slowly at a low heat.
4. Once the beans are soft, add in salt. Cook for 5 more minutes and remove from heat.

LEEK and JERUSALEM ARTICHOKE WITH OLIVE OIL

Ingredients

- 1 kg of fresh vegetables
- 6 tablespoons of oil
- 2 carrots
- 1 onion
- 2 cloves of garlic
- 1 long green pepper
- 1 teaspoon of sugar
- 1 teaspoon of salt
- 1 ½ tablespoons of rice

Directions

1. Wash, peel and chop vegetables, carrots, onion, garlic, and green pepper. Mix everything together in a pot and add sugar with 6 tablespoons of oil. Add in 1 cup of water.
2. Wash and soak rice for 10 minutes in hot water and sieve. When vegetables are cooked halfway through, add in rice.
3. Cook slowly for 5 minutes, then remove from heat and add salt.

ZUCCHINI IMAMBAYILDI WITH OLIVE OIL

Ingredients

- 8 small zucchinis
- 1 cup of oil
- 4-5 onions
- 7-8 cloves of garlic
- 3 tomatoes
- 2-3 long green peppers
- ½ a bunch of parsley
- ½ a bunch of dill
- 1-2 sprigs of fresh mint or 1 teaspoon of dried mint
- 2 teaspoons of sugar
- Salt
- Black pepper

Directions

1. Cut off the ends of the eggplants and peel. Soak them in salty water for half an hour. Then wash and dry the zucchinis and mar the peels.
2. Fry in oil until they turn pink, and set onto a plate.
3. Cut the zucchinis in half lengthwise.
4. Slice onions into half-circles, dice green peppers and garlic, and sauté them all in oil. Add in 2 grated tomatoes and stir. Add in diced parsley, dill, mint, salt, black pepper and sugar.
5. Fill zucchinis with the vegetable mixture and cover with sliced tomatoes.
6. Add half a cup of water to the edge of a tray and cook slowly on a low heat in an oven.

SOUR LEEKS WITH OLIVE OIL

Ingredients

- 1 kg of leeks
- 3 onions
- 3 cloves of garlic
- 6 tablespoons of oil
- 2 tomatoes or half a tablespoon of tomato paste
- ½ a bunch of parsley
- ½ a bunch of dill
- 1 teaspoon of sugar
- 1 lemon
- 2 teaspoons of salt

Directions

1. Wash and chop leeks into 5-6 cm long pieces.
2. Slice into thin pieces lengthwise and set in a pan.
3. Add in half a cup of water, cover and bring to a boil.
4. Slice onions into half-circles, dice garlic, and sauté them together in a pot with oil. Add in grated tomato or tomato paste and stir occasionally. Add in sugar, salt, diced parsley and dill.
5. Pour the vegetable mixture over the leeks. Add in half a cup of water to the edge of the pan and cook slowly on a stove.
6. Once cooked, pour lemon juice over and remove from heat after 5 minutes.

CELERY WITH OLIVE OIL

Ingredients

- 4 medium sized celery stalks
- 2 handfuls of baby onions or 3 onions
- 2 carrots
- 1 potato
- ½ a cup of fresh chickpeas
- ½ a cup of oil
- ½ a bunch of parsley
- ½ a bunch of dill
- 1 Lemon
- 1 teaspoon of sugar
- 1 teaspoon of salt

Directions

1. Sauté chopped onions, carrots, potato and chickpeas in oil for a short while.
2. Add in diced parsley, dill, sugar and salt and stir.
3. Wash and peel the celery stalks and cut them in half, making holes in the cut parts.
4. Set the celery pieces on an oven plate or shallow pot, holes facing up.
5. Fill the holes with the mixed vegetables, and pour the remaining mixture around the celery stalks.
6. Add two cups of water to the side of the pot and cover. Bring to a boil, then lower the heat and cook until the celery stalks are soft.
7. Sprinkle on lemon juice five minutes before removing from heat.

BROAD BEANS WITH OLIVE OIL

Ingredients

- 1 kg of broad beans
- 6 cups of oil
- 2 onions
- 2 cloves of garlic
- ⅓ tablespoon of flour
- ½ a bunch of dill
- 1 teaspoon of sugar
- 2 teaspoon of salt
- 2 cups of yogurt

Directions

1. Wash beans and put them in a pot.
2. Add chopped onions and garlic, sprinkle in sugar and salt, pour in oil by the spoonful, and mix everything together.
3. Add in 1 ½ cups of water to the side of the pot and cover.
4. Bring to a boil, then lower the heat and cook for half an hour.
5. Add salt and continue cooking until the beans are soft.
6. Sprinkle diced dill over the beans.
7. Serve with yogurt.

EGGPLANT WITH OLIVE OIL

Ingredients

- 6 eggplant
- 1 cup of oil
- 8-9 cloves of garlic
- 3 tomatoes
- ½ a bunch of parsley
- 1 teaspoon of sugar
- 2 tablespoons of lemon juice
- Salt
- Black pepper

Directions

1. Cut off the ends of the eggplants and peel. Divide into three pieces. Mar each piece lengthwise and breadthwise and soak for half an hour in salty water.
2. Wash and dry eggplants and sauté until they turn pink. Remove from the pan with a sieved ladle and place into a shallow pot.
3. Cook chopped garlic in the leftover oil, stirring occasionally. Add in 2 grated tomatoes, salt, black pepper, sugar, and diced parsley. Pour mixture over the eggplants and cover with sliced tomatoes.
4. Add in half a cup of water to the edge of the pot and cover. Cook for 15-20 minutes at a low heat, stirring occasionally. Pour lemon juice on top. Remove from heat after a few minutes, partially uncover and let cool.

SPINACH PATTIES

Ingredients

- 1 kg of spinach stalks
- 2 onions
- 2-3 tablespoons of flour
- 3 eggs
- Parsley
- Dill
- Salt
- Black pepper
- 1 cup of olive oil or sunflower oil (for frying)

Directions

1. Wash spinach stalks and simmer in 1/6 cup of water. Then sieve and dice them, and place in a shallow pot.
2. Add in diced onions, parsley, dill, salt, black pepper, eggs and flour, and stir.
3. Spoon the mixture onto a pan with hot oil and fry.
4. Remove fried pieces onto paper towels to absorb excess oil.

Note: *If desired, add 3-4 tablespoons of fried, lean, ground beef into the mixture.*

ZUCCHINI PATTIES

Ingredients

- 3 medium sized zucchinis
- 5-6 sprigs of scallions or 2 onions
- 2-3 long green peppers
- 3 eggs
- ½ a bunch of parsley
- ½ a bunch of dill
- 3-4 tablespoons of flour or breadcrumbs
- Salt
- Black pepper
- 1 cup of oil (for frying)

Directions

1. Wash and peel zucchinis, cut off edges and finely grate.
2. Add in chopped onions, green peppers, parsley, dill, eggs, flour, salt and black pepper, and stir.
3. Spoon the mixture onto a pan with hot oil and slightly flatten. Fry until both sides turn pink.
4. Remove cooked pieces onto a plate with paper-towels to absorb excess oil.

Note: *Replace zucchinis with 5 medium-sized grated potatoes, and follow the same directions to make Potato Patties.*

LEEK PATTY

Ingredients

- 3 medium sized leeks
- 2 small carrots
- 2 onions
- 2 long green peppers
- 3 eggs
- ½ bunch of parsley
- ½ bunch of dill
- 3-4 tablespoons of flour or breadcrumbs
- Salt
- Black pepper
- 1 cup of oil (for frying)

Directions

1. Clean and chop leeks into 5-6 cm long pieces. Then slice the pieces lengthwise into thin slivers.
2. Boil leeks with ⅙ cup of water until the water disappears and the leeks are cooked halfway through.
3. Once cooled, add in grated carrots, chopped onions and green peppers, and diced parsley and dill. Then add in salt, black pepper.
4. Add in eggs and flour, and mix together.
5. Spoon mixture onto a pan with hot oil and slightly flatten. Fry until both sides turn pink.
6. Remove cooked pieces onto a plate with paper-towels to absorb excess oil.

Note: Replace leeks and carrots with 1 kg of parboiled spinach stalks, and follow the same directions to make Spinach Stalk Patties.

FRIED ZUCCHINI

Ingredients

- 3 medium-sized zucchinis
- 1/3 cups of milk
- 3 tablespoons of flour
- Salt
- 1 cup of oil (for frying)

Directions

1. Wash and peel zucchinis, cut off the ends, and divide into three pieces. Slice into thin slivers and place onto paper-towels until the water is absorbed.
2. One by one, dip zucchini slices into milk, and then dredge in flour, shaking to remove loose flour.
3. In a small pot, heat oil and fry zucchini pieces until they turn pink. Remove with a sieved ladle.

Note: *If desired, serve with a yogurt and pulverized garlic mixture.*

ONION RINGS

Ingredients

- 2 large onions
- 3 tablespoons of flour
- 2 eggs
- 4 tablespoons of bread crumbs
- 1 cup of oil (for frying)
- Salt
- Black pepper

Directions

1. Peel onions and chop them breadthways into ½ cm wide, ring-shaped slices.
2. Sprinkle them with salt and black pepper.
3. Dredge onion slices in flour, dip into whisked eggs, and then cover with bread crumbs, and shake off excess crumbs.
4. Place rings in a pot with heated oil and fry until they turn pink. Remove with a sieved ladle onto paper-towels to absorb excess oil.

CARROT PUREE WITH OLIVE OIL

Ingredients

- ½ kg of carrots
- 2 onions
- ½ cup of oil
- ½ kg of yogurt
- 2 cloves of garlic
- ½ bunch of parsley leaves
- Salt

Directions

1. Peel and grate carrots.
2. Sauté diced onions in a small pot with oil and add in grated carrots.
3. Close the lid and cook in low heat by stirring occasionally.
4. Once cooled, mix wit a mixture of yogurt and pulverized garlic and put on a serving plate. Garnish with parsley leaves.

Note:

1) *Replace carrots with celery to make "CELERY PUREE WITH OLIVE OIL."*
2) *Variate recipe by using celery and carrots together.*
3) *Replace carrots with the same amount of zucchinis to make "ZUCCHINI PUREE."*

SPINACH PUREE

Ingredients

- 1 kg of spinach leaves (make spinach with rice dish with stalks and roots)
- 1 tablespoon of oil
- 1 tablespoon of flour
- 1 cup of milk
- Salt
- Black pepper

Directions

1. Wash and sieve spinach leaves. Boil in its own water for a short while. Once cooled, press with spinach hands and dice them. (Save stock for soup.)
2. In a separate pot, lightly fry flour with oil until it turns light pink. Add in diced spinach and milk, and cook for 2-3 minutes while stirring. Sprinkle with salt and black pepper.

Note:

1) *If desired, use spinach puree as a garnish for meat dishes, or mix with thick vermicelli. Also, it is can be served as a healthy, low-fat dish.*
2) *Mix spinach puree with pulverized garlic and yogurt and pour red pepper and oil mixture over it for a variation.*
3) *Use in an egg-dish, by placing the spinach puree in an oven plate, making holes according to the number of eggs that will be used. Put the eggs in the holes and add grated yellow cheese on top. Cook in the oven and remove before the eggs get too hard. Serve hot.*

MASHED POTATOES

Ingredients

- 6-7 potatoes
- 1 tablespoon of oil
- 1 cup of milk
- Salt

Directions

1. Wash potatoes and place in a pot of water. Bring to a boil.
2. Once cooked, peel while still hot and puree or grate to a pulp.
3. Put in a pot and add in oil, milk and salt. Cook again on a low heat, stirring occasionally.
4. Serve hot with meat dishes.

BAKED POTATO WITH CREAM

Ingredients

- 8 medium potatoes
- 1 ½ cups of cream
- 4-5 cloves of garlic
- 1 ½ teaspoons of salt
- ½ teaspoon of black pepper
- ½ teaspoon of grated coconut

Directions

1. Wash and peel the potatoes. Cut into 2-3 mm wide slices and dice the garlic.
2. Set the potato slices onto an oven plate, and sprinkle diced garlic, salt and black pepper on top.
3. Lastly, pour the cream over the potatoes and cook in a hot oven for 20 minutes.
4. Serve potatoes alone or with meat dishes.

BAKED POTATO WITH CHEESE

Ingredients

- 4 large potatoes
- 1 egg
- 5 tablespoons of unsalted goat's cheese
- 1 tablespoon of yogurt
- 1 tablespoon of oil
- 1 scallion sprig
- 1-2 long green peppers
- 7-8 sprigs of parsley
- 2 tablespoons of grated or slivered yellow cheese
- Salt
- Black pepper

Directions

1. Wash and dry potatoes. Wrap them in aluminum foil and cook in an oven on medium heat for 30-35 minutes. Test with a knife to see if it is ready; if the knife does not puncture easily, cook longer.
2. Cut the cooked potatoes in half, lengthwise. Carve out the inside of the potatoes, preserving the skins, and place in a separate bowl. Sprinkle with salt and black pepper.
3. Mash the potatoes with a fork. Mix with goat's cheese, yogurt, oil, diced scallions, green peppers, parsley, salt and black pepper.
4. Fill potato skins with the potato mixture. Pour a mixture of whisked eggs and grated or slivered yellow cheese on top. Set stuffed potatoes on an oiled oven plate and cook in an oven on medium heat.
5. Serve hot.

FRESH SAUTÉD VEGETABLES

Ingredients

- ½ kg of vegetables (green beans, chickpeas, carrots, zucchini, Brussels sprouts, etc.)
- 2 tablespoons of oil or 1 tablespoon of butter
- 1 teaspoon of sugar
- 1 teaspoon of salt

Directions

1. Clean and chop the vegetables. Remove the roots and some leaves of the Brussels sprouts, but do not chop.
2. Boil Brussels sprouts lightly with less then half a cup of water.
3. Heat oil in a pan and put in the dried vegetables. Sauté for 3-5 minutes, then add in sugar and salt.
4. Sautéed vegetables can be served alone, as a healthy meal, or with meat dishes.

SAUTÉD MUSHROOMS

Ingredients

- 300 grams of mushrooms
- 2 tablespoons of oil
- 1 tablespoon of butter
- 7-8 sprigs of parsley
- 1 tablespoon of lemon juice
- 1 teaspoon of sugar
- Salt
- Black pepper

Directions

1. Wash mushrooms and cut them into two or three pieces lengthwise.
2. Heat oil and lemon juice in a pan. Add mushrooms and sauté until the water evaporates. Add in sugar, salt and black pepper.
3. Place mushrooms onto a serving plate and pour melted butter on top. Sprinkle with diced parsley leaves.
4. Sautéed mushrooms can be served alone or with meat dishes.

GRAPE LEAVES STUFFED WITH MEAT

Ingredients

- 400 grams of ground beef
- 300 grams of fresh grape leaves or 250 grams of pickled grape leaves
- ½ cup of rice
- 2 onions
- 1-2 cloves of garlic
- 1 tomato or ½ tablespoon of tomato paste
- 2 tablespoons of oil
- ½ bunch of parsley
- ½ bunch of dill
- 1 teaspoon of dried mint
- Salt
- Black pepper

Directions

1. Wash fresh grape leaves, place in a pot with hot, salty water, and cover. Let sit for 1-2 minutes, and then shake. Remove the leaves once they change color. (For pickled grape leaves, follow the same directions, but let them sit longer in the water, and sieve.)
2. Mix ground beef with diced onions, parsley, dill, dried mint, grated tomato, 1 tablespoon of oil, salt and black pepper, and knead.
3. Lastly add in washed rice which has been soaked in hot water for 10-15 minutes, to avoid crushing.
4. Cut off the stalks and large veins of the grape leaves. (If desired, cut large grape leaves in half to make smaller stuffed grape leaves.) Put meat mixture onto the leaves, wrap, and set into a pot.
5. Add in half a grated tomato and 1 tablespoon of oil, and pour in half a cup of water from the side of the pot. Cook on a low heat until the leaves soften. Serve with yogurt.

OTHER VEGETABLES STUFFED WITH MEAT

CABBAGE STUFFED WITH MEAT

Soften smooth parts of the cabbage leaves in hot water and remove the stalk. Divide into a couple of pieces, place the meat mixture on each piece and wrap. Cook the same way as the grape leaves and serve plain.

CHARD STUFFED WITH MEAT

Wash and soak chard for a very short time and remove the stalk. Layer pieces on top of each other, stuff with the meat mixture and wrap. Cook the same way as the grape leaves and serve with yogurt.

MALLOW STUFFED WITH MEAT

Since Mallow leaves are very thin, only soak them for a short time to soften. Place meat mixture on the leaves and wrap. Cook the same way as the grape leaves and serve with yogurt.

LEEKS STUFFED WITH MEAT

Remove the heads of thick leek stalks. Make long strips by cutting down the middle lengthwise. Place in a pot with hot water until they soften. Cut the strips into 15-20 cm long pieces, and put meat mixture at the edges. Then wrap the leeks into a triangle-shape. Set into a pot and cook the same way as the grape leaves. Lastly, whisk 1 egg yolk with the juice from 1 lemon, dilute with 3 tablespoons of water and add into the pot. Mix together by shaking the pot in different directions.

GREEN PEPPERS, TOMATOES, AND ZUCCHINI STUFFED WITH MEAT

Ingredients

- 8 medium green peppers for stuffing
- 4 medium zucchini
- 4 medium hard tomatoes
- 20 grape leaves
- 500 grams of ground mince
- ½ cup of rice
- 2 onions
- 2 cloves of garlic
- 3 tablespoons of oil
- ½ bunch of parsley
- ½ bunch of dill
- 1 teaspoon of dried mint
- Salt
- Black pepper

Directions

1. Wash peppers, zucchini and tomatoes. Remove pepper stalks by pressing. Cut off the ends of the zucchini, cut in half lengthwise, and carve out the insides. Cut tomatoes in half and remove the insides to be used later.
2. Mix ground beef with diced onions, garlic, parsley, dill, half of the tomato insides, dried mint, 1 tablespoon of oil, salt, and black pepper, and knead.
3. Lastly add in washed rice which has been soaked in hot water for 10-15 minutes, to avoid crushing.
4. Fill carved vegetables with the meat mixture. Fill the grape leaves with the remaining meat mixture, and wrap. Set stuffed peppers and zucchinis in a pot, and then place in stuffed tomatoes and stuffed grape leaves. Add in 2 tablespoons of oil. Pour the rest of the tomato insides into the pot, and add half a cup of water to the side of the pot. Bring to a boil, then lower the heat, cook slowly until ready, and serve.

STUFFED GREEN PEPPERS (EGGPLANT, GRAPE LEAVES OR CABBAGE WRAPS)

Ingredients

- 18-20 medium green peppers for stuffing
- 2 cups of rice (1 tablespoon per green pepper)
- 1 cup of oil
- 7-8 onions
- 1 tablespoon of pine nuts
- 2 tablespoons of currants
- ½ bunch of parsley
- ½ bunch of dill
- 2 teaspoons of dried mint
- 2 teaspoons of salt
- 2 teaspoons of sugar
- 1 teaspoon of black pepper
- 1 teaspoon of cinnamon
- 1 teaspoon of allspice
- 1 lemon
- 1 tomato

Directions

1. Wash the rice and soak it in tepid water for 20 minutes.
2. Sauté diced onions, parsley, dill stalks and pine nuts in a pot. Add in sieved rice and stir occasionally.
3. Add in two cups of water and bring to a boil. Once boiling, lower the heat and cook until the water evaporates. Cover and let steep for 10-15 minutes.
4. Add in diced parsley, dill, mint, washed currants, cinnamon, allspice, black pepper, salt, sugar and lemon juice, and stir.
5. Stuff green peppers with the mixture. Cover with tomato pieces and set into a pot. Add 1 cup of water from the side of the pot and bring to a boil. Once boiling, lower the heat and cook until the water evaporates. Partially uncover and let cool before serving.

Note: *For variation, follow the same directions and use eggplant, grape leaves or cabbage instead of peppers.*

CAULIFLOWER (OR ZUCCHINI) AU GRATIN WITH BÉCHAMEL SAUCE

Ingredients

- 1 medium sized cauliflower
- 2 tablespoons of oil
- 2 tablespoons of flour
- 2 cups of milk
- 2 eggs
- 3-4 tablespoons of grated or slivered yellow cheese
- Salt
- Black pepper

Directions

1. Wash each stalk of cauliflower. Boil them with salted water until they begin to soften.
2. Fry flour in oil in a separate pot until it turns light yellow. Add in milk and let the mixture thicken while stirring. Let cool, stirring occasionally to prevent coagulation on the surface, and add in salt.
3. Add in eggs and 1 tablespoon of grated yellow cheese.
4. Oil the base of an oven plate and lay in ⅓ of the sauce. Set the cauliflowers on top and sprinkle on salt and black pepper.
5. Pour the remaining béchamel sauce over the cauliflowers and sprinkle with grated yellow cheese. Put in a hot oven and fry until the top is pink. Serve hot.

Note: *To make Zucchini Au Gratin, cut off the ends of 3 zucchinis and cut into two pieces lengthwise. Boil lightly with a little water and continue from direction 2.*

COLD WHITE BEANS VINAIGRETTE WITH OLIVE OIL

Ingredients

- 2 cups of dried beans
- 6 tablespoons of oil
- 2 carrots
- 1 small celery stalk
- 2 onions
- 5-6 cloves of garlic
- 2 long green peppers
- 2 tomatoes or ½ tablespoon of tomato paste
- ½ bunch of parsley leaves
- 1 teaspoon of sugar
- 2 teaspoons of salt

Directions

1. Wash and soak the beans overnight.
2. The following day, boil them halfway through.
3. Sauté chopped onions, carrots, and diced celery in a pot with oil.
4. Add in grated tomato or tomato paste and stir occasionally. Add in sieved beans and sugar, and two cups of beans stock and cover.
5. Bring to a boil and then lower the heat. Add in long green peppers, chopped into large pieces, and cook until the beans are soft.
6. Partially uncover the lid and let cool. Remove onto a serving plate and sprinkle parsley leaves on top.

Note: Dried kidney beans can replace dried beans but the stock should not be used. Fresh red beans can also replace dried beans, yet its stock should not be used.

ARTICHOKE WITH BROAD BEANS AND OLIVE OIL

Ingredients

- 6 artichokes
- ½ a kg of shelled broad beans
- ½ cup of oil
- 2 onions
- ½ bunch of dill
- 1 lemon
- 1 teaspoon of sugar
- 1 teaspoon of salt

Directions

1. Remove the outer leaves of the artichokes, and cut the bottom of the stalks.
2. Cut the thin leaves near the inside of the artichoke and peel without piercing too deep.
3. Remove the inner part of the artichoke with a spoon and place into salty water and lemon juice.
4. Peel the stalks until the inner parts are exposed, and chop into small pieces.
5. Sauté chopped onions in oil for a short while, then add in the artichokes and whole stalks. Stir occasionally, then add in 2-3 cups of water and cook halfway through.
6. Add in shelled broad beans, sugar and salt. Cover and cook slowly.
7. Partially uncover the pot and let cool. Remove artichokes onto a serving plate, and fill the carved part with beans. Sprinkle diced dill on top and serve.

IV

SALADS AND PICKLES

MAMZANA

Ingredients

- 5 eggplants
- 2 tomatoes
- 4 long green peppers
- ½ bunch of parsley
- 500 grams of yogurt
- 2-3 cloves of garlic
- 2 tablespoons of oil or 1 to 1 ½ tablespoons of butter
- 1 teaspoon of dried red pepper
- Salt

Directions

1. Grill eggplants, then peel and dice them into pieces.
2. Peel dice tomatoes, and dice green peppers and parsley.
3. In a bowl, mix together eggplants, tomatoes, peppers and parsley.
4. Place onto a serving dish and pour yogurt and pulverized garlic over.
5. Pour a mixture of oil (or melted butter) and red pepper on top.

Note: *If desired grill, peel and chop the long green peppers.*

MAYONNAISE

Ingredients

- 2 egg yolks
- 1 ½ cups of oil
- Juice of 1-2 lemons
- 1 teaspoon of mustard powder
- 1 teaspoon of salt

Directions

1. Put egg yolks in a bowl, slowly drip in a few drops of oil, and mix together in the same direction.
2. Slowly stir in the rest of the oil and 1 teaspoon of lemon juice.
3. Then add in the salt and mustard. Continue stirring, and slowly mix in the rest of the lemon juice until the mixture thickens to the appropriate consistency.

Note:

1) *Mayonnaise is an interesting chemical mixture that consists of egg yolks, oil, lemon and salt.*
2) *Lesitin in the egg yolk keeps the oil from separating out of the mixture.*
3) *By mixing the mayonnaise in the same direction, negative electrons are collected.*
4) *This electricity causes the oil particles to attract under equal constraints to the mayonnaise, and prevents spoiling.*
5) *Once the mayonnaise and the oil are successfully blended, add in some more lemon juice and whisk quickly, since the chemical solution requires more acid.*
6) *If desired, make mayonnaise by putting one egg into the same bowl, add in oil, drop by drop, occasionally add in spoiled mayonnaise and mix together.*
7) *If mayonnaise spoils, starch pudding can be added to recover it, however this can no longer be considered mayonnaise.*

RUSSIAN SALAD

Ingredients

- 1 small bowl of mayonnaise (see previous recipe)
- 2-3 boiled potatoes
- 2 carrots (diced and boiled in some water)
- ½ cup of boiled or canned peas
- 10-12 small baby corns
- 3-4 slices of Hungarian salami
- Salt

Directions

1. Chop potatoes, pickles and salami into quarter-sized pieces. Add in peas, carrot and salt.
2. Sparing 2-3 tablespoons of mayonnaise to decorate over the salad, add mixed vegetables into the remaining mayonnaise and mix.
3. Put into a salad bowl, and smooth over. Decorate with the remaining mayonnaise.
4. Russian salad can be served with tomatoes, which is weaved together.

CELERY SALAD WITH MAYONNAISE

Ingredients

- 5-6 tablespoons of mayonnaise
- 2 medium celery stalks
- 1 lemon
- Olives, red radishes, pickles, parsley leaves etc. (for garnish)
- Salt

Directions

1. Peel celery stalks.
2. Grate into medium-sized pieces. Add in salt and lemon juice.
3. Add mayonnaise and stir lightly.
4. Remove onto a serving plate and garnish with olives, red radishes, pickles and parsley leaves.

Note: *For best results, add 1-2 tablespoons of fresh milk cream (Chantilly cream) to the Celery Salad with mayonnaise.*

HUMMUS WITH MAYONNAISE

Ingredients

- 1 ½ cups of chickpeas
- ½ cup of sesame oil
- ½ cup of oil
- 4-5 cloves of garlic
- 3 teaspoons of dried red pepper
- 2-3 lemons
- 1 teaspoon of salt
- 4 tablespoons of mayonnaise
- Olives, pickles and parsley leaves (for garnish)

Directions

1. Wash the chickpeas and soak them overnight.
2. Boil and shell them.
3. Ground chickpeas into a fine paste.
4. Place mixture into a bowl and add in pulverized garlic with salt and dried red pepper.
5. Slowly add in oil and lemon juice and stir.
6. Lastly add mayonnaise into the mixture by the spoonful, and remove onto a serving plate. Garnish with olives, pickles and parsley leaves

CELERY and MUSHROOM SALAD WITH PEANUTS

Ingredients

- 1 medium celery stalk
- 200 grams of mushrooms
- 1 ½ cups of yogurt
- 2 cloves of garlic
- 2 tablespoons of oil
- 3 tablespoons of lemon juice
- ¼ cup of fried and peeled peanuts
- Salt
- Black pepper
- 5-6 sprigs of parsley leaves
- 5-6 black or green olives

Directions

1. Wash and peel celery stalk, and grate or sliver into matchstick size pieces.
2. Wash mushrooms and cut each one into 4-5 pieces lengthwise. Mix with celery pieces.
3. In a large bowl mix together yogurt and pulverized garlic with salt, oil, lemon juice, salt, black pepper and 3-4 sprigs of diced parsley. Stir celery and mushroom pieces into the yogurt mixture.
4. Remove into a salad bowl. Sprinkle peanuts on top and garnish with parsley, a few lemon slices, and green and black olives.

CELERY and RADISH SALAD WITH APPLES

Ingredients

- 1 red apple
- 1 small celery stalk
- 1 bunch of small red radishes
- 1 small onion
- 1 tablespoon of seedless raisins
- 1 tablespoon of diced walnuts

FOR SAUCE:

- 1 cup of yogurt
- 1 clove of garlic
- 2 tablespoons of mayonnaise
- 1 tablespoon of apple vinegar
- Salt
- Black pepper

Directions

1. In a large bowl, mix together pulverized garlic with salt, yogurt, mayonnaise, apple vinegar and black pepper.
2. Wash apple, celery and radishes. Chop the apple into quarters and remove the core. Peel the apples. Peel celery stalk and grate into the largest slices possible. Slice the radishes. Slice the onion into circles and separate the rings.
3. Spare 3-4 pieces of all the vegetables for garnishment. Mix the rest of the vegetables into the yogurt sauce.
4. Remove mixture into a salad bowl and garnish with apple, celery, radish and onion slices. Sprinkle diced walnuts and raisins on top.

CARROT and POTATO SALAD WITH YOGURT

Ingredients

- 5-6 medium potatoes
- 3 medium carrots
- 50 grams of yogurt
- 3-4 cloves of garlic
- ½ cup of oil
- 1 teaspoon of dried red pepper
- 6-7 sprigs of parsley
- Salt

Directions

1. Wash and boil potatoes and peel and puree once cooled.
2. Wash and peel carrots. Boil with a little bit of water until the water evaporates. Then mash and add to the potatoes.
3. Add pulverized garlic, salt and oil to the potato and carrot mixture and mix together.
4. Remove mixture into a salad bowl, and smooth the top. Garnish with parsley leaves and dried red pepper.

SALAD WITH YOGURT

Ingredients

- 1 cup of yogurt
- 2 cloves of garlic
- 1 tablespoon of sugar
- 2/3 a tablespoon of mustard powder
- 2 tablespoons of lemon juice
- ½ a tablespoon of diced fresh mint
- 1 teaspoon of salt

FOR THE GARNISH:

- 2 small tomatoes
- 4 long green peppers
- 8-10 parsley leaves
- 2 tablespoons of oil

Directions

1. In a bowl, mix pulverized garlic with salt, mustard powder, sugar, lemon juice and diced mint.
2. Add in yogurt, mix briefly and remove onto a plate.
3. Set sliced tomatoes around the edge of the plate. Put grilled green peppers and two tablespoons of olive oil on top. Garnish with parsley leaves, and serve.

POTATO SALAD

Ingredients

- 6 potatoes
- 1 onion
- 2 scallions
- 2 long green peppers
- 4 tablespoons of oil
- 3 tablespoons of apple vinegar
- 5-6 sprigs of parsley
- 2 teaspoons of dried red pepper
- 2 teaspoons of sumac powder
- Salt

Directions

1. Wash and boil potatoes. Once cooled, peel and cut them into cubes.
2. Chop onions into half-circle shape pieces, rub with 2 teaspoons salt, and wash. Add to the potatoes.
3. Add diced scallions, green peppers, parsley leaves, dried red pepper, sumac and salt to the potatoes, and mix together.
4. In a bowl, whisk together apple vinegar and oil, and mix into the potatoes.
5. Remove mixture into a salad bowl, and garnish with olives.

DRY BEAN PIYAZ WITH EGGS

Ingredients

- 1 cup of dry beans
- 1 onion
- 1-2 scallion sprigs
- 1-2 long green peppers
- 2 tomatoes
- 2 boiled eggs
- 6-7 olives
- 6-7 sprigs of parsley
- 2 teaspoons of dried red pepper
- 2 teaspoons of sumac powder
- 4 tablespoons of oil
- 3 tablespoons of apple vinegar
- Salt

Directions

1. Clean the beans and soak them overnight. The following day, boil them slowly in water to prevent them from cracking, and once cooked, let them cool in their own stock.
2. Chop onions into half-circle shape pieces, rub with 2 teaspoons of salt, and wash. Add to the beans with diced scallions, parsley and green peppers. Add in dried red pepper, sumac and salt, and mix.
3. In a bowl, whisk together apple vinegar and oil, and add to the beans.
4. Remove mixture into a salad bowl, and garnish with eggs (sliced lengthwise), tomato slices and olives.

CAULIFLOWER SALAD

Ingredients

- 1 small cauliflower
- 2 scallions
- 6-7 sprigs of parsley
- 3 tablespoons of oil
- 1 lemon
- Salt
- Black pepper

Directions

1. Separate and wash cauliflower branches. Boil in hot salty water with parsley stalks, and remove before they get too soft.
2. In a bowl, mix together oil, lemon juice, salt and black pepper and pour over cauliflower branches. Garnish with parsley leaves, salami, and green and black olives.

ARTICHOKE SALAD WITH POTATO

Ingredients

- 6 big artichokes
- ½ a tablespoon of flour
- 3 potatoes
- ⅓ cup of oil
- 1-2 lemons
- 5-6 sprigs of parsley
- 6 olives

Directions

1. Peel and remove the outer leaves of the artichokes. Cut the ends of the stalks off and peel the outer layer. Remove the insides with a spoon.
2. Mix ½ a tablespoon of flour with a little water and add into boiling, salty water. Add artichokes into the boiling water and cook until tender, but not too soft.
3. Remove artichokes with a sieved ladle and put into a salad bowl. Pour oil, salt and lemon juice over them.
4. Boil potatoes and puree them. Add in diced parsley, oil, lemon juice and salt, and mix together.
5. Fill empty artichokes with potato mixture and garnish with olives and parsley leaves.

FAVA (Mashed Broad Beans)

Ingredients

- 1 ½ cups of dry broad beans
- ½ a cup of oil
- 2 onions
- 2 cloves of garlic
- ½ a bunch of parsley
- ½ a bunch of dill
- 1 lemon
- 1 teaspoon of salt
- 1 teaspoon of sugar
- 1 teaspoon of dried red pepper
- 6-7 olives (for garnishment)

Directions

1. Clean and soak broad beans overnight.
2. Sauté chopped onions, garlic, parsley and dill stalks with oil for a short while.
3. Add in sieved broad beans and stir occasionally.
4. Add in salt, sugar and 3 cups of water and bring to a boil. Then lower the heat, and cook until the beans soften.
5. Sieve beans with a spoon into a deep salad bowl. Add in the juice from 1 lemon, and mix together.
6. Pour 1 tablespoon of oil over the beans. Garnish with dried red pepper, olives, lemon slices, parsley and dill.

HIBES

Ingredients

- 1 cup of sesame oil
- Juice of 2 lemons
- ⅙ cup of oil
- 2-3 cloves of garlic
- 2 teaspoons of cinnamon
- 1 teaspoon of salt
- 1 teaspoon of dried red pepper

FOR GARNISH:

- 6-7 olives
- 1-2 small pickles

Directions

1. Mix together sesame oil, cinnamon, and dried red pepper in a bowl.
2. Slowly add in lemon juice and oil, and stir. Lastly add in pulverized garlic with salt.
3. Remove into a salad bowl and garnish with olives and pickles.

Note: *Hibes can be used as a sauce for some salads.*

TARATOR (NUT AND GARLIC SAUCE)

Ingredients

- 1 cup shelled walnuts
- 2 slices of fried and flattened bread
- 4 tablespoons of sesame oil
- 3 cloves of garlic
- Juice of 2 lemons
- 1 teaspoon of dried red pepper
- ½ a teaspoon of cinnamon
- ½ a teaspoon of salt
- 5-6 sprigs of parsley leaves
- 5-6 olives
- 5-6 pickles

Directions

1. Slowly pulverize walnuts in a mortar.
2. Mix together crushed walnuts, sesame oil, pulverized garlic, salt, dried red pepper and cinnamon in a bowl.
3. Slowly add in lemon juice and stir.
4. Add in diced parsley leaves
5. Remove into a salad bowl and garnish with olives and pickles.

Note: *If desired tarator can be used as a spread for bread.*

TARAMA

Ingredients

- 100 grams of fish eggs
- 2 slices of crust-less stale bread
- ⅓ cup of milk
- 1 cup of oil
- 1-2 teaspoons of dried red pepper
- Juice of 1-2 lemons
- ½ a teaspoon of salt

Directions

1. Break the bread slices into small pieces in a bowl. Add in ⅓ of a cup of hot milk and mix together.
2. Remove the outer membranes of the fish eggs and then add them to the milk and bread mixture. Mix until they are completely covered.
3. Add olive oil and lemon juice in by the spoonful.
4. Add salt and dried red pepper and remove into a salad bowl.
5. Garnish as desired.

KISIR

Ingredients

- 2 cups of fine bulgur
- ½ a cup of oil
- 2 onions
- 5-6 scallions
- 3 tomatoes
- 4-5 long green peppers
- 1 tablespoon of pepper paste or 2 teaspoons of dry red pepper
- 2 lemons
- 1 bunch of parsley
- 1 bunch of dill
- 2 teaspoons of salt

Directions

1. Wash and dice tomatoes, green peppers, scallions, parsley, and dill.
2. Dice onions and sauté in 2 tablespoons of oil.
3. Put bulgur into a shallow pot with 1-2 cups of water and cover.
4. Once bulgur swells, add in sautéed onions, pepper paste and salt, and knead mixture together.
5. Add in diced vegetables, oil and lemon juice and mix.
6. Remove onto a service plate and garnish with lettuce leaves.

Note: *If desired, add 2-3 cloves of diced garlic and 2-3 pickles to the vegetables while prepraring.*

KETCHUP

Ingredients

- 2 ripe tomatoes
- 4 onions
- 4-5 cloves of garlic
- 2 bay leaves
- 1 cup of vinegar
- 5-6 cloves
- 2-3 teaspoons of dried red pepper
- 2-3 teaspoons of sugar
- 1 teaspoon of black pepper
- 1 teaspoon of cinnamon
- 1 teaspoon of salt

Directions

1. Wash and chop tomatoes, onions and garlic. Put all of them into a pot and cover. Cook on a low heat for 30-40 minutes.
2. Sieve with a spoon and add in bay leaves, vinegar, cloves, dried red pepper, sugar, black pepper, cinnamon and salt and mix.
3. Cook uncovered on a low heat, stirring occasionally, until the mixture thickens, but is still in liquid form. Then sieve again.
4. Once slightly cooled, remove into jars and let sit until completely cooled, then refrigerate.

EGGPLANT SALAD

Ingredients

- 6 eggplants
- 2 tomatoes
- 4 tablespoons of oil
- Juice of 1 lemon
- 2 cloves of garlic
- 5-6 sprigs of parsley leaves
- 1 teaspoon of salt

Directions

1. Grill eggplants and green peppers, turning occasionally. Remove skin and chop into pieces.
2. Place into a bowl and add in garlic, pulverized with salt, lemon juice, and oil. Mix together.
3. Remove onto a serving plate and garnish with tomato slices and parsley leaves.

Note: *If desired, serve with olive oil dressing that can be used for such salads or olives. To make the dressing, put 1 kg of olive oil into a jar with 5-6 whole, peeled garlic cloves, 3-4 small dried red peppers, 1 pinch of rosemary, and 2 bay leaves, and close the lid. Then cover the jar with paper, and leave in a cool part of the kitchen for 15 days. This dressing has an appealing scent and taste.*

MIXED PICKLED VEGETABLES

Ingredients

- 250 grams of long green peppers
- 250 grams of fresh beans
- ½ a kg of small green tomatoes
- 4-5 small cucumbers or Russian cucumbers
- 3-4 small carrots
- 2-3 red peppers for paste
- 1 apple
- 1 quince
- 1 garlic bulb
- 1 bunch of parsley
- 1 bunch of celery leaves
- 2-3 cups of vinegar
- Salt (1 tbsp for 4 ½ cups of water)
- 1-2 tablets of aspirin

Directions

1. Wash and sieve the vegetables. Remove the ends of the beans. Slice apple and quince, and leave unpeeled. Cut the red peppers into 4 pieces for paste. Pierce the other peppers in a few places.
2. Set the vegetables in a large jar, layering them with garlic (chopped in half), parsley and celery stalks.
3. Put 9 cups of water, 2 tablespoons of salt, 2-3 cups of vinegar and 2 aspirin tablets in a pot, and heat until they have all melted together.
4. Pour mixture over the vegetables. If there is not enough salty water, prepare more until all of the vegetables are covered.
5. Put a clean, heavy object on top of the vegetables, and close the lid.
6. Leave in a cool place.

PICKLED CABBAGE

Ingredients

- 1 medium cabbage
- 1 garlic bulb
- 2-3 hot red peppers
- 1 tablespoon of chickpeas
- 1/3 of a tablespoon of sugar
- Salt (1 tbsp for 5 cups of water)

Directions

1. Remove the outer leaves of the cabbage, and divide into 6-8 pieces. Place cabbage, hot red peppers, chopped garlic, and chickpeas into a jar or enameled container, forming different layers.
2. Add 1 tablespoon of salt into 5 cups of water, sprinkle in sugar, and mix together. Pour this mixture over the cabbage. If there is not enough salty water, prepare more until all of the cabbage is covered. Close the lid.
3. To ensure the best quality of pickled cabbage, mix the water everyday with a ladle.
4. Let sit for 10-15 days, until sufficiently pickled (varies depending on climate).

Note: To shorten the pickling process, add 1 teaspoon of brewers yeast to the water.

PICKLED BEETS

Ingredients

- 1 kg of red beets
- 1 cup of vinegar
- 1 cup of water
- 5-6 cloves of garlic
- ½ a tablespoon of salt

Directions

1. Wash the beets, put them in a pot and cover with water. Boil until cooked, but not too soft.
2. Let beets cool slightly, then chop them into 0.5 cm-wide slices, and put into jars.
3. Add pulverized garlic, salt, and vinegar into a bowl. Add in 1 cup of water, mix together and pour over beets.
4. Tilt the jars in different directions and close the lids. Shake the jars every 1-2 hours.
5. Let sit overnight. Pickled beets can be served the following day.

QUICK PICKLED CUCUMBERS AND PEPPERS

Ingredients

- ½ a kg of long green peppers
- 10-15 small cucumbers
- 6-7 cloves of garlic
- ½ bunch of parsley or a few celery stalks
- 2 cups of vinegar
- Salt (1 tbsp for every 4-5 cups of water)

Directions

1. Wash and pierce cucumbers in a few places.
2. Add 2 tablespoons of salt into 9 cups of water and boil.
3. Dip peppers and cucumbers into the hot salty water and take out immediately after.
4. Put into jars with chopped garlic (in halves), parsley and celery stalks.
5. Once the salty water gets tepid add in vinegar. Pour over the cucumbers and peppers until they are completely covered. Put a clean, heavy object on top, close the lids and let sit.
6. The vegetables are pickled, and ready to eat when they turn yellow.

PICKLING VARIATION

Ingredients

- 2 kg of cucumbers
- 7-8 cloves of garlic
- 7-8 sprigs of parsley
- 3 cups of vinegar
- 5 tablespoons of salt
- 9 cups of water

Directions

1. Wash and pierce cucumbers in a few places, and set into a jar. Put washed garlic and parsley sprigs over them.
2. Mix 9 cups of water, 5 tablespoons of salt and 3 cups of vinegar together in a pot and pour over the cucumbers. Close the lid of the jar.
3. Let sit for 10-12 days, until pickled. If desired, once pickles are ready, remove them and add new cucumbers to the water and continue pickling.

HOW TO MAKE YOUR OWN APPLE VINEGAR

Ingredients

- Washed apple peels
- Salt
- Water

Directions

1. Fill a jar with apple peels. Add salt and fill with water. Leave at room temperature with the lid off. If desired, add in grapes.
2. Let sit until it smells like vinegar. Then sieve out apple peels and grapes. Apple vinegar can be used for salads or pickling.

HOW TO MAKE YOUR OWN YOGURT

Ingredients

- 1 liter of milk
- 1 tablespoon of yogurt (as yeast)

Directions

1. Boil the milk while stirring, and slowly pour into a pot or a jar. Cover and cool until tepid.
2. Put your pinkie finger into the milk and count until 20, if it is bearable (not scalding), whisk 1 tablespoon of yogurt with 2-3 tablespoons of milk and add into the tepid milk. Mix together, cover and let sit for 3 hours. Uncover and check to see if the yogurt is ready. When ready, uncover and let sit for half an hour, then refrigerate.

V

RICE, MACARONI AND EGGS

PLAIN RICE

Ingredients

- 2 cups of rice
- 4 tablespoons of oil
- 3 cups of beef stock (1 ½ cups of beef stock for 1 cup of rice)
- 1 teaspoon of salt

Directions

1. Wash rice and sprinkle with 2 teaspoons of salt. Soak for 20-30 minutes in tepid water.
2. In a pot, bring 3 cups of water to a boil with oil.
3. Add sieved rice and stir. Cover and boil on a high heat for 2-3 minutes. Lower the heat and boil until the water is absorbed.
4. Cover and let steep for 10 minutes. Stir and partially uncover for a short while.

Note:

1) *If there is no time to soak rice, you can cook it by adding an extra half a cup of water.*
2) *If you use a beef stock tablet, then do not add salt into the cooking water.*
3) *You can add 2-3 tablespoons of milk to the cooking water to change the taste of the rice.*
4) *RICE WITH CARROTS: Prepare plain rice. Peel and chop carrots, and boil in a little water until the water evaporates. Sauté carrots with 1 tablespoon of oil and add to the rice.*

   RICE WITH PEAS: Boil 1 cup of peas and sauté with 1 tablespoon of oil and add to the rice.

   RICE WITH CHICKPEAS: Wash and soak half a cup of chickpeas in water overnight. Add chickpeas in their water to the rice while it is cooking.

PLAIN RICE (Roasting)

Ingredients

- 2 cups of rice
- 4 tablespoons of oil
- 3 ½ cups of beef stock
- 1 teaspoon of salt

Directions

1. Wash rice and sprinkle with 2 teaspoons of salt. Soak for 20-30 minutes in tepid water.
2. Heat oil in a pot. Add sieved rice, stirring occasionally to prevent the rice from cracking.
3. Add 3 ½ cups of beef stock, stir and cover.
4. Boil for 2-3 minutes, then lower the heat and boil until the water is absorbed.
5. Remove from heat and let steep for 10 minutes. Stir and partially uncover for a short while.

Note: *If the rice is fried with oil, add slightly more than 1 ½ cups of water for each cup of rice.*

RICE WITH VERMICELLI

Ingredients

- 2 cups of rice
- 4 tablespoons of oil
- 2 tablespoons of barley vermicelli
- 3 cups of beef stock (1 ½ cups of beef stock for 1 cup of rice)
- 1 teaspoon of salt

Directions

1. Wash the rice, sprinkle with 2 teaspoons of salt, and soak for 20-30 minutes in tepid water.
2. Fry vermicelli in oil until it turns yellow. Add 3 cups of water and salt, and boil.
3. Add sieved rice, stir and cover.
4. Boil for 2-3 minutes, then lower the heat and boil until the water is absorbed.
5. Remove from heat and steep for 10 minutes. Stir and partially uncover for a short while.

RICE WITH TOMATOES

Ingredients

- 2 cups of rice
- 4 tablespoons of oil
- 1 tomato
- 3 cups of beef stock (1 ½ cups of beef stock for every cup of rice)
- 1 teaspoon of salt

Directions

1. Wash the rice and sprinkle with 2 teaspoons of salt. Soak for 20-30 minutes in tepid water.
2. Fry grated tomato in a pot with oil, stirring occasionally.
3. Add 3 cups of beef stock and salt, and bring to a boil. Then add in sieved rice and cover.
4. Boil for 2-3 minutes, then lower the heat and boil until the water is absorbed.
5. Remove from heat and steep for 10 minutes. Stir and partially uncover space for a short while.

RICE WITH EGGPLANT

Ingredients

- 2 cups of rice
- 4 tablespoons of oil
- 1 onion
- 1 small tomato
- 3 cups of beef stock
- 3-4 eggplants
- 4-5 tablespoons of oil (for frying)
- Salt
- Black pepper

Directions

1. Wash the rice, sprinkle with 2 teaspoon of salt, and soak for 20-30 minutes in tepid water.
2. Sauté chopped onion in 4 tablespoons of oil. Add in grated tomatoes and stir occasionally. Then add in 3 cups of beef stock and salt and bring to a boil.
3. Add in sieved rice, stir and cover.
4. Boil for 2-3 minutes, then lower the heat and boil until the water is absorbed.
5. Remove from heat and steep for 10 minutes.
6. Wash the eggplants and cut into four parts lengthwise and cube. Sprinkle with 2 teaspoons of salt and let sit for 10 minutes. Wash, dry and fry eggplants in hot oil until they turn light pink. Place on paper towels and cover to remove excess oil.
7. Add fried eggplants into steeped rice. Sprinkle with black pepper and stir. Serve tepid or cold.

IC RICE

Ingredients

- 2 cups of rice
- 3 cups of meat stock
- 5 tablespoons of oil
- ½ of a lamb's liver (diced and skinless)
- 2 carrots (diced and boiled)
- ½ cup of boiled peas
- 2 tablespoons of pine nuts
- 2 tablespoons of currants
- Salt
- Black pepper

Directions

1. Wash the rice, sprinkle with 2 teaspoons of salt and soak for 20-30 minutes in tepid water.
2. Fry pine nuts with a little bit oil until they turn light pink, then remove. Fry carrots and peas in the same oil. Then fry the liver and add in the carrots and peas.
3. Add remaining oil into a pot with the meat stock. Sprinkle with salt and bring to a boil. Add in sieved rice, stir and cover.
4. Boil for 2-3 minutes, then lower the heat and boil until the water is absorbed.
5. Remove from heat and let steep for 10 minutes.
6. Add in salt, black pepper, pine nuts, currants, carrots and peas, and stir lightly.

PERDE RICE (From Siirt)

Ingredients

- 2 cups of rice
- 3 ½ cups of fat-free chicken stock
- 1 boiled chicken
- 4 tablespoons of oil
- 1 tablespoon of pine nuts
- 2 tablespoons of currants
- 1-2 tablespoons of almonds (boiled and shelled)

FOR DOUGH:

- ½ a package of margarine (125 g)
- 1 egg
- 250 grams of flour
- 1 teaspoon of salt

Directions

1. Sieve the flour in a bowl and put the margarine, salt and egg into the middle. Mix into dough, flour both sides and flatten until it is 2-3 mm thick. Place dough in a lightly oiled pot, letting the edges hang over the sides, and refrigerate.
2. Wash the rice and soak for 20-30 minutes in tepid, salty water.
3. Fry almonds and pine nuts in a pot until they turn light pink, then remove onto a plate.
4. Put sieved rice in the same pot and fry briefly while stirring. Add 3 ½ cups of chicken stock and boil on a high heat for 2-3 minutes. Lower the heat and wait until the water is absorbed. Remove from heat and steep for 10 minutes.
5. Add nuts, currants, diced chicken, salt, and black pepper and stir.
6. Once cooled, add rice into the dough pot, press with a spoon and cover by folding the edges of the dough over the rice.
7. Place in an oven on medium heat until the dough is cooked. Serve upside down on a plate and slice into pieces.

KEBAB WITH RICE

Ingredients

- 2 cups of rice
- ½ kg of cubed mutton
- 4 tablespoons of oil
- 1 onion
- 1 tomato
- 1 long green pepper
- Salt
- Black pepper

Directions

1. Wash rice, and soak for 20-30 minutes in tepid, salty water.
2. Sauté meat and chopped onion with oil in a pan. Add grated tomato, slowly pour in hot water and cook until the meat softens.
3. Put meat into a heat-resistant container. Add in pepper and sprinkle with salt and black pepper. Turn the container upside down into a saucepan, and add weight on top to secure it.
4. In a separate pot, bring oil and 3 cups of water to a boil. Add in half a teaspoon of salt.
5. Sieve the rice and add it into the pot. Cover and lower the heat. Cook until the water is absorbed.
6. Steep for 10 minutes. Stir the rice, and then remove the case over the meat.

RICE WITH CHICKEN AND VEGETABLES

Ingredients

- ½ kg of cubed chicken
- 2 cups of rice
- 6 tablespoons of oil
- 1 tablespoon of pine nuts
- 2 tablespoons of currants
- 2 onions
- 2 long green peppers
- ½ cup of shelled peas (lightly boiled)
- 2 carrots (chopped and lightly boiled)
- ½ a teaspoon of black pepper
- ½ a teaspoon of cinnamon
- ½ a teaspoon of allspice
- 2 teaspoons of salt

Directions

1. Wash the rice, and soak it in tepid, salty water for 20 minutes.
2. Heat oil in a pot, add in pine nuts, fry until they turn light pink, and remove onto a plate.
3. In the same oil, fry cubed chicken for 5 minutes. Add in chopped onions and green peppers and cook until the water is absorbed and the meat turns light red. Add salt, black pepper, cinnamon, allspice and stir. Then remove meat onto a plate.
4. Sieve rice and heat with the same oil from the chicken. Cook on high heat while stirring, and then lower the heat until the water is absorbed.
5. Add pine nuts, currants, carrots, peas and cooked chicken meat over the rice. Cover and let steep for 20 minutes.
6. Mix and serve.

RICE WITH ANCHOVIES

Ingredients

- 1 kg of anchovies
- 1 cup of rice
- 3 tablespoons of oil
- 2-3 onions
- 6-7 sprigs of parsley
- 1 tablespoon of pine nuts
- 2 tablespoon of seedless raisins
- 1 teaspoon of salt
- 1 teaspoon of sugar
- ½ a teaspoon of cinnamon
- ½ a teaspoon of black pepper

Directions

1. Wash anchovies, remove bones, sieve and refrigerate.
2. Wash the rice and soak for 20-30 minutes in tepid, salty water.
3. Sauté chopped onions, parsley stalks and pine nuts in oil. Add in sieved rice and stir. Pour in 1 ½ cups of hot water and cook until the water is absorbed.
4. Steep for 10 minutes and add washed raisins, diced parsley leaves, sugar, cinnamon, salt, and black pepper and stir.
5. Set more than half of the anchovies back-to-back on a small oiled tray, hanging them over the edge of the tray.
6. Put rice over the anchovies and press with a spoon. Turn hanging anchovies over the rice, and set the remaining anchovies on top.
7. In a heated oven, fry the anchovies until they turn red. Place on a serving plate upside down and serve hot.

BURYAN (From Edirne)

Ingredients

- ½ kg of mutton meat with bones.
- 2 cups of rice
- 5 tablespoons of oil
- 2 onions
- 1 tomato
- 1 long green pepper
- Salt
- Black pepper

Directions

1. Wash the rice, add 2 teaspoon of salt and soak in tepid water for 20 minutes.
2. In a pot, sauté chopped onions, pepper and meat.
3. Grate tomato, add 1 cup of water and cook the meat slowly until the water evaporates. Add sieved rice and stir occasionally, without cracking the rice.
4. Add 3 cups of water and salt. Cook on a high heat for 2-3 minutes and then on a low heat until the water is absorbed. Let steep for 10-15 minutes.
5. Uncover and stir the rice. Sprinkle with black pepper.

Note: Chicken can be substituted for mutton.

CRACKED WHEAT KESKEK

Ingredients

- 1 mutton neck
- 2 cups of cracked wheat
- ½ cup of chickpeas
- 2 - 2 ½ tablespoons of butter
- 1 teaspoon of dried red pepper
- Salt
- Black pepper

Directions

1. Wash cracked wheat and chickpeas and soak overnight in separate pots.
2. Boil 7 cups of water in a pressure cooker. Add washed mutton neck, sieved chickpeas and 2 teaspoon of salt and cover.
3. Once the pressure cooker steams, release the pressure, lower the heat and cook for 30-40 minutes.
4. Once cooled, uncover, pour meat stock into another pot and add in cracked wheat.
5. Cook slowly while uncovered until the wheat softens. Add in salt and black pepper.
6. Remove the neck meat from the bones, cut them into small pieces and mix into the wheat pot with a spoon.
7. Add cooked chickpeas and stir. When serving, pour melted butter over the dish and sprinkle with dried red pepper.

Note: *In the Aegean region, this meal is cooked in a cauldron and served with rice that is cooked with the meat stock.*

VERMICELLI WITH MILK

Ingredients

- 2 eggs
- 4 tablespoons of milk
- 1 teaspoon of salt
- Flour (as needed)

FOR VERMICELLI:

- 1 cup of milk
- 1 ½ - 2 tablespoons of butter
- ¼ cup of grated yellow or white cheese

Directions

1. In a pot, stir together eggs, milk, and salt. Add flour until it reaches a dough-like consistency. Knead the dough, cover and let rest.
2. Flour the dough and flatten until it is 5-1 mm thick. Let dry.
3. Divide the flattened dough into four pieces. Flour the pieces, pile them up, and cut them into strips that are about 1 inch wide.
4. Cut the strips into 2-3 mm wide pieces and cover with a cloth to dry.
5. Boil water (the same amount as vermicelli) with 1 teaspoon of salt. Add vermicelli and bring to a boil while uncovered. Add 1 cup of milk and stir occasionally.
6. Remove from heat once the vermicelli is soft. Pour melted butter over, and sprinkle with grated cheese.

MACARONI WITH TOMATO SAUCE

Ingredients

- 1 package (500 g) of macaroni
- 4 tablespoons of oil (2 tbsp for macaroni, 2 tbsp for sauce)
- 1-2 onions
- 2 cloves of garlic
- 3 ripe tomatoes
- 1 tablespoon of tomato paste
- 1 carrot
- 1 celery stalk
- Parsley stalks
- 1 ½ tablespoons of flour
- 2-3 cups of beef stock or water
- 1 teaspoon of salt
- 1 teaspoon of sugar
- 1 teaspoon of black pepper

Directions

1. TOMATO SAUCE: Sauté chopped onions, garlic and parsley stalks until they turn yellow.
2. Add diced carrots and celery and stir occasionally.
3. Add flour and stir occasionally.
4. Add grated tomato, 2-3 cups of beef stock (or wine, if desired). Cook slowly.
5. Sieve with a spoon. Add salt, black pepper and sugar.
6. Boil macaroni in a pot with the lid partially uncovered and sieve when cooked. Wash with cold water, and pour in 2 tablespoons of oil.
7. Pour hot tomato sauce on top and stir. Keep warm in an over until served.

CRACKED WHEAT RICE WITH TOMATO

Ingredients

- 2 cups of bulgur.
- 4 cups of beef stock
- 2 onions
- 1-2 tomatoes
- 1 long green pepper
- 5 tablespoons of oil
- Salt

Directions

1. Sauté chopped onions and green pepper.
2. Add in grated tomatoes and stir. Add 4 cups of beef stock and bring to a boil.
3. Add in bulgur, stir and cover. Cook for 4-5 minutes on a high heat and then lower heat until the water is absorbed.
4. Remove from heat and let steep. Stir and serve.

Note: *For a healthier meal, prepare the bulgur pilaf with more sauce.*

MACARONI WITH BAKED FILO DOUGH

Ingredients

- 1 package of ziti macaroni
- 1 package of filo dough
- 4 tablespoons of oil
- 3 eggs
- 2 cups of milk
- 1 cup of grated yellow or white cheese
- Salt
- Black pepper

Directions

1. Break macaroni in half and boil in salty water. Sieve and wash with cold water.
2. In a bowl whisk together eggs, salt and black pepper. Add oil and milk, and stir.
3. Oil a tray to cook the macaroni in, and spread the filo dough out onto the tray, letting the edges hang over the tray.
4. Mix sieved macaroni, eggs, milk and oil mixture with 1/3 of the cheese.
5. Spread half of the macaroni over the filo dough, and sprinkle on 1/3 of the remaining cheese.
6. Spread the remaining macaroni over and press lightly. Sprinkle on the rest of the cheese and pour over the rest of the egg, oil and milk mixture. Fold the hanging filo dough over the macaroni.
7. Fry in the oven until it turns pink on both sides.
8. Slice and serve upside down.

BAKED MACARONI AU GRATIN

Ingredients

- 1 package of ziti macaroni
- 3 tablespoons of oil
- Salt
- Black pepper

FOR BÉCHAMEL SAUCE:

- 2 tablespoons of oil
- 2 tablespoons of flour
- 2 eggs
- ½ liter of milk
- 4-5 tablespoons of grated or slivered yellow cheese
- Salt
- Black pepper

Directions

1. Break macaroni in half and boil in salty water. Sieve and wash with cold water. Mix with 3 tablespoons of oil, 2 tablespoons of grated yellow cheese, salt and black pepper.
2. BÉCHAMEL SAUCE: Lightly fry flour with oil. Add milk and cook until it reaches a pudding-consistency, then remove from heat. Once cooled, add in egg, sprinkle with salt and black pepper and mix.
3. Oil a small tray, and spread some béchamel sauce out onto it. Set boiled macaroni over the sauce and press with a spoon.
4. Pour over the remaining sauce. Sprinkle with grated cheese, and fry in the oven until it turns pink.
5. Serve hot, sliced or with a spoon.

MEAT PASTRY WITH CHICKEN and RICE (From Thrace Region)

Ingredients

FOR DOUGH:

- 1 egg
- 1 cup of water
- 1 teaspoon of salt
- Flour (as needed)

FOR MEAT PASTRY

- 1 cup of rice
- 3 chicken's liver or a small mutton liver.
- 3 tablespoons of oil
- 1 piece of chicken breast with bones
- 1 onion
- Salt
- Black pepper

Directions

1. Boil 3 cups of water in a pot. Wash the chicken breast, sprinkle with salt and pepper, and chop into quarters. Boil with a whole onion.
2. Wash the rice and soak in salty, tepid water.
3. Fry small, chopped liver with oil and remove to a plate.
4. Sieve the rice and fry with the same oil from the liver.
5. Add 1 cup of chicken stock and cook until the water is absorbed. Steep for 10 minutes, add liver, salt, black pepper and stir.
6. PREPARATION OF DOUGH: Whisk together one egg, 1 cup of water and 1 teaspoon of salt. Add flour and form into tough dough. Flour and spread out the dough until it is 1-2 mm thick. Cut dough into 3-4 cm squares.
7. Put liver mixture onto the dough pieces. Close by bringing the edges together and sticking them closed. Set on an oiled tray. Fry until they turn pink. Remove bones from the chicken meat and put over the pastry.
8. Pour 2 cups of chicken stock on top. Remove from the oven and serve hot, preventing the pastry to get soggy.

MEAT PASTRY

Ingredients

- 3 cups of flour
- 1 egg
- Salt
- 1/3 cups of water

FOR INGREDIENTS:

- 250 g of ground beef
- 1 onion
- 4-5 sprigs of parsley
- Salt
- Black pepper

FOR UPPER PART:

- ½ kg of yogurt
- 2 cloves of garlic
- 5 tablespoons of oil
- 1 tablespoon of tomato paste
- 1 teaspoon of dried red pepper

Directions

1. Sieve flour in a pot. Put one egg, salt and ⅓ cup of water in the middle, and knead the mixture into dough. Cover and let rest.
2. Mix ground beef, onion, parsley leaves, salt and black pepper and knead.
3. Divide the dough into two parts and spread out until it is 1-2 mm thick. Cut into 3 cm squares.
4. Put the meat onto the dough pieces and cover by sticking the edges of the dough together.
5. Boil 8 cups of water in a pot. Add in 2 teaspoons of salt and the stuffed dough.
6. Boil the dough for 7-8 minutes and remove to a container.
7. Serve onto plates, pour yogurt and garlic mixture over and lastly pour oil with tomato paste on top.

Note: *The meat pastry can be roasted in an oven on an oiled tray instead of boiled. Afterwards it can be cooked by adding 6-7 cups of hot beef stock. Remaining beef stock can be used to make soup.*

ITALIAN MEAT PASTY

Ingredients

FOR DOUGH:
- 2 cups of flour
- 1 egg
- 1 teaspoon of salt
- 3-4 tablespoons of water

FOR MEAT PASTRY:
- 1 chicken breast
- 2 onions
- 1 tablespoon of oil
- 1 tablespoon of flour
- 1 cup of milk
- 6-7 sprigs of parsley
- Salt
- Black pepper (if available a pinch of grated coconut)

FOR UPPER PART:
- 4 tablespoons of oil
- ½ cup of grated yellow cheese
- 3 ladles of tomato sauce (home made)

Directions

1. PREPARATION OF THE MEAT: In a pot, boil breast meat, one quartered onion, salt and black pepper. Once cooked, let cool and quarter the meat.
2. Dice an onion, and fry with 1 tablespoon of oil until it turns yellow. Add diced chicken meat and 1 tablespoon of flour and stir. Add 1 cup of milk and cook. Add salt, black pepper, grated coconut and chopped parsley leaves.
3. PREPARATION OF DOUGH: Sieve flour into a pot. Put egg, salt and water in the middle and form into tough dough. Let sit for 15-20 minutes while covered.
4. Flour the dough and spread out until it is 1-2 mm thick. Put the meat mixture on half of the dough by the spoonful with some water, covering it with the other half of the dough as you go along. Cut the dough into a rectangular shape, bringing the stuffed meat into the middle.
5. Boil 6-7 cups of water and add 2 teaspoon of salt. Slowly add dough into the water, and boil for 10 minutes. Take out with a sieved ladle, first dipping into cold water before removing.
6. Heat 4 tablespoons of oil in a pot. Pass the pastry through the heated oil and then place onto a tray. Sprinkle with grated cheese and put into an oven. Heat until the cheese is melted, pour tomato sauce over it, and serve.

OMELETTE WITH CHEESE

Ingredients

- 2 eggs
- 2 tablespoons of oil
- 1 tablespoon of grated cheese
- 5-6 sprigs of parsley leaves
- A pinch of salt
- Black pepper

Directions

1. Wash and dice parsley leaves and mix with eggs. Sprinkle with salt and black pepper.
2. Heat oil in a pan. Pour in egg and parsley mixture and tilt pan to spread out the mixture. Turn upside down when the underside is pink, and fry both sides.
3. Sprinkle grated cheese on top and fold in half. Remove onto a service plate.
4. If desired, pour tomato sauce on top.

Note:

OMELETTE WITH POTATO: Peel 2 potatoes, chop into small pieces, and fry with oil. Put this over the fried omelette with parsley, sprinkle with salt and black pepper and fold in half.

OMELETTE WITH MUSHROOM: Wash and slice 6-7 mushrooms lengthwise. Sauté and put the mushroom over the fried omelette with parsley, sprinkle with salt and black pepper, and fold in half.

OMELETTE WITH VEGETABLE MIXTURE:

1. *Boil 1 small zucchini, 1 small carrot and 1/3 cup of shelled peas in some water. Add in 3-4 mushrooms, sliced lengthwise, 1 chopped long green pepper and a slice of salami.*
2. *Sauté this mixture in oil, and sprinkle with a pinch of salt, black pepper and sugar.*
3. *Put this mixture over the fried omelette with parsley, sprinkle on grated yellow cheese and fold in half.*

EGGS WITH ONION (Mıklama)

Ingredients

- 5 onions
- 4 tablespoons of oil
- 4 eggs
- 1 bunch of parsley stalks
- Salt
- Black pepper

Directions

1. Dice parsley stalks, chop onions and put them into a pan.
2. Add oil and cover. Fry on a low heat while stirring until the onions soften. Add in salt and black pepper.
3. Puncture 4 large holes into 4 onions and put 1 egg into each hole. Sprinkle with salt and black pepper. Add 2-3 tablespoons of water from the side of the pan and cover.
4. When the egg-whites are cooked, remove from heat and serve.

Note: *If desired, after frying the onions, add 2-3 tablespoons of ground beef and in place of the eggs.*

MENEMEN

Ingredients

- 3-4 tablespoons of oil
- 3-4 onions
- 3-4 long green peppers
- 3-4 tomatoes
- ½ bunch of parsley
- 4 eggs
- Salt
- Black pepper

Directions

1. Dice parsley stalks, chop onions and green peppers and put them into a pan.
2. Add oil and sauté on a low heat until they turn yellow while stirring occasionally.
3. Peel the tomatoes, chop into small pieces and add into the pan. When the tomato starts to disintegrate, add parsley. Sprinkle with salt and black pepper.
4. Whisk eggs in a bowl, add into the pan and stir.
5. Once the egg is cooked, remove from heat.

Note: Eggs can also be cooked by breaking into the pan without stirring.

CILBIR (Poached Eggs With Yogurt)

Ingredients

- 2 tablespoons of oil
- 4 eggs
- 1 ½ cups of yogurt
- 2 cloves of garlic
- Salt
- Black pepper
- Red pepper
- 2 tablespoons of vinegar

Directions

1. Beat garlic with salt and add into yogurt. Mix and divide onto four plates.
2. Boil 7-8 cups of water in a pot. Add in salt and vinegar.
3. Break the egg over a sieved ladle and slowly sink into the boiling water until the egg is cooked.
4. Before the egg gets hard, remove from the pot, immerse in a cup of cold water, and remove.
5. Put the egg on the plate with yogurt. Sprinkle with black pepper and cover the egg with yogurt. Cook the other eggs the same way.
6. Pour oil over the eggs and sprinkle with dried red pepper.

Note: Eggs can be fried with oil softly and placed on the yogurt plates.

BAKED TOMATO WITH EGGS

Ingredients

- 4 large, hard tomatoes
- 4 eggs
- 2 tablespoons of oil
- 2 long green peppers
- 1 tablespoons of grated cheese
- Salt
- Black pepper

Directions

1. Wash tomatoes. Slice the top of the tomatoes with a knife, leaving the end so the slices remain attached, like lids.
2. Remove the insides of the tomatoes, and put ⅓ tablespoon of oil, chopped green peppers and cracked eggs into each tomato.
3. Add in salt, black pepper and grated cheese and close the tops.
4. Oil an oven plate, set the tomatoes in it, and cook on a low heat until cooked.

VI

PASTRIES, BUNS AND PIZZAS

PASTRY WITH GROUND BEEF

Ingredients

- 1 egg
- 1 cup of milk
- ½ a cup of oil
- 1 tablespoon of salt
- 1 teaspoon of baking powder
- Flour (as needed)
- 1 cup of starch

PASTRY FILLER

- 150 grams of ground beef
- 2 onions
- 2 long green peppers
- 2 tablespoons of oil
- 1 small tomato
- 1 bunch of parsley
- Salt
- Black pepper

FOR THE TOP OF THE PASTRY

- 1 cup of oil
- 1 teaspoon of black cumin

Directions

1. Mix together 1 egg, 1 cup of milk, half a cup of oil, salt and baking powder in a pot. Add in sieved flour and mix until the dough is fairly tough. Divide into 24 pieces. Cover and let rest for a while.
2. Dredge each piece of dough in starch. Roll out until each piece is 12-15 cm in diameter. Dredge with starch again, and pile into two groups of 12.
3. Roll out each pile until the dough is 30-35 cm in diameter. Lay the first pile onto a greased tray. Place ground beef filling over (see direction 5) and cover with the second layer of dough. Press with a spoon and then slice as desired.
4. Heat 1 cup of oil, and pour over the pastry by the spoonful. Sprinkle black cumin on top. Cook in an oven until it turns pink.
5. PREPARATION OF THE GROUND BEEF FILLING: Sauté diced onions, green peppers, and parsley stalks with 2 tablespoons of oil until they turn yellow. Add in ground beef, and fry together until cooked.
6. Grate the tomato, and add to the meat. Remove from heat once all the water is absorbed. Add in salt, black pepper and diced parsley leaves.

PASHA PASTRY WITH GROUND BEEF

Ingredients

FOR THE DOUGH
- 3 eggs
- 2 teaspoons of salt
- 1/12 a cup of water
- Flour (as needed)

FOR THE GROUND BEEF FILLING
- ½ a kg of lean ground beef
- ½ a bunch of parsley
- 1/3 a cup of almonds (soaked in hot water and peeled)
- 1 teaspoon of salt
- ½ a teaspoon of black pepper

FOR THE TOP AND FILLING
- 2 cups of yogurt (stir well)
- ½ cup of melted butter
- 1 teaspoon of dried red pepper
- 1,5 cups of oil (for frying)

Directions

1. Mix together 3 eggs and 2 teaspoons of salt in a pot by hand. Add in 1/12 a cup of water and stir. Add in flour, and knead together until the dough is soft. Divide into 6 pieces. Cover and let rest for 15-20 minutes.
2. Fry ground beef with 2 tablespoons of oil. Add in almonds (with skins removed), and fry for 5 minutes. Add in salt and black pepper and remove from heat. Divide the mixture in half.
3. Roll out the dough until each piece is 1 mm thick. Fry in a big pan or tray with oil, then dip into hot water and remove immediately. Layer 3 pieces of dough on top of each other, pouring melted butter with dried red pepper in between each piece. Put half of the ground beef over the layers, and pour 1 cup of yogurt on top. Pour melted butter with dried red pepper over everything.
4. Oil the other 3 pieces of dough and put them over the filling, making a total of 6 layers of borek.
5. Put the remaining ground beef mixture on top, and spread yogurt over it. Lastly, pour melted butter with dried red pepper on top and serve.

SAVOURY BUN PASTRY WITH LEEKS

Ingredients

FOR THE DOUGH

- 4 cups of flour
- 1 egg (egg white for the dough, yolk for the top)
- 3 tablespoons of yogurt
- 3 tablespoons of oil
- 1 teaspoon of salt (for the top)
- 1 teaspoon of black cumin

FOR THE LEEK FILLING

- 5-6 leeks
- 1 bunch of parsley
- 2 onions
- 2-3 long green peppers
- 1 teaspoon of salt
- 1 teaspoon of black pepper
- 3 tablespoons of oil

FOR THE OILING

- ½ a package of margarine (125 g)
- 5 tablespoons of oil

Directions

1. Sieve flour into a pot, leaving a hole in the middle, and add in egg white, yogurt, oil, salt and a cup of water. Mix together and knead into dough. Divide into 12 pieces. Cover and let rest for a while.
2. Mix soft margarine with 4 tablespoons of oil until it turns white and has a creamy consistency.
3. Wash and peel leeks. Dice them with the onions, green peppers and parsley stalks. Sauté vegetables in 3 tablespoons of oil, until they are soft and the water is absorbed. Remove from heat and add in salt, black pepper and diced parsley leaves.
4. Roll out dough until it is 15-20 cm in diameter. Separate into 2 groups of 6 pieces and spread the oil and margarine mixture over them. Pile each piece on top of each other, leaving the top piece unoiled. Cover and refrigerate for a while.
5. Flour the dough and lay one pile on the tray. Put the leek filling over it. Cover with the other half of the dough, press lightly, and slice as desired.
6. Mix egg yolk with 1 tablespoon of oil and half a tablespoon of milk. Pour mixture on top of the borek and sprinkle on black cumin. Cook in a hot oven.

KETE (From Erzincan)

Ingredients

- ½ a liter of milk
- ½ a cup of oil
- 1 egg (egg white for the dough, and yolk for the top)
- ⅔ a tablespoon of yeast
- ⅓ a tablespoon of sugar
- ⅓ a tablespoon of black cumin
- Flour (as needed)

FOR KETE FILLING

- ½ a package of margarine (125 g)
- 2 ½ cups of flour

Directions

1. Dissolve the sugar and yeast with tepid milk in a pot. Add in half a cup of oil, egg white, salt and flour and mix until the dough is soft but not sticky. Cover and set in a warm place until the dough has risen.
2. PREPARATION OF THE KETE FILLING: Blend together half a package of margarine with 2 ½ cups of flour in a pot.
3. Divide risen dough into 2 egg-sized pieces. Divide Kete filling into the same quantity.
4. Flour the dough and roll out until it is 3 mm thick. Place the kete filling on the edge of the dough and twist it together to form it into a bun.
5. Set into a greased tray. Mix egg yolk with half a tablespoon of oil and a few drops of milk. Spread over the dough, and sprinkle black cumin on top.
6. Put into a warm oven and cook slowly, without drying out the bread. Remove from the oven, let cool, and cover.

LEAF DOUGH VARIATION

Ingredients

- 4 ½ cups of flour (and extra for kneading)
- 1 large package of margarine (250 g)
- 3 tablespoons of oil
- 3 tablespoons of yogurt
- 1 tablespoon of vinegar
- 1 teaspoon of salt
- ½ a cup of water

Directions

1. Sieve flour into a pot, leaving a hole in the middle. Add in oil, yogurt, vinegar and salt, and mix together. Add in ½ a cup of water and mix until the dough is soft. Knead, cover and let rest for 10-15 minutes.
2. Flour the dough and roll out into large pieces, 25-30 cm in diameter, with the thickness larger in the centre and thinner around the edges.
3. Soften margarine, put into the center of the dough, and wrap up like a bundle. Let rest for 10 minutes while covered.
4. Flour the dough and roll it out until it is 25-30 cm in diameter. Fold up the edges, leaving an inch-wide space in the middle, and fold it together like a book into the flour. Cover and refrigerate for 15-20 minutes.
5. Flour, roll out and fold two more times, waiting 15-20 minutes after each time.
6. Lastly, flour and roll out the dough again until it is ½ a cm thick.
7. This dough can be used for a variety of pastries.

LEAF DOUGH

Ingredients

- 3 ½ cups of high quality flour
- 1 large package of margarine (250 g)
- 1 teaspoon of salt
- 1 tablespoon of vinegar or lemon juice
- ½ a cup of water

Directions

1. Sieve flour into a pot, leaving a hole in the middle. Add in salt, vinegar, and water, and knead into dough. On a table, spread into a long, thin piece, and fold in three. Repeat this a few times, then cover and let rest for 10 minutes.
2. Roll out dough until it is 25 cm in diameter. Put softened margarine in the middle, and roll up like a bundle. Cover and let rest for 10 minutes.
3. Flour both sides of the dough and roll out until it is ½ a cm thick. Fold in three, cover and let rest for 15-20 minutes.
4. Roll out the dough again lengthwise, and fold into four. Let rest for 15-20 minutes.
5. Again, fold the dough into threes and fours, two times each, every 15-20 minutes.
6. Lastly, roll the dough out until it is ½ a cm thick.
7. This dough can be used for a variety of buns and pastries.

DILBER PASTRY WITH CHEESE MADE WITH LEAF DOUGH

Ingredients

- 1 portion of leaf dough (page 239-240-241)
- ½ a portion of white cheese
- ½ a bunch of parsley
- ½ a bunch of dill
- 1 egg (egg white for the cheese, yolk for the top)
- 1 tablespoon of oil
- 1 teaspoon of black cumin

Directions

1. Grate the cheese, and mix with diced parsley (with stalks), dill, and egg yolk.
2. Roll out the leaf dough until it is ½ a cm thick. Cut into 8 x 10 cm rectangles.
3. Place an even amount of the cheese mixture on the edge of each dough piece, and fold in half like a book.
4. Spread 1 tablespoon of oil and half a tablespoon of oil and egg yolk mixture on top of the dough, and then sprinkle black cumin on top.
5. Cook in a preheated oven for 20-25 minutes without opening the oven door.

CUBUK PASTRY

Ingredients

- 1 portion of leaf dough (page 239-241)
- 1 cup of grated yellow cheese
- 1 egg yolk
- ½ a tablespoon of oil (for spreading on the upper part)

Directions

1. Roll out the leaf dough until it is 3 mm thick.
2. Put grated yellow cheese onto half of the dough. Fold the other part over and press until the dough is 4 mm thick.
3. Cut the dough into pieces 2 cm wide by 10-12 cm long, and place onto a tray.
4. Mix together egg yolk, oil and half a tablespoon of milk together. Spread mixture on top of the dough, and cook in a preheated oven for 20-25 minutes without opening the door.

TALAS PASTRY WITH LEAF DOUGH

Ingredients

- 1 portion of leaf dough (page 239-241)
- ½ a kg of small cubed mutton
- 6 onions
- 2 long green peppers
- 2 tablespoons of oil
- 1 tomato or a ½ a tablespoon of tomato paste
- 1 egg yolk
- ½ a tablespoon of oil (for spreading on the upper part)
- Salt
- Black pepper

Directions

1. Sauté meat cubes with one chopped onion and 2 tablespoons of oil. Add in grated tomato or tomato paste and stir occasionally. Add in 1 cup of water. Chop the other 5 onions and add into the meat. Cook on a low heat until the meat and onion soften and the water evaporates. Add in salt and black pepper, and let cool.
2. Roll out the leaf dough until it is 4 mm thin, and cut into 10-12 cm rectangles.
3. Place the meat mixture onto the dough pieces, and wrap up like a bundle. Set onto a tray, edges facing down.
4. Mix together the egg yolk, oil and half a tablespoon of milk together. Spread the mixture over the dough, and cook in a preheated oven for 25-30 minutes without opening the door.

SARIYER PASTRY

Ingredients

- 5 cups of flour (½ a cup for flouring the dough)
- 200 g of margarine
- 7 tablespoons of oil (3 tablespoons for the dough)
- 3 tablespoons of yogurt
- 1 tablespoon of vinegar
- 1 egg (egg white for the cheese, and yolk for the top part)
- 1 teaspoon of salt
- ½ a portion of white cheese
- ½ a bunch of parsley
- ½ a bunch of dill

Directions

1. Sieve flour into a pot, leaving a hole in the middle. Add in yogurt, vinegar, 3 tablespoons of oil, salt and ¾ cup of water. Mix until the dough is soft and knead. Divide into 16 pieces, cover and let rest for a while.
2. Soften the margarine and beat until it is white and creamy.
3. Grate the cheese. Wash and dice the parsley and dill, including the stalks. Mix cheese, parsley, dill and egg white together, and divide mixture into 16 parts.
4. Roll out dough until each is 12-15 cm in diameter. Grease the dough with the margarine and fold it together like a bundle. Cover and refrigerate.
5. Once the margarine has hardened, remove the dough from the refrigerator and roll out each piece. Grease the dough and put the cheese mixture in the middle. Bring the edges of the dough together, until the cheese is covered. Lightly roll the dough until it is 1 ½ - 2 inches in width. Place on a tray with the folded part facing down.
6. Spread a mixture of the yolk, oil, and ½ a tablespoon of the milk over the dough and cook in a preheated oven.

AFYON CURL WITH GREEN LENTILS

Ingredients

FOR DOUGH

- 5 cups of flour
- 200 g of margarine
- 7 tablespoons of oil (3 tbsp for dough)
- 3 tablespoons of yogurt
- 1 tablespoon of vinegar
- 2 teaspoons of salt
- 2 eggs (1 egg and egg white for the dough, and one egg yolk for the top)

FOR LENTIL FILLING

- 1 cup of green lentils
- 3 onions
- 3 tablespoons of oil
- 1-2 long green peppers
- Parsley stalks

Directions

1. Wash and soak the lentils overnight.
2. Chop onions, peppers, and parsley stalks and sauté with 3 tablespoons of oil. Add in sieved lentils and 1 ½ cups of water and cook until the water evaporates. Add in salt and black pepper.
3. Soften margarine and stir in 4 tablespoons of oil.
4. Sieve flour into a pot, leaving a hole in the middle. Add in 3 tablespoons of oil, yogurt, vinegar, 1 egg, 1 egg white and salt, and mix together. Add in ¾ of a cup of water and mix until the dough is soft. Divide in half, cover and let rest for 15 minutes.
5. Roll out the dough until it is 35-40 cm in diameter. Grease both sides of the dough, and fold each piece together like a bundle. Refrigerate until the margarine hardens.
6. Roll out one piece of dough again until it is 40 cm in diameter. Place the second bundle on top and fold the rolled out dough over it into a bundle. Refrigerate for 20 minutes to let settle.
7. Flour the dough and roll out until it is 40 cm wide by 65 cm long. Cut into 25 pieces, each 9 by 13 cm in length.
8. Put lentil mixture onto each piece of dough and fold into three. Set each piece onto a tray. Mix together egg yolk, ½ a tablespoon of oil, and a few drops of milk together and spread over the dough. If desired, sprinkle black cumin over the dough and cook in an oven.

RUSSIAN PASTRY

Ingredients

- 1 cup of milk
- 1 cup of water
- 2/3 a tablespoon of yeast
- 1/3 a tablespoon of sugar
- 5 tablespoons of oil
- 1/3 a tablespoon of salt
- Flour (as needed)
- 2 cups of oil (for frying)

FOR FILLING

- 250 g of ground beef
- 2 onions
- 1 long green pepper
- ½ a bunch of parsley
- Salt
- Black pepper
- 2 tablespoons of oil

Directions

1. Dissolve sugar and yeast in tepid milk. Add in 1 cup of tepid water, 5 tablespoons of oil and salt and stir together.
2. Add in flour until the dough is soft, but not sticky. Leave covered in a warm place for the dough to rise.
3. While the dough is rising, sauté chopped onions and green pepper in oil until they turn yellow. Add in ground beef and stir until the stock of the meat evaporates. Add in salt, black pepper, ad diced parsley (with stems).
4. Once the dough has risen to twice its size, knead again and divide into egg-sized pieces. (Divide the meat filling into the same amount of portions.)
5. Spread the dough out with your palms, and put some of the meat filling into each piece. Fold up the pieces and shape them into eggs. Cover dough with a cloth, and wait for them to rise more.
6. Heat oil in a small pot, and put dough pieces in. Fry while shaking the pot lightly.
7. Remove onto paper towels to absorb excess oil.

ENTEKKE PASTRY

Ingredients

- 1 cup of water
- ⅓ a cup of milk
- ⅓ a tablespoon of dry yeast
- ⅓ a tablespoon of sugar
- 1 tablespoon of yogurt
- 1 egg
- 1 teaspoon of salt
- 1 ½ cups of oil (for frying)
- Flour (as needed)

FOR FILLING:

- 250 g of ground beef
- 2 tablespoons of oil
- 2 onions
- 1 long green pepper
- ½ a bunch of parsley
- Salt
- Black pepper

Directions

1. Add ⅓ cup of milk to 1 cup of water and heat slowly. Add in yeast and sugar and stir lightly to dissolve.
2. Mix in 1 egg, 1 tablespoon of yogurt and salt. Add in flour until the dough is soft.
3. Cover dough and let rest in a warm place until it rises to twice its size.
4. While the dough is rising, sauté chopped onions and green pepper in oil. Add in ground beef and continue to sauté. Add in salt, black pepper and diced parsley (with stems).
5. Knead risen dough and divide into egg-sized pieces. (Divide the meat filling into the same amount of portions).
6. Flour and spread the dough in your palms. Put meat filling into each piece, and fold together, pressing the edges. Cover dough with a cloth and let rise again.
7. Fry dough in a pot with hot oil, shaking occasionally. Remove onto a paper towel to absorb excess oil.

Note: *If desired, replace ground beef with a grated cheese and diced parsley mixture.*

CIG PASTRY (From Eskisehir)

Ingredients

- 1 cup of water
- ½ a cup of milk
- 2 tablespoons of oil
- 2 teaspoons of salt
- Flour (as needed)
- 1 ½ cups of oil (for frying)

FOR GROUND BEEF FILLING:

- 250 g of ground beef
- 2 onions
- 1-2 long green peppers
- 1 small tomato
- 1 egg
- ½ a bunch of parsley
- Salt
- Black pepper

Directions

1. Mix ground beef with diced onions, peppers, parsley, grated tomato, 1 egg, salt and black pepper.
2. Pour milk, water, oil and salt into a pot and mix together. Add in flour until the dough is soft. Knead, cover and let rest.
3. Divide dough into egg sized pieces. (Divide the meat filling into the same amount of portions). Roll out the dough until it is 2-3 mm thick. Put the meat filling onto half of the dough, spread, and then cover with the other half of the dough, pressing the edges together.
4. Heat oil in a small pot, and fry the dough. Remove onto paper towels.
5. To keep the borek soft, place it in a pot and cover until serving.

PANCAKES

Ingredients

- ½ a cup of milk
- 1 cup of water
- 1 teaspoon of salt
- Flour (as needed)

FOR OILING:

- 125 g of margarine
- 5 tablespoons of oil

Directions

1. Mix together milk, water and salt in a pot. Add in sieved flour until the dough is soft. Knead, cover and let sit for 10-15 minutes.
2. Roll out the dough and divide into 16 pieces. Flour each piece and roll out to 15 cm in diameter.
3. Soften margarine, and mix with oil until it is whitish.
4. Grease the rolled dough pieces with the oil mixture, and pile them into 4 groups, with 4 stacks in each group, leaving the top piece ungreased. Cover and refrigerate for 15-20 minutes.
5. Roll out each group of dough and oil the top. Fold the dough from one side into a 2 inch width. Then cut the dough into four pieces.
6. Spread each piece out until it is 15 square cm and fry both sides in a lightly oiled pan.
7. Pile up the dough to keep them soft.

AKITMA (From Edirne)

Ingredients

- 1 cup of milk
- 1 cup of water
- 2 tablespoons of dry yeast
- 1 tablespoon of sugar
- 1 ½ teaspoons of salt
- Flour (as needed)
- 125 g of margarine
- 1 egg (for the pan)

Directions

1. Pour milk and water in a pot. Heat lightly, add in yeast and sugar, gently stirring until it dissolves.
2. Add in sieved flour and salt, and mix until the dough has a consistency like whisked yogurt.
3. Let the dough rise in a warm place until it doubles in size.
4. Preheat an earthenware cooker. Spread an egg yolk in the cooker.
5. Pour the risen dough into the cooker with a cup, ⅔ a cup at a time. Spread the dough out until it is 10-12 cm in diameter, using the bottom of the cup.
6. Cook both sides of the dough. Remove from the cooker and oil. Pile the bread on top of each other to keep them soft. Cover once cooled.

BREAD PASTRY WITH SAUSAGE

Ingredients

- 3 eggs
- 1 slice of toasted bread (without crusts)
- 10 peeled sausages
- ½ a cup of oil
- 2 slices of yellow cheese
- 1 bunch of chopped dill
- 2 onions
- 1 can of corn
- 1 small package of cream (without sugar)
- 3 tablespoons of breadcrumbs

Directions

1. Mix with blender 2 eggs, toast bread, sausages, oil, yellow cheese and dill.
2. Fry lightly with 2 tbsp of oil large chopped onion. Add this with sieved canned corn into the blended mixture and stir.
3. Oil a tray and flour with dried bread flour. Pour the mixture and smooth.
4. Mix an egg with a fork. Add a small package of cream and a few tbsp of milk and make a thinner mixture. Pour the mixture over
5. Cook in a medium heated oven and serve hot.

güneşler açar,
İstediği kadar geç gelsin,
onsuz ev, ev değil,
Elimde değil, seviyorum.
OSCAR HAMMERSTEIN

SPINACH PASTRY WITH YUFKA

Ingredients

- 1 kg of spinach leaves (stalks and roots can be used in a rice dish)
- 3 tablespoons of oil (for frying the spinach)
- 2 onions
- 2 long green peppers
- ½ a bunch of parsley
- 4 pieces of yufka
- ⅚ a cup of oil (for oiling the yufka)
- 1 egg yolk
- 1 tablespoon of oil (for the top)
- ½ a teaspoon of salt
- ½ a teaspoon of black pepper
- 1 teaspoon of black cumin

Directions

1. Wash and chop the spinach leaves.
2. Sauté diced onions, green peppers and parsley stems with 3 tablespoons of oil. Add in spinach leaves and fry while stirring. Add in salt, black pepper and diced parsley leaves. Divide mixture into 16 portions.
3. Mix half a cup of oil with half a cup of water in a cup and mix together. Spread oil mixture over each yufka piece and fold it together like a bundle. While folding, oil in between the layers.
4. Cut each folded yufka into four pieces (making 16 total pieces). Put the spinach filling in the middle of each piece and bring the four edges of the yufka together. Place into a tray upside down, folded edges underneath.
5. Spread oil and yolk mixture over the dough, and sprinkle black cumin on top.
6. Cook in an oven and serve hot.

Note: *If desired, add sausage or strips of cheese into the borek.*

POT PASTRY WITH READY-TO-USE YUFKA

Ingredients

- 4 pieces of yufka
- 4 eggs
- 5/6 a cup of oil
- 1 cup of milk
- 1 cup of grated white cheese
- 1 cup of grated yellow cheese
- ½ a bunch of parsley
- ½ a bunch of dill
- 1 teaspoon of black pepper
- 1 teaspoon of dried red pepper

Directions

1. Grease a pot 25-30 cm in diameter. Put one piece of yufka in the pot, letting it hang over the edge.
2. Tear up the other 3 pieces of yufka into small pieces.
3. Mix the yufka with grated white and yellow cheese, diced parsley and dill, black pepper and dried red pepper.
4. Set the mixture into the pot, layer by layer.
5. Whisk eggs in a bowl. Add in oil and milk, sparing 5 tablespoons for spreading on the top. Pour the whisked eggs over the yufka by the spoonful.
6. Fold the hanging part of the yufka over the top. Spread the saved 5 tablespoons of egg mixture over the top.
7. Cook yufka on a medium heat for a long time, until the inside is cooked.
8. Once cooked, remove onto a serving plate upside down and slice.

ZUCCHINI PASTRY WITH YUFKA

Ingredients

- 4 pieces of yufka
- 6 medium zucchinis
- 3-4 onions
- 2 long green peppers
- 1 bunch of dill
- 1 ½ cups of milk
- ¾ cups of oil
- Salt
- Black pepper

Directions

1. Wash zucchinis, green peppers and dill. Grate the unpeeled zucchinis, using the largest grate size.
2. Mix milk and oil together. Cut 3 pieces of yufka to fit the tray.
3. Set the 4th piece of yufka on the tray, with the sides hanging over. Pour some of the milk and oil mixture over it. Put a trimmed yufka piece on top. Spread some of the milk and oil mixture on top, and add on zucchinis. Sprinkle over with salt and black pepper.
4. Repeat this, layering the other yufka pieces, milk-oil mixture, salt, and black pepper over each other. Fold the hanging edges on top, making 6 layers of borek.
5. Spread the milk and oil mixture on top. Cook slowly in the oven, to allow the zucchinis to cook properly.
6. When serving, place upside down in a serving dish and slice.

CHINESE PASTRY WITH VEGETABLES AND YUFKA

Ingredients

- 6 pieces of yufka
- 3 eggs
- 1 cup of milk
- ¼ a cup of melted margarine
- ¼ a cup of oil
- 1 teaspoon of baking powder

FOR FILLING:

- 1 onion
- 5/6 a cup of lentils
- 2 medium carrots (diced and lightly boiled)
- 1 medium zucchini (diced)
- 200 g of mushroom (sliced thin, lengthwise)
- 3 scallions (diced)
- 1 teaspoon of salt
- 1 teaspoon of black pepper

FOR TOP:

- 1 cup of bread crumbs

Directions

1. PREPARATION OF FILLING: Clean and soak the lentils overnight. Boil and sieve them the following day.
2. Sauté chopped onions with 4 tablespoons of oil. Add in washed and sliced mushrooms, carrots, and zucchini, stirring occasionally. Add in sieved lentils and continue frying. Remove from the heat and add in scallions, salt and black pepper. Divide the mixture into 24 pieces.
3. In a large bowl, mix together eggs, milk, melted margarine, oil, and baking powder.
4. Spread out one piece of yufka, and spread some of the egg and milk mixture on top. Put another piece of yufka on top, and again spread with the egg and milk mixture. Cut the yufka into 8 pieces. Put the filling on one edge, and bring two sides of the yufka together, rolling loosely into 1 inch wide pieces.
5. Prepare the other yufkas in the same way. Cover the 24 pieces with the remaining oil, milk and egg mixture and top with bread crumbs. Set them onto a tray and fry in the oven. Serve hot.

SAUSAGE PASTRY WITH YUFKA

Ingredients

- 3 pieces of yufka
- 6 tablespoons of oil
- 2 tablespoons of yogurt
- 2 eggs (1 egg yolk for the top)
- 6 sausages
- 2 long green peppers
- 1 small tomato
- 1 teaspoon of thyme
- ½ a teaspoon of salt
- ½ a teaspoon of black pepper

Directions

1. Wash sausages and pierce them with a fork. Boil them on low heat.
2. Dice the boiled sausages, green peppers, and tomato and mix in thyme, salt and black pepper.
3. In a bowl, mix the oil, yogurt and egg together.
4. Spread out one piece of yufka, and pour ⅓ of the egg mixture over it. Repeat this with rest of the yufka, spreading the egg mixture in between each layer, and on top.
5. First divide the yufka into four pieces, and then divide each piece into 3, totaling 12 pieces.
6. Put the sausage filling on the edge of each piece and loosely roll it together.
7. Set pieces onto a tray, spread a mixture of egg yolk and half a tablespoon of oil over the top, and cook in the oven. If desired, sprinkle with black cumin.

EASY-TO-MAKE STUFFED BALLS WITH YUFKA

Ingredients

- 500 g of lean ground beef
- 3-4 onions
- 6 yufkas
- 3 eggs (egg whites for yufka layers and yolks for frying)
- 1 cup of fine bulgur (cooked with ½ a cup of hot water)
- 1 cup of grated carrots
- ½ a cup of diced walnuts
- 1 cup of bread crumbs
- 2 cups of oil for frying (4 tablespoons for the filling)
- Salt
- Black pepper

Directions

1. Sauté chopped onions with 4 tablespoons of oil in a pot until they turn light yellow. Add in ground beef and fry while stirring until the water evaporates. Add in grated carrots, cook for 4-5 minutes, and remove from heat. Add in cooked bulgur, walnuts, salt and black pepper. Divide the mixture into 24 portions.
2. Cut each piece of yufka into 8 pieces (totaling 48 pieces). Spread egg white mixture over one piece, and stick a second piece on top, putting the meat mixture in the middle. Loosely roll yufka into 1 inch wide pieces, totaling 24 pieces.
3. Whisk the remaining egg whites with the egg yolks. Dredge each yufka piece in the egg, and then the bread crumbs. Fry in a small, deep pot with hot oil until they turn pink. Serve hot.

POTATO PASTRY WITH YUFKA

Ingredients

- 3 pieces of yufka
- 6 tablespoons of oil
- ½ a cup of grated white cheese
- 3 eggs (one egg yolk will be for the top)
- 6 medium potatoes
- 1 cup of milk
- 1 teaspoon of salt
- 1 teaspoon of black pepper
- 1 teaspoon of black cumin

Directions

1. Boil potatoes, then peel and grate them. Mix together with oil, cheese, egg, milk, salt, and black pepper, and divide the mixture into three portions.
2. Roll out one piece of yufka. Spread ⅓ of the potato mixture onto the dough. Add the other yufka pieces on top, layering the potato mixture in between each one, as well as on the top.
3. Cut the yufka into 4 pieces, and then cut each piece into 4 more pieces, making 16 total pieces.
4. Loosely roll each piece together, starting at a wide edge.
5. If cooking immediately, set the pastry onto a tray. Spread a mixture of egg yolk and 1 tablespoon of oil over the pastry. Sprinkle black cumin on top and cook in an oven.
6. If cooking later, refrigerate while covered. When ready to cook, set the pastry onto a tray, spread over with a mixture of egg yolk and 1 tablespoon of oil. Sprinkle black cumin on top and cook in an oven.

Note: *If desired, egg yolk and oil mixture can be kept in a covered container, frozen, and used when needed.*

BAZLAMA

Ingredients

- 2 cups of water
- 1 tablespoon of dry yeast
- 2/3 a tablespoon of sugar
- 2 teaspoons of salt
- Flour (as needed)

Directions

1. Dissolve yeast and sugar in a pot with tepid water. Add in flour and salt until the dough is soft, but not sticky.
2. Let the dough rise in a warm place until it is twice its size.
3. Knead the dough again, and divide into egg-sized pieces.
4. Lightly flour each piece and roll out until they are 1 cm thick. Again let the dough rise while covered.
5. Grease a metal, earthenware or Teflon cooker, and heat. Put the dough in one by one, and close the lid. Turn once one side is cooked.
6. Remove from the cooker once both sides are pink. The Bazlama pastry should be 1 ½ - 2 cm thicker than before.

Note: *Bazlama is also referred to as Tapil in Eskişehir, Bezdirme in Aydın, Bazdirma in Isparta and Denizli, and Bazlamac in Middle Anatolia.*

KARAKOY PASTRY WITH MEAT AND CHEESE FILLING

Ingredients

- 1 cup of milk and yogurt mixture
- ⅔ a tablespoon of yeast
- ⅓ a tablespoon of sugar
- 1 ½ cups of oil
- 1 egg (egg white for the dough and yolk for the top)
- Flour (as needed)
- ½ a portion of white cheese
- ½ a bunch of parsley
- ½ a bunch of dill
- 1 teaspoon of black cumin

Directions

1. Dissolve the yeast and sugar with milk in a pot. Add in oil, and salt, and whisk together. Add in flour until the dough is soft but not sticky. Let the dough rise in a warm place until it is twice its size.
2. Mix together grated cheese, washed and diced parsley and dill.
3. Knead the risen dough and divide into egg-sized pieces.
4. Divide the cheese mixture into the same number of pieces as the dough. Spread out the dough with your palms, and put the filling in the middle, closing the dough around it. Set the dough onto an oiled tray.
5. After the dough has risen slightly more, spread a mixture of egg yolk and a few teaspoons of milk over the pastry. Sprinkle black cumin on top and cook in a preheated oven.

SWEET BUNS WITH SESAME OIL AND YUFKA

Ingredients

- 3 pieces of yufka
- 9 tablespoons of sesame oil
- 9 tablespoons of sugar
- FOR TOP:
- 1 egg yolk
- ½ a tablespoon of oil
- 2 tablespoons of sesame oil

Directions

1. Roll out one piece of yufka. Pour 2 tablespoons of sesame oil on top. Then sprinkle 2 tablespoons of sugar on top, and fold the yufka in half.
2. Pour 1 tablespoon of sesame oil over the folded yufka, and sprinkle 1 tablespoon of sugar on top.
3. Fold the yufka in 5 cm from the edges and smooth out. Roll the dough starting from the rounded side, and cut into 4-5 slices, smooth side down.
4. Prepare the other two yufkas the same way, and set them all on a tray with aluminum foil.
5. Spread a mixture of egg yolk, oil and a few teaspoons of milk on the pastry, and sprinkle sesame oil on top. Cook in an oven.
6. If desired, sprinkle powdered sugar over the pastry once it cools.

ANATOLIAN BUNS WITH SESAME OIL (From Eskişehir)

Ingredients

FOR DOUGH:

- 1 cup of yogurt
- 1 cup of water
- 2 tablespoons of yeast
- 2 tablespoons of sugar
- 2 eggs (1 for dough and 1 for top)
- 2 teaspoons of salt
- Flour (as needed for soft dough)
- Crushed walnuts

FOR TOP:

- ½ a cup of sesame oil
- 1 cup of oil
- 1 teaspoon of allspice

Directions

1. Dissolve sugar and yeast in tepid water. Mix in yogurt, one egg and salt. Add in flour until the dough is soft. Let the dough rise in a warm place until it is twice its size.
2. Cut the dough in half. Flour one half, and spread out using palms. Dredge with a mixture of sesame oil and oil, and fold over like a bundle. Let rest while covered.
3. Roll out the dough again, and dredge with sesame oil and oil mixture. Sprinkle crushed walnuts and allspice on top. Roll up in 1 inch wide increments from the edge.
4. Twist one edge of the dough left, in the opposite direction of the rolled dough.
5. Starting from one edge of the dough, wrap it around into a circle bun. Hide the last edge underneath. Prepare the second half of the dough in the same way.
6. Place the dough onto an oiled tray and let rise again for half an hour.
7. Spread the one yolk and oil mixture over the pastry and cook in a preheated oven.

Note: *If desired, sprinkle sesame and black cumin on top.*

POPPY BUNS (From Amasya-Merzifon)

Ingredients

- 1 cup of milk
- 1 cup of water
- 2/3 a tablespoon of yeast
- 2/3 a tablespoon of sugar
- 1 egg (egg white for the dough and yolk for the top)
- 1 cup of poppy seeds
- 1 cup of oil
- 1 cup of crushed walnuts
- 2 teaspoons of salt

Directions

1. Fry poppy seeds in a pot on low heat while stirring. Let cool, then pulverize in a mortar or blend in a mixer. Then mix with oil.
2. Heat water in a pot with milk, add in sugar and yeast, and let dissolve.
3. Add in an egg white, salt and sieved flour, and mix together until the dough is soft but not sticky. Knead and let the dough rise in a warm place until it is twice its size.
4. Divide the dough into 6 pieces. Roll 3 of the pieces until they are 2-3 mm thick. Spread poppy and oil mixture, and crushed walnuts on each one and pile them on top of each other, spreading the poppy and oil mixture on top as well.
5. Cut the piled dough into 1 ½ inch strips. Twist each strip like a corkscrew by turning the edges on opposite sides. Set the twisted strips onto an oiled tray.
6. Prepare the other 3 dough pieces the same way, and set them onto a tray.
7. Spread an egg yolk, diluted with half a tablespoon of milk, over the dough. Cook slowly in an oven on low heat.

MRS. NIMET PASTRY (WITH GROUND BEEF)

Ingredients

FOR DOUGH

- 3 egg yolks
- ½ a cup of oil
- 2 tablespoons of lemon juice
- 2 teaspoons of salt
- 1-1 ½ cups of water
- 5-5 ½ cups of flour
- 1 package of margarine (250 g)

FOR GROUND BEEF:

- 250 g of ground beef
- 2 tablespoons of oil
- 2 onions
- 1 long green pepper
- ½ a bunch of parsley
- Salt
- Black pepper

Directions

1. Mix 3 eggs yolk, ½ a cup of oil, 2 tablespoons of lemon juice, and 2 teaspoons of salt together in a pot. Spare 2 tablespoons for spreading on the top.
2. Slowly add in water and flour until the dough is soft but not sticky. Knead the dough and divide into 6 pieces. Cover and let sit for a while.
3. Roll out each piece of dough, and spread margarine on top. Oil each layer and fold together like a bundle.
4. Cover and refrigerate until the margarine hardens.
5. Stack two bundles together, so that the 6 pieces become 3. Roll out until it is 2 cm thick. Cut into rectangular pieces, put ground beef mixture into each piece, and fold it in half.
6. Set dough onto a tray, and spread a leftover egg yolk mixture on top. Cook in a preheated oven.

   PREPARATION OF THE GROUND BEEF FILLING: Sauté diced onions, green pepper, and parsley stems with 2 tablespoons of oil. Add in ground beef and remove from heat once the water from the meat evaporates. Add in salt, black pepper, and parsley leaves.

TRAY BUNS WITH CHEESE

Ingredients

- 1 cup of milk
- 2 tablespoons of yeast
- ⅓ a tablespoon of sugar
- 3 ½ cups of flour
- 1 package of margarine (250 g)
- 2 eggs (1 for dough, 1 egg yolk for the top)
- ½ a portion of white cheese
- ½ a bunch of dill
- 1 teaspoon of salt
- 1 teaspoon of black cumin

Directions

1. Dissolve yeast and sugar in tepid milk in a pot.
2. Add in margarine, 1 egg, 1 egg yolk and salt and mix together.
3. Add in sieved flour until the dough is soft but not sticky. Cover and let the dough rise in a warm place until it is twice its size.
4. Knead the dough again. Put half of the dough in an oiled tray that is 25-30 cm in diameter and spread out by pressing with your hands.
5. Sprinkle grated cheese mixed with diced dill over the dough. Roll out the second half of the dough by hand, put cheese over the top and press down.
6. Spread a mixture of an egg yolk, half a tablespoon of oil, and a few teaspoons of milk over the pastry and sprinkle with black cumin. Cook in an oven at medium heat.
7. Once cooled, serve.

CRESCENT BUNS WITH POTATO AND SALT

Ingredients

- 3 cups of flour
- 3 medium potatoes (boiled and pureed)
- ½ a cup of oil
- 2 eggs (1 egg for dough, 1 egg yolk for the cheese and the top)
- ⅓ a cup of milk
- ⅔ a tablespoon of yeast
- ⅓ a tablespoon of sugar
- 2 teaspoons of salt
- ½ a portion of white cheese
- ½ a bunch of parsley

Directions

1. Warm milk in a pot, and dissolve yeast and sugar. Add in 1 egg, oil, potato purée and salt. Mix together and add in sieved flour. Cover and let the dough rise in a warm place until it is twice its size.
2. Knead again and divide into egg-size pieces. Roll out until it is 10 cm in diameter and add a mixture of cheese, parsley, and egg whites to the edge. Roll and twist into a crescent shape.
3. Set dough onto an oiled tray and spread a mixture of half a tablespoon of oil and egg yolk on top. Cook in an oven on medium heat.

PITA BREAD WITH CHEESE

Ingredients

- 1 cup of water
- 2 tablespoons of yeast
- ⅓ a tablespoon of sugar
- 1 cup of oil
- 1 small portion of white cheese
- 1 egg (egg white for cheese, egg yolk for the top)
- ½ a bunch of parsley
- ½ a bunch of dill
- 2 teaspoons of salt
- Flour (as needed)

Directions

1. Dissolve yeast and sugar in tepid milk.
2. Add in oil, salt, and flour, as necessary, until the dough is soft but not sticky.
3. Cover and let rise in a warm place until it is twice its size.
4. Knead dough again and divide into egg size pieces. Spread out the dough into an oval shape on a floured surface, and put a mixture of cheese, parsley, dill and an egg white onto each one.
5. Bring two edges of the dough together, closing the dough, but still being able to see the cheese inside. Set the dough on an oiled tray and let rise again in a warm place.
6. Spread a mixture of half a tablespoon of oil, a few teaspoons of milk and an egg yolk over the dough. Cook in an oven on medium heat, removing before it gets too dry.
7. Immediately after removing the dough from the oven, brush butter over the tops of the dough. Put the pastry in a pot with the lid spaced to keep it soft.

PITA BREAD WITH GROUND BEEF

Ingredients

FOR GROUND BEEF FILLING:

- 500 g of ground beef
- 5 tablespoons of oil
- 3-4 onions (500 g)
- 3 tomatoes (500 g)
- 4 long green peppers (2 for filling, 2 for garnishment)
- ½ a bunch of parsley leaves
- 1 teaspoon of salt
- 1 teaspoon of black pepper
- 1 teaspoon of dried red pepper

FOR DOUGH:

- ½ a cup of milk
- 1 cup of water
- 1 tablespoon of yeast
- ⅓ a tablespoon of sugar
- 2 teaspoons of salt
- 2 tablespoons of oil
- Flour (as needed)

Directions

1. Warm milk and water together in a pot, add in sugar and yeast and let dissolve. Add in 2 tablespoons of oil, salt and sieved flour and mix together until the dough is soft but not sticky. Knead until the dough as a homogeneous consistency.
2. Cover and let the dough rise in a warm place until it is twice its size.
3. Once the dough is raised, add in ground beef, chopped onions, green peppers, salt and black pepper and knead together. Add in grated tomatoes, oil and diced parsley leaves to make a more watery consistency.
4. Knead the dough again and let sit for 10 minutes. Flour the dough and roll out until it is 35-40 cm in diameter or larger than the tray. Set onto a greased tray with the ends rolled into a crust. Spread 2 tablespoon of oil over the dough and let it rise again in a warm place for half an hour.
5. Add the ground beef mixture onto the dough. Cut a long green pepper in half and add on top. Cook in a preheated oven, removing before it gets too dry.

Note: *Preparation for one serving.*

Flour the dough and roll out it as a big egg size. Add the ground beef mixture on to the dough. Put together the two heels of dough. Add a long green pepper on top. Put the tray and cook in an oven.

EASY-TO-MAKE PIZZA

Ingredients

FOR DOUGH:

- 2 ½ cups of flour
- ½ a cup of oil
- 1 egg
- 2 tablespoons of yogurt
- 1 teaspoon of baking powder
- 1 teaspoon of salt

FOR THE TOP:

- 1 small piece of sausage
- 2-3 long green peppers
- 1-2 small tomatoes
- 1 egg
- ½ a cup of milk
- 5-6 sprigs of parsley leaves

Directions

1. Mix 1 egg, yogurt, baking powder and salt together in a pot. Add in sieved flour and knead. Cover and let rest for a while.
2. Roll out the dough until it is 35-40 cm in diameter, or lager than the tray. Set the dough onto a greased tray, with the edges rolled into a crust.
3. Dice up the sausage, green pepper and parsley and spread it over the dough.
4. Whisk 1 egg with half a cup of milk. Pour over the pizza and cook in a preheated oven on medium heat.

PERFECT PIZZA

Ingredients

FOR THE DOUGH:

- 5 cups of flour
- 1 tablespoon of yeast
- $2/3$ a tablespoon of sugar
- 1 ½ cups of milk
- 1 egg
- 2 teaspoons of salt

FOR THE TOP:

- 10-12 sausages
- 2-3 green peppers
- $1/3$ a cup of oil
- 1 tablespoon of tomato paste
- 3 cloves of garlic
- 2 teaspoons of thyme
- 1 teaspoon of salt
- 1 teaspoon of black pepper
- 4-5 tablespoons of grated yellow cheese

Directions

1. Pierce the sausages with a fork, and boil them for 15-20 minutes. Dice the green peppers. Mix together the pulverized garlic, salt, black pepper, thyme, oil, and tomato paste (diluted with 3-4 tablespoons of water).
2. Warm the milk, add in the yeast and sugar and let them dissolve. Mix in oil, egg and salt. Add in sieved flour until the dough is soft but not sticky. Cover and let the dough rise in a warm place until it is twice its size.
3. Knead the dough again and roll it out until it is 35-40 cm diameter. Place it on an oiled tray the same size, and smooth it over. Spread oil over the dough and let rise for 15-20 minutes.
4. Spread the sauce mixture on top, sprinkle with grated cheese and cook in a preheated oven on medium heat.

VEGETABLE PIZZA

Ingredients

- 5 cups of flour
- 1 tablespoon of yeast
- 2/3 a tablespoon of sugar
- 1 ½ cups of milk
- ½ a cup of oil
- 1 egg
- 2 teaspoons of salt

FOR THE TOP:

- 200 g of mushrooms
- 3 zucchinis
- 20 black or green olives
- 5-6 scallions or 2 onions
- 4 green peppers
- 1 bunch of parsley leaves
- 5-6 slices of salami
- ⅓ a cup of oil
- 1 teaspoon of salt
- 1 teaspoon of black pepper
- 1 ½ cups of grated yellow cheese

Directions

1. PREPARATION OF THE TOPPINGS: Wash the vegetables. Cut the mushrooms, zucchinis and onions into thin slices. Mix together with chopped olives, parsley, salt, black pepper and oil.
2. Warm milk in a pot, add in sugar and yeast and let dissolve. Add in oil, egg, salt and sieved flour until the dough is soft but not sticky. Cover and let rise in a warm place until it is twice its size.
3. Knead the dough again and roll out until it is 35-40 cm in diameter. Set the dough onto a tray the same size, rolling the edges up into a crust. Spread oil over the dough and let rise for 15-20 minutes.
4. Put half of the grated yellow cheese and all of the vegetable mixture over the dough and spread out. Then sprinkle the other half of the cheese over the vegetables. Set quartered salami slices on top. Cook in a preheated oven on medium heat.

SOUFFLÉ WITH YUFKA (FAT-FREE)

Ingredients

- 2 pieces of yufka
- 3 cups of milk
- 3 eggs
- 4 tablespoons of grated white cheese
- 4 tablespoons of grated yellow cheese
- ½ a teaspoon of black pepper

Directions

1. Whisk the eggs in a bowl. Add in grated cheeses, black pepper and milk.
2. Cut the yufka into small pieces and mix it into the egg mixture.
3. Pour the mixture into an oven-safe glass tray, and refrigerate overnight. Cook in an oven and serve hot.

PASTRY WITH YOGURT

Ingredients

- 5 cups of flour
- 1 package of margarine (250 g) or 1 cup of oil
- 3 tablespoons of yogurt
- 3 eggs (1 egg white for the cheese, 1 egg yolk for the top)
- 1 teaspoon of baking powder
- 2 teaspoons of salt
- ½ a portion of white cheese
- ½ a bunch of parsley
- ½ a bunch of dill
- 1-2 teaspoons of black cumin

Directions

1. Sieve flour into a pot, making a hole in the middle. Put margarine, 2 eggs, yogurt, baking powder and salt in the middle and mix into dough. Knead, cover and let rest for 15-20 minutes.
2. Mix grated cheese, diced parsley, dill and one egg white together.
3. Divide the dough into large walnut size pieces, and divide the cheese mixture portions accordingly.
4. Roll out the dough with your palms, put the cheese filling inside, and close. Spread a mixture of one egg yolk, a few teaspoons of milk and half a tablespoon of oil over the dough, and sprinkle black cumin on top.
5. Set the dough onto a greased tray and cook in a preheated oven on medium heat.

BOREK PASTRY VARIATION

Ingredients

- 2 eggs (1 for dough, 1 egg white for the cheese and 1 yolk for the top)
- 1 cup of oil
- ½ a cup of yogurt
- 1 teaspoon of baking powder
- 1 teaspoon of salt
- Flour (as needed)
- ½ a portion of white cheese
- ½ a bunch of parsley
- ½ a bunch of dill
- 1 tablespoon of sesame
- 1 teaspoon of black cumin

Directions

1. Mix 1 egg, yogurt, oil, baking powder and salt together in a pot by hand.
2. Add in sieved flour until the dough is slightly tough. Divide into three pieces, cover and let rest for 15-20 minutes.
3. Grate the cheese. Add washed and chopped parsley, dill and 1 egg white to the cheese and mix together. Divide mixture into 24 pieces.
4. Roll out the dough until it is 3 mm thick and cut it into 8 pieces (totaling 24 pieces of dough).
5. Put the cheese mixture onto the larger part of the dough, and loosely roll together. Set on a greased tray, and spread a mixture of egg yolk, ½ a tablespoon of oil and a few teaspoons of milk over the dough. If desired, sprinkle sesame and black cumin over the pastry, and cook in a preheated oven on medium heat.

EASY-TO-MAKE PASTRY

Ingredients

- 2 cups of yogurt
- 3 eggs
- A small portion of cheese
- 2 teaspoons of baking powder
- 2 teaspoons of salt
- Flour (as needed)
- 1 ½ - 2 cups of oil (for frying)

Directions

1. Mix yogurt, egg, grated cheese, baking powder and salt together in a pot.
2. Add in flour until the dough is soft. Flour the dough and roll out until it is 1 cm thick. Cut into 1 ½ inch size squares.
3. Heat oil in a small pot, and place in dough pieces, leaving enough room for each. Fry while shaking, then remove onto a paper towel to remove any excess oil.

PUFF PASTRY

Ingredients

- 4 cups of flour
- 1 egg
- 2 tablespoons of yogurt
- 1 teaspoon of salt
- ½ a package of margarine (125 g)

CHEESE FILLING:

- 1 small portion of cheese
- 1 egg
- ½ a bunch of parsley
- ½ a bunch of dill
- 2 cups of oil (for frying)

Directions

1. Sieve flour in a pot, leaving a hole in the middle. Add 1 egg, yogurt, salt and half a cup of water to the middle of the pot, and knead into dough. Divide into 15 pieces, cover and let rest for a while.
2. Grate cheese, and mix with washed and chopped parsley, dill and 1 egg.
3. Soften the margarine and mix until creamy.
4. Flour and roll out the dough until it is 10-12 cm in diameter. Oil the dough, and pile them into 3 groups of 5. Do not oil the top piece, and refrigerate until the oil hardens.
5. Roll out the piled dough until it is 2-3 mm thick. Place the cheese mixture at the edge of the dough, leaving 1 ½ inch spaces in between each filling. Cover with dough, lightly pressing the empty spaces, and cut.
6. Heat oil in a small pot, and add in pastry, leaving enough room for each piece. Fry until they turn pink.
7. Remove with a sieved ladle onto paper towels to absorb any excess oil.

EASY-TO-MAKE PUFF PASTRY

Ingredients

- 1 egg
- 1/3 a cup of melted margarine
- 2/3 a cup of water
- 1/3 a cup of oil
- 1/3 a cup of vinegar
- 1 teaspoon of salt
- Flour (as needed)
- 1 portion of white cheese
- ½ a bunch of parsley
- ½ a bunch of dill
- 1 ½ cups of oil

Directions

1. Mix egg, water, oil, margarine, vinegar, and salt together in a pot. Add in flour until the dough is slightly tough. Divide into 40 pieces.
2. Grate the cheese and mix with washed and chopped parsley and dill. Divide into 40 portions.
3. Roll out the dough until it is 6-7 cm in diameter, fill with cheese and close, pressing the edges of the dough with your fingers.
4. Fry dough in hot oil and remove with a sieved ladle to drain any excess oil.

Note: *For a variation of the dough, add less salt and add in crushed walnut, sugar and cinnamon, then shape. After frying, cover with powdered sugar.*

BREAD WITH MILK

Ingredients

- 1 cup of milk
- 1 cup of water
- 1 tablespoon of yeast
- 2/3 a tablespoon of sugar
- 2 tablespoons of oil
- 2 teaspoons of salt
- Flour (as needed)
- 1 teaspoon of black cumin

Directions

1. Lightly heat milk and water in a pot, add in yeast and sugar and let dissolve.
2. Add in oil, salt and sieved flour until the dough is slightly tough, but not sticky.
3. Cover and let rise in a warm place until it is twice its size.
4. Knead again, and divide into 2 egg sized pieces. Shape into round or long pieces by hand. Set onto a greased tray, and let rise in a warm place again.
5. Spread milk over the dough and sprinkle on black cumin. Cook in a preheated oven on medium heat.
6. Remove from heat and place into a pot to keep the pastry soft. Cover with a paper towel and close the lid.

CORN BREAD

Ingredients

- 1 cup of milk
- 1 cup of flour
- 1 cup of corn flour
- ½ a cup of oil
- 1 teaspoon of baking powder
- 1 teaspoon of salt

Directions

1. Mix milk, oil, baking powder, salt, corn flour and flour together in a pot.
2. Grease a tray 25-30 cm in diameter. Place dough on the tray and spread it out. Cook in a preheated oven on medium heat.
3. Once cooked, remove and let cool before slicing.

VII

DESSERTS

LOR DESSERT (MADE WITH GOAT'S MILK CURD)

Ingredients

- 3 eggs
- ½ kg of goat's milk curd
- 1 cup of milk
- ½ a cup of semolina
- ½ a cup of flour
- 65 g of margarine
- 2 tablespoon of sugar
- ½ a lemon peel (grated)
- 1 package of baking powder

FOR SYRUP:

- 2 ½ cups of sugar
- ⅛ of a lemon

Directions

1. Boil 2 ½ cups of sugar with 3 cups of water in a pot. Squeeze a piece of lemon (⅛) into the pot and cover. Remove from heat after 10 minutes.
2. Grease a tray (25 cm in diameter) with soft margarine, and sprinkle 1 tablespoon of sugar over it.
3. Mix baking powder and flour together and add in sieved semolina.
4. Whisk together 3 eggs, grated lemon peel and a tablespoon of sugar together in a pot.
5. Add in goat's milk curd and mix. Then add in melted margarine, milk, and the semolina and flour mixture. Mix together and slowly pour onto the oiled tray.
6. Smooth out in the tray, leaving the edges higher, and cook in an oven on medium heat for 30-35 minutes.
7. Remove the tray from the oven and pour cold sauce over it with a ladle. Cover the tray to let the sauce absorb into the dessert.
8. Slice and serve once cooled.

FAT-FREE SWEET SEMOLINA PASTRY

Ingredients

- 6 eggs
- 1 cup and 2 tablespoons of semolina
- 1 cup of flour
- 4 ½ cups of sugar
- 1 lemon peel (grated)
- 2 tablespoons of lemon juice
- 1 teaspoon of baking powder
- ½ a package of vanilla

Directions

1. Melt 4 cups of sugar with 4 ½ cups of water in a pot, stirring occasionally. Bring to a boil, and then add in 1 tablespoon of lemon juice and half of the grated lemon peel. Boil for 10 more minutes and then remove from heat.
2. Separate the yolks and whites from the eggs. In a bowl, add in half a cup of sugar and the rest of the grated lemon peels to the egg yolks, and mix until the sugar dissolves.
3. Mix flour, baking powder and vanilla together and sieve. Add in semolina and mix with a spoon.
4. Grease a tray that is 25-30 cm wide in diameter.
5. Whisk egg whites in a pot, and add in yolk and sugar mixture, stirring occasionally.
6. Slowly add in flour and semolina mixture to the eggs, stirring occasionally. Add in lemon juice and mix.
7. Pour mixture onto a greased tray and smooth with a spoon, leaving the edges higher. Cook for 25-30 minutes in a preheated oven until it turns pink.
8. Remove from heat and immediately pour syrup over it with a ladle by the spoonful. Cover to let the sauce absorb into the dessert. Once cooled, slice and serve.

SWEET SEMOLINA PASTRY

Ingredients

- 5 eggs
- 2/3 cups of sugar
- 1 cup of semolina
- 1/3 cups of flour
- ½ a teaspoon of baking powder
- 1/6 cup of oil
- 1 tablespoon of lemon juice
- ½ a lemon peel (grated)

FOR SYRUP:

- 2 ½ cups of sugar
- Juice from ¼ a lemon

Directions

1. Boil 2 ½ cups of sugar with 3 cups of water in a pot. Squeeze lemon juice from ¼ a lemon into the pot, and cover. Boil for 10 more minutes and remove from heat.
2. Separate egg whites and yolks into separate bowls. Whisk yolks with 2/3 cups of sugar until the sugar melts, and add in grated lemon peel.
3. In a pot mix together 1 cup of semolina, 1/3 cup of flour and baking powder.
4. Whisk egg whites. Stir in egg yolks with sugar.
5. Add the flour and semolina mixture to the eggs. While mixing, add in 1/6 cup of oil and 1 tablespoon of lemon juice.
6. Pour mixture onto a greased tray, and spread out, leaving more at the edges. Cook in an oven on medium heat for 25-30 minutes.
7. Remove from heat and immediately pour sauce over the dessert in a ladle by the spoonful. Cover to let the sauce absorb into the dessert. Once cooled, slice and serve.

FAT-FREE YOGURT DESSERT

Ingredients

- 3 eggs
- 1 cup of sugar
- 1 cup of yogurt
- 1 cup of semolina
- 1 ½ cups of flour
- 1 teaspoon of baking powder
- ½ a lemon peel (grated)
- 1 tablespoon of lemon juice

FOR SYRUP:

- 4 cups of sugar
- Juice from ¼ a lemon

Directions

1. Melt 4 cups of sugar in 4 ½ cups of water, and bring to a boil. Squeeze lemon juice from ¼ a lemon into the pot and cover. Boil for 10 minutes and remove from heat.
2. Sieve flour and baking powder mixture over semolina.
3. Whisk together 3 eggs, 1 cup of sugar and grated lemon peels. Add in 1 cup of yogurt and mix together.
4. Slowly add in flour and semolina mixture and add in lemon juice. Stir gently and pour onto a tray, 30 cm in diameter. Smooth with a spoon leaving more at the edges.
5. Cook in an oven on medium heat for 30-35 minutes, until it turns pink.
6. Remove from heat and immediately pour sauce over the dessert in a ladle by the spoonful. Cover to let the sauce absorb into the dessert.
7. Let cool, then slice and serve.

YOGURT DESSERT

Ingredients

- 4 eggs
- 1 ½ cups of yogurt
- 1 cup of sugar
- 1 cup of flour
- 1 cup of semolina
- ⅓ cup of oil
- ⅓ cup of lemon juice
- ½ a lemon peel (grated)
- 1 teaspoon of baking powder

FOR SYRUP:

- 3 ½ cups of sugar
- Juice from ¼ a lemon

Directions

1. Boil 3 ½ cups of sugar with 4 cups of water and mix until the sugar dissolves. Add juice from ¼ of a lemon, and cover. Boil for 10 more minutes and remove from heat.
2. Separate the yolks and egg whites into separate bowls. Add 1 cup of sugar and grated lemon peels to the yolks, and mix until the sugar dissolves. Add yogurt and mix everything together.
3. Sieve flour and baking powder mixture over semolina and mix together.
4. Whisk egg whites. Add egg yolk, sugar and yogurt mixture, and semolina, baking powder and flour mixture. Lastly add in oil and lemon juice and stir gently.
5. Pour onto a greased tray (30 cm in diameter) and spread out. Cook in an oven on medium heat for 30-35 minutes.
6. Remove from heat and immediately pour sauce over the dessert with a ladle by the spoonful. Cover to let the sauce absorb into the dessert. Let cool, then slice and serve.

KADAYIF WITH MILK

Ingredients

- 750 g of kadayif
- 250 g of margarine
- 1-2 cups of crushed walnuts or hazelnuts
- 5 cups of sugar
- 2 cups of milk

Directions

1. In a pot, boil 5 cups of sugar with 3 cups of water. Stir until the sugar dissolves. Once it comes to a boil and the mixture thickens, lower the heat. Add in 2 cups of milk and stir. Remove from heat.
2. Spread out half of the kadayif onto a tray (35-40 cm in diameter) greased with margarine. Sprinkle crushed walnuts or hazelnuts over the kadayif and press gently.
3. Cover the nuts with the remaining kadayif and press down.
4. Melt the remaining margarine and pour over the kadayif by the spoonful. Cook in an oven until it turns pink.
5. Remove from the oven and pour prepared milk sauce over it with a ladle. Cover until tepid, then slice and serve.

Note: To avoid pasty kadayif, make sure the sauce or kadayif is cold before combining.

BAKLAVA

Ingredients

- 1 cup of milk
- 3 cups of sugar
- 3 cups of water
- Half a cup of oil (for dough)
- 2 eggs
- 1 teaspoon of salt
- 1 teaspoon of baking powder
- 1 tablespoon of lemon juice
- ¼ a lemon
- Flour (as needed)
- 1-2 cups of crushed walnuts or hazelnuts
- FOR TOP PART: 375 g of margarine
- FOR DOUGH: 2 cups of starch

Directions

1. Heat 3 cups of sugar with 3 cups of water in a pot until the sugar dissolves. Squeeze in the lemon juice from ¼ of a lemon and cover. Remove from heat once the mixture begins to thicken.
2. Mix together milk, oil, eggs, salt, baking powder and lemon juice in a pot by hand.
3. Add in flour until the dough is slightly tough, roll into a long round shape, and cut into 24 pieces. Cover and let sit for 15-20 minutes.
4. Roll out the dough with starch until it is 15 cm in diameter. Make 2 groups of 12 layers of dough, flouring each layer.
5. Roll each layer of dough out evenly to 30-35 cm in diameter. (Turn the dough occasionally to ensure even rolling.) If desired, dough can be rolled out separately with starch.
6. Set the first pile of dough into a tray and sprinkle crushed walnuts on top. Put the second pile of dough over the nuts, and press gently. Slice into long horizontal strips.
7. Pour melted margarine over the dough by the spoonful.
8. Cook in the oven on a medium heat until the top layer turns pink and becomes crusted.
9. Remove from the oven and pour sugar syrup over it while still hot.

BREAD KADAYIF

Ingredients

- 1 bread kadayif
- 4 ½ cups of sugar
- 2 tablespoons of lemon juice
- Grated peel of 1 lemon
- Cream

Directions

1. Heat 4 ½ cups of sugar with 5 cups of water in a pot and stir until the sugar dissolves. Bring to a boil, then add in lemon juice and lemon peel. Boil for 5 minutes, then remove from heat.
2. Bread kadayif has two layers. Remove from second layer, turn it upside down and put it back on top of the other layer.
3. Put the kadayif in a deep tray. Pour hot water over kadayif until it is completely covered. Place a heavy plate on top to prevent the kadayif from rising above the water. Cover the tray and let sit to allow the water to be absorbed.
4. Once the water turns tepid, gently press the kadayif to sieve out any excess water. Pour prepared syrup over it, and cook on a low heat, occasionally turning the tray and pouring in more syrup from the edge of the tray until the kadayif absorbs the syrup and gets thicker.
5. Let cool, then slice and remove onto serving plates. Top each slice with cream.

KUNEFE (KADAYIF WITH FRESH CHEESE)

Ingredients

- 300 g of kadayif
- 2 ½ cups of sugar
- ⅓ cups of melted margarine
- 2 cups of grated, salt-free, fresh white cheese
- ½ a tablespoon of lemon juice
- Grated peel of 1 lemon

Directions

1. Heat 2 ½ cups of sugar with 2 ½ cups of water in a pot and stir until the sugar dissolves. Bring to a boil, then add in lemon juice and lemon peels. Let boil for 5 minutes then remove from heat.
2. Grease a tray (25 cm in diameter) with half of the margarine.
3. Put half of the kadayif into the tray. Sprinkle grated cheese over, and press gently.
4. Put the remaining kadayif on top and press gently.
5. Pour the remaining melted margarine on top with a spoon. Cook in an oven until it turns pink. Remove from the oven, and pour sugar-water on top.
6. Slice and serve while hot.

SARAY LOKMASI

Ingredients

- 3 cups of flour
- ⅔ tablespoons of yeast
- 2 tablespoons of oil (for dough)
- ½ a teaspoon of salt
- 2 cups of oil (for frying)

FOR SYRUP:

- 3 cups of sugar
- 1 tablespoon of lemon juice
- Grated peel from 1 lemon

Directions

1. Heat half a cup of water in a pot on low heat. Add in ⅓ a tablespoon of sugar and ⅔ a tablespoon of yeast and melt together.
2. In a separate bowl, sieve flour, add in salt and 2 tablespoons of oil, and then slowly add in tepid water. Mix together to form dough with a yogurt-like consistency.
3. Whisk dough by hand. Cover and let sit in a warm place until the dough doubles in size.
4. Heat 3 cups sugar with 3 ½ cups of water in a pot, stirring until the sugar dissolves. Bring to a boil, then add in lemon juice and lemon peel. Remove from heat after 5 minutes.
5. Heat oil in a small pot. Form dough into walnut-size pieces, and fry, leaving enough room for each piece.
6. Once the pieces harden, stir with a ladle. Remove once fried, and put in prepared syrup while hot.

FLAT KADAYIF

Ingredients

- 8 flat kadayıfs
- 2 eggs
- 1 cup of oil (for frying)
- 2 cups of sugar
- ½ a tablespoon of lemon juice
- 2 tablespoons of crushed walnuts or hazelnuts

Directions

1. Heat 2 cups of sugar with 2 cups of water in a pot, and stir until the sugar dissolves. Add lemon juice and lemon peels and boil for 10 minutes.
2. Whisk eggs. Dredge kadayıfs in eggs and remove, letting excess egg fall off. Put kadayıfs into a pan with hot oil, porous side up. Flip over once the bottom side is fried.
3. Remove onto a paper towel, to absorb excess oil. Then put into sugar syrup.
4. Cook on a very low heat, flipping over occasionally, to absorb the syrup.
5. Remove to a plate once cooled, and sprinkled with crushed nuts.

HANIM HANIMCIK DESSERT

Ingredients

- 1 egg
- 2 tablespoons of oil (for dough)
- 2 tablespoons of yogurt
- 1 tablespoon of lemon juice
- 1 teaspoon of baking powder
- A pinch of salt
- Flour (as needed)
- 1 ½ cups of oil (for frying)

FOR SYRUP:

- 3 cups of sugar
- ¼ a lemon

Directions

1. Boil sugar with 3 cups of water by stirring. Add in lemon juice and its peel. Let thicken, and then remove from heat.
2. Put egg, 2 tablespoons of oil, yogurt, lemon juice, baking powder and salt in a pot and mix by hand.
3. Add in flour until the dough becomes soft and not sticky. Cover and let sit for 10-15 minutes.
4. Flour the dough and roll out until it is 2 mm thick. Cut into square pieces, 5 cm in length. Bring the two edges of each piece together and stick.
5. Heat oil in a pot and fry dough squares, leaving enough room for each piece. Shake the pot gently, and flip over each piece once they harden.
6. Remove with a ladle and put into prepared syrup.

HANIM GOBEGI

Ingredients

- 2 ½ cups of flour
- ⅓ a cup of oil (for dough)
- 4 eggs
- 2 pinches of slat
- 2 cups of oil (for frying)

FOR SYRUP:

- 3 cups of sugar
- Juice from ¼ a lemon

Directions

1. Heat sugar with 3 cups of water in a pot, stirring until the sugar dissolves. Bring to a boil, remove foam, and add in lemon juice and lemon peel. Cook until the syrup thickens, and test with a spoon (the syrup should fall slowly from the spoon). Remove from heat.
2. Boil 2 cups of water in a pot with ⅓ a cup of oil and salt. Add in sieved flour and stir while cooking. Once it does not stick to the pot, remove from heat.
3. Let cool until tepid, and then add eggs in one at a time. Knead together and divide into golf-ball sized pieces.
4. Oil your palms, and use hands to flatten each piece, making holes in the centres.
5. Heat oil in a pan, and add in dough pieces, leaving enough room for each piece. Gently shake the pan, and fry until both sides of the dough is pink and crusted. Remove onto paper towels to absorb the excess oil.
6. Put pieces into prepared syrup while they are still hot. Turn them occasionally to absorb the syrup, and then remove onto a serving plate.

Note: *If desired, the flour can be reduced to 2 tablespoons and the rest can be replaced with semolina.*

HAZELNUT DESSERT

Ingredients

- 2 eggs
- 2 tablespoons of yogurt
- 250 g margarine
- 2 teaspoons of baking powder
- ½ a teaspoon of salt
- Juice from ½ a lemon
- Flour (as needed)
- ½ a cup of diced hazelnuts or walnuts

FOR SYRUP:

- 3 cups of sugar
- ¼ of a lemon

Directions

1. Boil 3 cups of sugar with 3 cups of water. Add juice from ¼ a lemon and its peel to give a nice scent. Boil for 5 minutes and remove from heat.
2. In a pot, mix together eggs, yogurt, margarine, baking powder, salt, and lemon juice.
3. Add in flour until the dough is soft but not sticky. Cover and let sit for 10 minutes.
4. Divide the dough into 3 pieces. Flour each piece and roll out until it is 3 mm thick. Cut each piece into four parts, and then cut those pieces into three, making a total of 36 pieces. Put a pinch of diced nuts onto the largest edge of each piece, and roll it up. Set the pieces onto a tray and cook in an oven until they turn pink.
5. Remove from the oven and put into syrup. Turn occasionally to allow the syrup to absorb into the pastry.

SEKERPARE (SMALL CAKES WITH SYRUP)

Ingredients

- 2 ½ cups of flour
- 125 g of margarine
- 2 eggs
- 2 tablespoons of sugar (For dough)
- 1 teaspoon of baking powder
- ½ a teaspoon of salt
- ½ a lemon peel (grated)
- Half a package of vanilla[1]

FOR SYRUP:

- 2 ½ cups of sugar
- ¼ a lemon

FOR TOP PART:

- 10 almonds or hazelnuts

Directions

1. Heat 2 ½ cups of sugar with 2 ½ cups of water, stirring until the sugar dissolves. Bring to a boil, and add in lemon juice and lemon peel. Boil for 5 minutes and then remove from heat.
2. In a bowl, mix margarine with 2 tablespoons of sugar. Add in 2 eggs, grated lemon peel, vanilla and baking powder and mix together.
3. Add in flour and knead. Divide dough into walnut size pieces.
4. Pressing gently, flatten each piece with your palms. Put peeled almonds or hazelnuts in the centre.
5. Set dough into a tray and cook in an oven until they turn pink. Remove from heat and pour syrup over it. Place back into warm oven (with the heat off) to let the cakes absorb the syrup.

Note: *If desired, the flour can be reduced to 2 tablespoons and replaced with semolina.*

FLOUR HALVA

Ingredients

- ½ a cup of oil or 125 g of margarine
- 2 cups of flour
- 1 tablespoon of pine nuts
- 1 ½ cups of sugar
- 1 cup of milk
- 1 cup of water

Directions

1. Heat oil in a pot and add in sieved flour. Fry on a medium heat until the flour turns dark pink.
2. Add in pine nuts and stir occasionally. Once they turn pink, add in water, milk and sugar.
3. Stir on a medium heat until the mixture thickens, but does not stick to the pot. Press with a spoon and smooth over. Remove onto a plate by the spoonful.

KALBURABASTI DESSERT

Ingredients

- ½ a cup of oil
- ½ a cup of melted margarine
- ½ a cup of milk
- ½ a cup of sugar
- ½ a lemon peel (grated)
- ½ a tablespoon of lemon juice
- ½ a teaspoon of baking soda
- ½ a teaspoon of baking powder
- Flour (as needed)

FOR SYRUP:

- 2 ½ cups of sugar
- ⅛ of a lemon

Directions

1. SYRUP: Boil 2 ½ cups of sugar with 3 cups of water. Stir until the sugar dissolves. Bring to a boil, then add in lemon juice and grated peel. Boil for 10 minutes and remove from heat.
2. In a pot put the first 8 ingredients and mix by hand. Add in flour until the dough is soft but not sticky.
3. Cover and refrigerate for half an hour.
4. Divide dough into golf-ball size pieces. Shape in to oval pieces half a cm thick with palms. Lightly press a grater onto each piece, twisting from one end to make an impression.
5. Set pieces onto a tray and cook in an oven on medium heat until they turn light pink. Remove from heat and immediately dredge each piece into the cold syrup. Turn upside down and let sit in the syrup before serving.

SEMOLINA DESSERT

Ingredients

- 125 g of margarine
- 1 ½ cups of medium-sized semolina
- 1 tablespoon of pine nuts
- 1 ½ cups of sugar
- 3 tablespoons of sugar
- 1 cup of milk
- 1 cup of water

Directions

1. Melt margarine in a pot. Add in semolina and fry on a low heat until it turns light pink.
2. Add in pine nuts and stir occasionally until they turn pink. Then add in water and milk, and stir.
3. Leaving the lid partially open, let simmer on a low heat until the water evaporates.
4. Add in sugar, stir and cover. Cook on a very low heat for 5-6 minutes. Remove from heat and let steep longer until ready to serve.

KUYMAK (From Sivas-Divrigi)

Ingredients

- 1 cup of oil or butter
- 3 cups of flour
- 5-6 tablespoons of grape molasses or strained honey

Directions

1. Fry flour with oil until it turns light pink. Remove onto a small tray and spread out by pressing.
2. Cook molasses or honey while stirring on the stove or in the oven. Pour grape molasses or honey onto the flour by the spoonful. Serve with a spoon.

ASURE (NOAH'S PUDDING)

Ingredients

- 3 cups of wheat
- ½ a cup of rice
- ½ a cup of chickpeas
- ½ a cup of beans
- ½ a cup of grapes
- 5-6 figs and 5-6 apricots
- 2-3 slices of orange peels
- 6 cups of sugar
- ⅓ cups of rose water
- 1 cup of walnuts or hazelnuts
- 2 teaspoons of cinnamon
- 1 teaspoon of salt

Directions

1. Wash wheat, rice, chickpeas and beans. Soak the wheat and rice in a pot overnight, and soak the chickpeas and beans in a second pot overnight.
2. Dice orange peels and add into the rice and wheat with 10 cups of water. Boil on low heat until the wheat is soft. Boil the chickpeas and beans together in a separate pot.
3. Add the chickpeas and beans with their stock to the wheat and rice pot and boil everything together for a while.
4. Add in sugar and continue cooking. Then add in washed grapes and chopped apricots.
5. Add in diced figs, stir, and lower the heat. Let cook for 10 minutes and then remove from heat. Add in rose water, cover and let sit for half an hour.
6. Pour into serving bowls while still warm. Let cool, and then sprinkle crushed walnuts or hazelnuts and cinnamon on top.

Note: *Asure should be cooked slowly, and the stock should be at just the right consistency so that the grains do not sink to the bottom. Also, it should not get too hard once cooled.*

SUTLAC (RICE PUDDING)

Ingredients

- 1 liter of milk (plus an extra ½ cup for mixing the starch)
- ½ a cup of rice
- 1 cup of sugar
- 1 tablespoon of starch
- ½ a package of vanilla
- 1 teaspoon of cinnamon

Directions

1. Clean the rice and boil slowly in 1 cup of water.
2. Add milk and boil for 10 more minutes.
3. Add sugar and stir until it dissolves.
4. Mix the starch with half a cup of milk and then add it into the milk and rice mixture. Bring to a boil, then remove from heat and add in vanilla. Cover and let sit for 10 minutes.
5. Pour into serving bowls while it is still warm. Sprinkle cinnamon on top once it has cooled.

Note:

1) *If desired, make sütlaç in the oven during directions 1-3.*
2) *If desired, mix starch with 2 eggs and 1 cup of milk before adding it to the milk and rice mixture. Then add in vanilla.*
3) *If desired, put the pudding into oven-safe bowls, and set on a tray with water in it. Then put bowls in the oven, and use overhead heat to toast the tops of the pudding.*

GULLAC (Dessert for Ramadan)

Ingredients

- 5 layers of gullac
- 3 cups of milk
- 1 cup of sugar
- ½ a cup of crushed walnuts or hazelnuts
- 2 tablespoons of rose water

Directions

1. Boil the milk. Remove from heat and add in sugar, stirring until it dissolves.
2. Pour into a large tray and add in rose water once it gets tepid. Soften the gullac in the milk and sugar mixture. Divide the gullac into 8 pieces and remove them onto a plate one at a time.
3. Sprinkle crushed nuts on top of the gullac, and loosely roll it together. Place onto a serving plate, with the ends underneath.
4. Pour remaining milk and sugar mixture over and serve.

MURTAGA (From Van)

Ingredients

- ½ a cup of oil
- 2 cups of flour
- 2 eggs
- 3-4 tablespoons of strained honey

Directions

1. Fry flour with oil in a pan on medium heat until it turns pink.
2. Add in whisked eggs while the flour is still hot. Remove onto a serving plate and pour honey on top by the spoonful.

YELLOW TWIST (From Corum)

Ingredients

- 5 cups of flour
- 2 eggs
- 3 tablespoons of oil (for dough)
- 1 tablespoon of lemon juice
- 1 teaspoon of salt
- 1 teaspoon of baking powder

FOR FILLING:

- 1 cup of crushed walnuts or hazelnuts

FOR TOP:

- 375 grams of margarine
- 5 cups of sugar
- ¼ of a lemon

FOR DOUGH:

- 2 cups of starch

Directions

1. Boil 5 cups of sugar with 5 cups of water in a pot, stirring until the sugar dissolves. Bring to a boil and add in the lemon juice and grated lemon peel of ¼ of a lemon. Cook until the sauce thickens (once it is difficult to drip from a spoon) and remove from heat.
2. Put sieved flour in a pot, leaving a space in the middle. Add in eggs, oil, lemon juice, salt and baking powder and slowly pour in a cup of water. Knead until the dough is slightly tough, and then divide into 14-16 pieces. Cover and let sit.
3. Dredge each dough piece in starch one at a time, and roll out until they are as thin as possible. Sprinkle crushed walnuts over them. Roll the dough from one edge, and then the other. Gather rolled dough at the centre. Remove the rollers and set it into a 30-35 cm diameter tray.
4. Pour melted margarine over the dough by the spoonful. Cook in an oven on a low-medium heat until they turn pink and get crusty.
5. Remove from the oven, and pour cold syrup over them by the spoonful.

TEZ PISTI (QUICK COOKED)

Ingredients

- 1 liter of milk (plus an extra ½ cup for mixing the starch)
- 1 cup of sugar
- 3 tablespoons of rice flour
- 2 egg whites
- ½ a package of vanilla
- 2 tablespoons of powdered sugar

Directions

1. Boil sugar and milk in a pot while stirring.
2. Mix rice flour with half a cup of milk and slowly add into the sugar and milk.
3. Bring to a boil, remove from heat, and add in vanilla. Pour the pudding into 6-8 oven-safe bowls. Leave the remaining pudding in the pot, cover and lower the heat.
4. Whisk 2 eggs whites and mix with the remaining pudding in the pot.
5. Pour the mixture equally over the pudding bowls. Let cool, and then sprinkle powdered sugar on top.
6. Set bowls in a tray with water, and cook with overhead heat in an oven until the pudding turns pink. If desired, garnish with black cherries or black cherry jam.

KESKUL (MILK PUDDING WITH COCONUT)

Ingredients

- 1 liter of milk (plus an extra ½ cup for mixing the starch)
- 8 tablespoons of sugar
- 1 egg yolk
- 2 tablespoons of cornstarch
- 2 tablespoons of grated coconut
- ½ a package of vanilla

Directions

1. Boil sugar and milk in a pot while stirring.
2. Mix together egg yolk, starch, 1 tablespoon of grated coconut and half a cup of milk.
3. Slowly pour the mixture into the boiling milk and sugar.
4. Bring to a boil, remove from heat and add in vanilla. Let sit for 10 minutes while covered.
5. Pour pudding onto serving plates while still warm, and sprinkle remaining coconut on top.

FAKE CHICKEN BREAST

Ingredients

- 1 liter of milk
- 65 g of margarine
- 1 cup of flour
- 1 cup of sugar
- ½ a package of vanilla

Directions

1. Fry flour with oil in a pot until it turns light pink. Add in 1 liter of milk and sugar and boil while stirring. Remove from heat once it thickens, and add in vanilla.
2. Mix for 15-20 minutes with a blender. Wet a tray (20 cm in diameter) with rose water or regular water. Pour pudding onto the tray, spread out, and refrigerate.
3. Sprinkle cinnamon on top, slice and serve on plates.

LION'S MILK

Ingredients

- 1 liter of milk (plus an extra ½ cup for mixing the starch)
- 1 cup of sugar
- 2 tablespoons of vermicelli
- 1 tablespoon of starch
- 1 tablespoon of green pistachios
- 1 tablespoon of almonds
- 1 tablespoon of hazelnuts
- 1 tablespoon of grated coconut
- ½ a package of vanilla

Directions

1. Put almonds and green pistachios in hot water for a few minutes and then peel.
2. Dice almonds, pistachios and hazelnuts, or pulverize them in a mortar. Add nuts to the grated coconut and mix together.
3. Fry vermicelli in a pan on low heat until it turns pink.
4. Boil milk with sugar in a pot and add in fried vermicelli.
5. Mix starch with half a cup of milk and then add to the milk and sugar pot and let boil for a while.
6. Add in nut and coconut mixture last to the pot, and stir. Remove from heat.
7. Cover and let sit for 10 minutes. Pour mixture into bowls while it is still warm.

PUDDING WITH MILK AND SEMOLINA

Ingredients

- 1 liter of milk
- 9 tablespoons of sugar
- 9 tablespoons of semolina
- 30 g of margarine
- 1 tablespoon of grated coconut
- 2 tablespoons of rose water
- ½ a package of vanilla
- 1 teaspoon of cinnamon

Directions

1. Heat milk and sugar in a pot.
2. Add in semolina and cook while stirring
3. Remove from heat once it thickens. Add in margarine, coconut and vanilla, and stir.
4. Wet a tray (20 cm in diameter), pour the mixture onto it, and spread it out.
5. Let cool, then cover and refrigerate for 5-6 hours or overnight.
6. Before serving, turn upside down onto a large plate and sprinkle with cinnamon. Slice and serve onto plates.

Note: *If desired, the pudding can be made for single servings as well.*

CREAM CARAMEL

Ingredients

- 6 eggs
- 3 cups of milk
- 1 ½ cups of sugar
- ½ a package of vanilla

Directions

1. Boil half a cup of sugar with half a cup of water until it turns into caramel and is the colour of molasses.
2. Pour the caramel into small moulds while it is still hot.
3. Whisk eggs and 1 cup of sugar together in a pot.
4. Add milk and vanilla and mix until the sugar dissolves. Then pour the mixture into the moulds over the caramel.
5. Set the moulds in a large pot, and pour cold water from the side, until it covers half of the moulds.
6. Cover the pot with a paper towel, and cover partially. Cook on a medium heat until the cream softens, but do not bring to a boil. Occasionally add water to the edge.
7. Remove from heat and cool the cream in water. Then refrigerate.
8. Place moulds upside down onto serving plates when serving.

Note: *If individual moulds are unavailable, it is possible to use one large mould.*

CHOCOLATE WITH CREAM

Ingredients

- 1 liter of milk
- 12 tablespoons of sugar
- 3 eggs
- 3 tablespoons of flour
- 1 ½ tablespoons of cocoa
- ½ a grated lemon
- ½ a package of vanilla
- 2-3 tablespoons of crushed hazelnuts

Directions

1. Separate the egg yolks from the egg whites. Add sugar, flour, cocoa, grated lemon peel and some milk to the egg yolks, and stir.
2. Add to hot milk and cook while stirring. Lower the heat and cover.
3. Beat egg whites with a blender. Add in 2-3 tablespoons of hot cream with cocoa. Then add in the rest of the cream in with the vanilla.
4. Pour the mixture into 7-8 bowls. Sprinkle crushed hazelnuts on top or add Créme Chantilly.

BAVARIAN CREAM

Ingredients

- 6 eggs
- 1 ½ cups of sugar
- 1 tablespoon of flour
- 8 layers of gelatin
- 1 liter of milk
- 1 package of vanilla
- 2-3 apples
- 3-4 bananas
- 2 tangerines
- 1 orange
- 1 tablespoon of diced green pistachio nuts

Directions

1. Peel fruits and dice, removing any excess water.
2. Lightly grease a jello mould and refrigerate.
3. Separate the egg whites and yolks. Add sugar, flour and a few tablespoons of milk to the egg yolks and mix together. Pour the mixture into hot milk and boil while stirring.
4. Remove from heat and add in gelatin and vanilla. Cook while stirring until they dissolve. Cover and lower the heat to keep it hot.
5. Beat egg whites with 2-3 tablespoons of cream. Then add in the rest of the egg yolk mixture.
6. Let cool, then add in chopped fruits. Pour into the cooled mould and smooth over. Refrigerate for 5-6 hours or overnight.
7. Dip the mould a few times into tepid water and turn upside down onto a serving plate. Sprinkle diced green pistachio nuts on top.

Note: *Seasonal fruits can be used for Bavarian cream.*

PROFITEROLE

Ingredients

FOR DOUGH

- 125 g of margarine
- 2 cups of water
- 2 2/3 cups of flour
- 4 eggs
- 1 tablespoon of sugar
- ½ a teaspoon of salt

FOR CREAM

- 1 egg
- 1 cup of sugar
- 3 tablespoons of flour
- ½ a liter of milk
- Grated lemon peels
- Vanilla

Directions

1. PREPARATION OF DOUGH: Boil 2 cups of water, margarine, salt, and sugar together in a pot. Add in sieved flour and cook until the dough doesn't stick to the pot.
2. Cool until tepid, then add in 4 eggs, one at a time, and knead together. Using oiled palms, roll into walnut-sized pieces and set onto a tray. Cook slowly in an oven on medium heat until the dough puffs out and becomes hollow, and the outside is crusty.
3. Remove from heat and let cool. Fill the insides with cream using a cream filler. Remove onto a serving plate and pour chocolate sauce on top. If desired, add Créme Chantilly on top.
4. PREPARATION OF THE CREAM: Mix together 1 egg, 1 cup of sugar, 3 tablespoons of flour and grated lemon peels with a few tablespoons of milk. Add in hot milk, and boil together while stirring. Once the cream thickens, remove from heat. Stir occasionally as it cools.

CHOCOLATE SAUCE

Ingredients

- 2 egg yolks
- 1 cup of sugar
- 1 tablespoon of corn or potato starch
- 2 tablespoons of cocoa
- ½ a liter of milk
- ½ a package of vanilla
- 1 tablespoon of banana or orange liqueur

Directions

1. Mix together sugar, egg yolk, starch, cocoa, and a few tablespoons of milk in a pot.
2. Add in hot milk, and cook while stirring slowly.
3. Let cool while stirring to prevent cream from concentrating on the surface. Add in vanilla and liqueur.

SUP-ANGLE

Ingredients

- 24 Savayer biscuits (see page 415)
- ½ a portion of Crème Chantilly (see page 304)
- 1 portion of chocolate sauce (see page 324)
- 1 tablespoon of diced green pistachio nuts

Directions

1. Spread Crème Chantilly on the bottom of a savayer biscuit and place another one underneath to form a sandwich.
2. Put biscuits on plates, 2 per plate. Pour chocolate sauce on top, covering up the biscuits. Sprinkle diced pistachios on top.

Note: *If desired, use the remaining cakes to make sup-anglez.*

CRÈME CHANTILLY

Ingredients

- 1 cup of fresh milk cream
- 2 tablespoons of powdered sugar
- ½ a package of vanilla

Directions

1. In a bowl beat together cream, powdered sugar and vanilla.
2. Stop beating once it thickens, as it can loose its consistency if over-beaten.
3. Crème Chantilly is used in pastries and desserts.

CRÈME CHANTILLY IMITATION

Ingredients

- 3 egg whites (yolks are not used)
- About 1 cup of sugar
- ½ a package of vanilla

Directions

1. Heat 1 cup of sugar with 1 cup of water in a pot and stir until the sugar dissolves. Boil to thicken the consistency. Drop a spoonful of the syrup into cold water to check the consistency. It should disperse at a medium speed, not too quickly or too slowly.
2. Beat egg whites with either a blender or a whisker.
3. Add whisked egg whites into the sugar and water mixture and beat together. Add in vanilla, stirring occasionally, and let cool. Do not mix the syrup that has concentrated at the bottom of the pot.

SOUFFLÉ WITH CHOCOLATE

Ingredients

- 65 g of margarine
- 3 tablespoons of flour
- 4 tablespoons of sugar
- 2 cups of milk
- 4 eggs
- 1-1 ½ tablespoons of cocoa
- ½ a package of vanilla

Directions

1. Grease a large, deep, oven-safe glass tray with margarine.
2. Fry flour with oil in a pot until it turns light pink. Add in hot milk and sugar, and cook while stirring. Remove from heat and stir occasionally while it cools down.
3. Separate the egg yolks and whites. Mix egg yolks to the pot. Then mix in cocoa and vanilla.
4. Whisk egg whites. Add into the mixture and stir occasionally.
5. Pour the mixture into the greased tray and smooth over. Cook in an oven on medium heat (200-250°C) for 25 minutes. Remove from heat and sprinkle powdered sugar on top. Serve tepid. If desired, add on imitation Crème Chantilly (see page 327).

Note: *If desired, make soufflé with Nescafe instead of cocoa.*

CREPE SUZETTE

Ingredients

- 4 eggs
- 1 ½ cups of flour
- ½ a liter of milk
- 3-4 tablespoons of melted margarine (1 tbsp for dough)
- ½ a teaspoon of salt
- Grated peel of ½ a lemon
- ½ a package of vanilla
- 3-4 tablespoons of marmalade or honey
- 2-3 tablespoons of powdered sugar

Directions

1. Mix eggs, flour, salt, grated lemon peel, vanilla, 1 tablespoon of melted margarine and a few tablespoons of milk together in a pot.
2. Slowly add in milk and mix, making the dough watery.
3. Grease a Teflon or regular pan and pre-heat. Pour a small ladle of dough onto the pan and shake gently. Fry both sides by turning upside down.
4. Once both sides are cooked remove from the pan. Spread marmalade on one side of each crepe and fold in half. Place on serving plates back to back and sprinkle powdered sugar on top.
5. Place in a tepid oven to keep warm.

APPLES WITH CREAM

Ingredients

- 8 apples
- 1 ½ cups of sugar (half for the apples and the rest for the cream)
- 1 egg
- 1 tablespoon of starch
- ½ a liter of milk
- ½ a package of vanilla
- ½ a cup of crushed hazelnuts or walnuts
- 2 teaspoons of cinnamon

Directions

1. Mix together 1 egg, half of the sugar, starch and a few tablespoons of milk. Add in hot milk and cook while stirring. Let cool, stirring occasionally, and add in the vanilla.
2. Wash the apples, carve out the pits with a paring knife, and peel.
3. Set the apples in a pot and pour half of the sugar over them. Add in half a cup of water and boil slowly. Once the syrup thickens, remove the apples into bowls. Pour the syrup over them.
4. Fill the carved part of the apples with hazelnuts or walnuts, and cinnamon.
5. Pour the prepared cream over the apples. If desired, sprinkle diced green pistachios, almonds or coconuts on top.

APPLE WITH TURBAN

Ingredients

- 8 apples
- 1 ½ cups of sugar
- 3 egg whites
- ½ a cup of crushed hazelnuts or walnuts
- 1 ½ teaspoons of cinnamon
- ½ a teaspoon of allspice
- 1 tablespoon of seedless raisins

Directions

1. Wash and pit apples with a paring knife, and peel them.
2. Set apples into a pot and add in 1 cup of water. Pour in 1 ½ cups of sugar, cover and cook. Uncover and continue cooking until the syrup thickens.
3. Remove the apples into individual bowls. Fill each apple with cinnamon, allspice, raisins, and hazelnuts/walnuts mixture.
4. Beat 3 egg whites with a blender. Add in the apple syrup and continue to beat. Let mixture cool down. Add the cream to the apples, setting it on top like a turban.
5. Pour the syrup that concentrated from the cream on top by the spoonful.
6. Set the bowls onto a tray and cook on low heat in an oven until the cream turns light pink.

PUMPKIN DESSERT

Ingredients

- 2 kg of sweet pumpkin
- 2 ½ cups of sugar
- 4-5 pink cloves
- 1 cup of crushed walnuts or hazelnuts

Directions

1. Slice and peel the pumpkins. Remove the seeds, slice into pieces 3-4 cm in breadth and wash.
2. Layer the pumpkin pieces into a pot with sugar, and cover. Let sit for 4-5 hours or overnight.
3. During this time, the pumpkin will release water. Add 4-5 pink cloves and cook on medium heat without adding any water.
4. To thicken the syrup, cook for a while with the lid off.
5. Remove onto a serving plate, and sprinkle with crushed walnuts or hazelnuts.

Note: *The best pumpkins have a hard skin, and a dark orange color inside.*

QUINCE DESSERT WITH CREAM

Ingredients

- 3 quinces
- 9 tablespoons of sugar
- 6 slices of cream

Directions

1. Wash and cut the quinces in half. Remove the seeds and core.
2. Put the quinces in a pressure cooker, unpeeled, cored sides up. Fill the carved depressions with 1 ½ tablespoons of sugar.
3. Add 1 cup of water to the side of the pot and cover. Cook on a medium heat until it steams, then cook for 10 more minutes.
4. Uncover once cooled. If necessary, cook uncovered longer until the syrup has a thick consistency. Let the pot cool.
5. Place quinces on a serving plate, carved sides facing up. Pour syrup over them, then add on a slice of cream and serve.

ORANGE STARCH PUDDING

Ingredients

- 6 orange for juicing (2 cups of orange juice)
- 1 ½ cups of sugar
- 6 cups of water
- 3 ½ tablespoons of potato or corn starch

Directions

1. Wash and grate the oranges. Blend grated orange peels with 2 tablespoons of sugar and add in 1 cup of water. Stir until the sugar dissolves and sieve into a pot.
2. Add in starch and squeezed orange juice and stir.
3. Add in 5 cups of water and the remaining sugar and boil.
4. Slowly add in the orange juice and starch mixture and stir. Bring to a boil, then remove from heat and pour evenly into 8-9 bowls.
5. Starch pudding should have a slightly watery consistency.

Note:

1) *If desired, put orange slices into the bottom of the bowls before pouring in the starch pudding.*
2) *If desired, use the remaining syrup of jams to make starch pudding.*
3) *To make lemon starch pudding, use 4 lemons, 2 cups of sugar, 7 cups of water and 3 ½ tablespoons of starch, following the same directions.*

LEMON-SWEETENED JELLY

Ingredients

- 3 lemons
- 1 package of lemon or pineapple jello
- 6 cups of sugar
- 1 package of Crème Chantilly
- 1 cup of cold milk

Directions

1. Put jello into 2 cups of hot water and dissolve while stirring.
2. Wash and grate lemons with the smallest grate. Blend with 6 tablespoons of sugar. Add in juice from 3 lemons and 1 ½ cups of water. Stir until the sugar dissolves.
3. Sieve the lemonade into the jello.
4. Whisk 1 cup of Crème Chantilly with 1 cup of cold milk. Add lemon mixture to the Crème Chantilly and mix together with a blender for a while.
5. Pour the mixture onto a plate and freeze for 2 hours, then refrigerate.
6. Before serving, dip the plate into tepid water, and turn it upside down onto a serving plate.

STARCH PUDDING WITH BISCUITS AND LEMON

Ingredients

- 250 g of biscuit
- 1 cup of lemon juice
- 1 cup of sugar
- 2 tablespoons of starch
- 2 eggs
- 125 g of margarine

Directions

1. Wash and grate the lemons. Using a spoon, mix the lemon pulp with the sugar. Add in 2 cups of water, mix until the sugar dissolves, and sieve.
2. Whisk together the eggs and starch in a pot, adding in a few tablespoons of lemon juice. Add in lemon mixture, and cook while stirring. Remove from heat once the mixture thickens. Add in 125 grams of margarine.
3. Spread parchment paper or aluminum foil over a tray, 20-25 cm in diameter, and sprinkle with water.
4. Spread out 3-4 tablespoons of the mixture onto the tray.
5. Add crumbled biscuits into the remaining pudding, and pour onto the tray while stirring. Smooth over while pressing with a spoon.
6. Refrigerate overnight. Before serving, turn up the edges with a spoon, turn upside down onto a plate and remove the paper.

Note: *To make cream with cocoa, mix together 2 eggs, 1-2 tablespoons of cocoa, 1 cup of sugar, and 2 tablespoons of starch in a pot, blending with a few tablespoons of milk. Add in half a liter of hot milk and cook while stirring. Remove from heat, add in 125 g of margarine and mix. Add in vanilla and serve once it is tepid.*

FRUIT SALAD

Ingredients

- 3 apples
- 2 oranges
- 2 tangerines
- 2 bananas
- 1 pear
- 1 kiwi
- 2 tablespoons of powdered sugar
- 2 tablespoons of fruit or pear liqueur or vermouth
- ½ a cup of prepared Crème Chantilly
- 2 tablespoons of roasted pistachios or almonds

Directions

1. Wash, peel and dice the fruit. Lightly cook apples with 1 tablespoon of sugar.
2. Put fruit in a bowl with powdered sugar and mix together. Pour liqueur or vermouth over. Cover and refrigerate until cooled.
3. Pour evenly into serving dishes. Pour syrup concentrated at the bottom of the pot over the fruit. Top with 1 tablespoon of Crème Chantilly and sprinkle with diced pistachios or almonds.

Note:

1) *If desired, make fruit salad with the remaining fruit.*
2) *Use seasonal fruits such as peaches, apricots, strawberries, melons and raisins.*

APPLE AND ORANGE CUP

Ingredients

- 1 orange
- 3 tablespoons of seedless raisins
- 4 small apples
- 6 tablespoons of sugar
- 1 portion of salt-free, Labne cheese
- 6 sweetened bran biscuits
- 2 egg whites

Directions

1. Wash and squeeze the orange. Boil 2 slices of diced orange peel in water and sieve the stock. Cook the boiled orange peels on low heat with 1 tablespoons of sugar and 1 tablespoon of orange juice.
2. Wash and sieve the raisins, and soak them in 3 tablespoons of orange juice for 15 minutes. Mix with half of the cheese.
3. Wash and peel the apples, cut them into quarters, and dice. Add 2 tablespoons of sugar and remaining orange juice to the apples and cook on a low heat. Remove from heat while the consistency is still watery.
4. Beat egg whites with 3 tablespoons of sugar.
5. Crumble biscuits by hand and mix with the other half of the cheese.
6. Layer the ingredients in the following order, from bottom to top, into 6 oven-safe bowls: **a)** Cheese and raisin mixture. **b)** Cooked apple slices. **c)** Cheese with biscuits. **d)** Cooked apple slices. **e)** Whisked egg whites with sugar. Top with orange peels.
7. Heat the bowls for a short while in the oven until the egg whites turn pink. Let cool, then refrigerate and serve cold.

STEWED QUINCES

Ingredients

- 2 quinces
- 1 ½ cups of sugar
- Grated peel of ½ a lemon

Directions

1. Wash and cut the quinces into quarters. Remove the core and seeds and peel. Cut each quarter into three pieces.
2. Boil the core and seeds with 5 cups of water in a pot for 15-20 minutes and sieve the water for later use.
3. Put chopped quinces in a pot. Add in sieved stock and cover. Boil on a medium heat, without letting the quinces get too soft.
4. Add in sugar and boil slowly on a low heat for a while. Remove from heat and add in lemon juice. Uncover and let cool.

STEWED APPLES

Ingredients

- 5 small apples
- 1 cup of sugar
- Juice from ½ a lemon

Directions

1. Wash and chop the apples into quarters. Remove the core and peel.
2. Boil sugar with 5 cups of water. Add in apples and lower the heat. Cover and cook until the apples get soft.
3. Remove from heat and add in lemon juice. Keep covered and let cool.
4. Once cooled, remove into bowls. If desired, top with Crème Chantilly.

STEWED STRAWBERRIES

Ingredients

- ½ a kg of strawberries
- 1 cup of sugar

Directions

1. Put strawberries into a pot filled with water. Shake and sieve into another pot filled with water. Then wash and sieve again.
2. Boil sugar with 5 cups of sugar. Add in cleaned strawberries. Cover and lower the heat. Cook for 10 minutes without boiling. Remove from heat, and uncover to let cool.

STEWED BLACK CHERRIES

Ingredients

- ½ a kg of black cherries
- 1 ½ cups of sugar

Directions

1. Wash cherries and remove the stems.
2. Boil sugar in a pot with 5 cups of water. Add in cherries. Cover and bring to a boil. Lower the heat and cook for 10 more minutes then remove from heat. Uncover and let cool.

STEWED APRICOTS

Ingredients

- ½ a kg of apricots
- 1 cup of sugar

Directions

1. Wash apricots and remove the seeds.
2. Boil sugar with 5 cups of water. Add in apricots and cover. Lower the heat and cook until the apricots get soft, without boiling. Remove from the heat and let cool while covered.

Note: *To make stewed plums, follow the same directions and replace with plums, removing the seeds.*

VIII

CAKES AND COOKIES

CAKE WITH HAZELNUTS AND GRAPES

Ingredients

- 5 eggs
- 1 cup of sugar
- 2 cups of flour
- ½ a teaspoon of baking powder
- 1 tablespoon of lemon juice
- ½ a grated lemon peel
- 4 tablespoons of large chopped hazelnuts
- 3 tablespoons of seedless raisins

Directions

1. Grease a cake mould 25 cm in diameter with softened margarine. Sprinkle 1 tablespoon of large chopped hazelnuts over the bottom and sides of the mould and preheat the oven.
2. Separate egg whites into a pot and egg yolks into a bowl. Add in sugar and grated lemon peels to the egg yolks and mix until the sugar dissolves.
3. Whisk the egg whites. Add in lemon juice and the yolk, sugar and lemon peel mixture, and mix together.
4. Add in flour and baking powder and mix together. Stir in 3 tablespoons of raisins and 2 tablespoons of hazelnuts.
5. Pour the dough mixture into the mould and smooth it over. Sprinkle the remaining 1 tablespoon of hazelnuts on top. Put the mould on a tray and cook in a preheated oven on medium heat for 30-35 minutes, keeping the door closed. Remove from heat and take out of the mould once it cooled. Slice and serve.

QUICK SWEET CAKE

Ingredients

- 2 eggs
- 2 cups of sugar
- 3 cups of flour
- 1 cup of milk
- ½ a cup of oil
- 1 teaspoon of baking powder
- ½ a teaspoon of baking soda
- ½ a teaspoon of salt
- ½ a grated lemon peel
- 2 tablespoons of lemon juice

Directions

1. Mix 3 cups of flour, baking powder, baking powder and salt together and sieve.
2. Grease and flour a cake mould and preheat the oven.
3. Whisk sugar, oil, lemon peels and lemon juice together in a pot.
4. Sieve the flour mixture again into the pot.
5. While stirring, slowly add in 1 cup of milk to the flour and lemon mixture then pour it into the mould.
6. Put the mould onto a tray and cook on a medium heat in a preheated oven for 30-35 minutes.
7. Remove from the heat, let cool and slice.

Note:

1) *If desired, first pour half of the cake mixture into the mould, then mix 1 tablespoon of cocoa to the remaining dough and pour into the mould. Cook in a preheated oven on medium heat for 30-35 minutes.*
2) *If desired, replace lemon juice and peels with grapefruit.*

FIG CAKE WITH WALNUTS

Ingredients

- 3 eggs
- 1 cup of sugar
- 2 ½ cups of flour
- ½ a cup of oil
- 1 ½ teaspoons of baking powder
- 1 tablespoon of lemon juice
- ½ a grated lemon peel
- ⅓ a cup of milk
- ½ a cup of chopped walnuts
- 3 figs

Directions

1. Grease a cake mould with softened margarine, cover with flour, and preheat the oven.
2. Dice the figs and walnuts.
3. Sieve flour and baking powder together.
4. Mix oil and flour together. Add in egg yolks, grated lemon peels, and lemon juice, and stir until the sugar dissolves.
5. Whisk egg whites and add to the egg yolk and sugar mixture, stirring occasionally. Add in sieved flour and diced walnuts and figs. Slowly turn the cake mixture upside down and add in milk.
6. Pour the mixture into the mould. Cook in an oven on medium heat for 30-35 minutes. Remove from the oven and let cool. Once tepid turn upside down onto a serving plate.

CHOCOLATE CAKE WITH COFFEE

Ingredients

- 2 eggs
- 1 ½ cups of sugar
- 2 ½ cups of flour
- 1 tablespoon of cocoa
- ½ a tablespoon of instant coffee
- 200 g of margarine
- 1 ⅓ cups of milk
- 2 teaspoons of baking powder
- ½ a package of vanilla
- ½ a grated lemon peel
- ½ a teaspoon of salt

Directions

1. Grease a cake mould with softened margarine, cover with flour and preheat the oven.
2. Mix flour, ground coffee, cocoa baking powder, vanilla and salt together, and sieve.
3. Mix softened margarine with sugar and lemon peels until it is creamy. Add in egg yolks and milk.
4. Whisk egg whites, and then stir them into the lemon peels and egg yolks mixture.
5. Sieve the flour mixture into the egg mixture. Gently stir together and pour into the mould. Cook in the oven on medium heat for 35-40 minutes. Once cooled, remove from the oven.
6. FOR THE TOP: Mix 1 cup of powdered sugar, 3-4 teaspoons of lemon juice and 2-3 tablespoons of water together until it has a yogurt consistency. Pour and spread half of the mixture over the cooled cake. Add 1 tablespoon of cocoa and 1 tablespoon of coffee into the remaining mixture and stir. Pour the remaining mixture over the cake, and decorate as desired.

APPLE SAUCE CAKE

Ingredients

- 2 eggs
- 1 ½ cups of powdered sugar
- 2 cups of flour
- ½ a cup of oil
- 1 ½ cups of grated apples
- ½ a cup of seedless raisins
- ½ a cup of chopped walnuts
- ½ a tablespoon of cocoa
- 1 ½ teaspoons of cinnamon
- ½ a teaspoon of ground cloves
- ½ a teaspoon of allspice
- 1 ½ tablespoons of baking powder
- ½ a teaspoon of salt

Directions

1. Grease and flour a tray 25 cm in diameter and preheat the oven.
2. Mix flour, cocoa, baking powder, cinnamon, cloves, allspice and salt together and sieve.
3. Mix oil and sugar together in a large bowl. Add in eggs one at a time, and whisk together.
4. Add in grated apples, walnuts, raisins, and flour mixture. Stir and pour into the mould, leaving the edges higher.
5. Cook in an oven for 35-40 minutes on medium heat.
6. Remove from the oven, and take out of the mould once cooled.

APPLE CAKE

Ingredients

- 4 eggs
- 1 cup of sugar
- 3 cups of flour
- ½ a cup of milk
- 200 g of margarine
- 4 apples
- 1 ½ teaspoons of cinnamon
- ½ a grated lemon peel
- 1 ½ teaspoons of baking powder
- ½ a teaspoon of salt

Directions

1. Grease and flour a tray 25 cm in diameter, and preheat the oven.
2. Wash the apples and chop them into quarters. Peel and dice two apples, and slice the other two into 32 thin slices.
3. Whisk softened margarine with 1 cup of sugar until it is creamy. Add in lemon peels and egg yolks, and whisk again. Add in half a cup of milk and the sliced apples and mix together.
4. Whisk egg whites, and mix in the egg yolk and lemon peel mixture, baking powder, and a mixture of 1 teaspoon of cinnamon and flour.
5. Stir slowly and pour into the greased mould.
6. Place the apple slices on top, and sprinkle on a mixture of 1 tablespoon of powdered sugar and cinnamon. Cook in an oven for 40-50 minutes on medium heat.

APPLE AND CARAMEL CAKE

Ingredients

FOR CAKE:

- 2 eggs
- 2 cups of sugar
- 1 ½ cups of flour
- ½ a cup of orange juice
- 1 grated orange
- 1 teaspoon of baking powder

FOR THE TOP:

- 125 g of margarine
- 9 tablespoons of sugar
- 3 medium apples
- 9 walnuts
- 9 hazelnuts

Directions

1. Melt margarine in a tray 25 cm in diameter and freeze. Grease the edges of the tray with softened margarine.
2. Boil 5 tablespoons of sugar with 5 tablespoons of water in a small pot until a molasses-colored caramel forms. Then add in 8-9 tablespoons of water and cook until the syrup has a molasses consistency.
3. Pour 5-6 tablespoons of caramel syrup over the frozen margarine in the tray and sprinkle 4 tablespoons of powdered sugar on top.
4. Wash the apples, remove the cores, and divide into three parts breadth-wise. Set the 9 apple pieces into a pot, and put hazelnuts or walnuts in the middle.
5. Whisk together 2 eggs, 1 cup of sugar and the grated orange peel in a pot until the consistency thickens. Add in a mixture of 1 ½ cups of flower and baking powder and half a cup of orange juice. Mix together, pour over the apples, and spread evenly.
6. Cook apple cake in an oven on medium heat for 30-35 minutes. Let cool, then serve upside down.

ORANGE CAKE

Ingredients

- 4 eggs
- 10 tablespoons of sugar
- 10 tablespoons of flour
- 1 ½ teaspoons of baking powder
- 1 grated orange peel
- ½ a cup of orange juice

FOR SYRUP:

- 1 cup of orange juice
- 8 tablespoons of sugar
- 2 thinly grated orange peels

Directions

1. Grease a cake mould with softened margarine and cover with flour. Preheat the oven.
2. Separate the egg whites into a pot, and put the yolks in a bowl. Add in 10 tablespoons of sugar and the grated orange peel into the yolk and stir until the sugar dissolves.
3. Whisk the egg whites and whisk in the yolk and orange peel mixture.
4. Mix together the flour and baking powder, add into the pot and stir together. Lastly add in half a cup of orange juice and stir.
5. Pour the cake mix into the mould. Cook in an oven on medium heat for 35-40 minutes. Remove from the oven and let cool. Then remove the mould and set onto a plate.
6. SYRUP: Boil 2 grated orange peels, 8 tablespoons of sugar and 1 cup of orange juice in a pot. Pour over the cake by the spoonful.

BLACK CHERRY CAKE

Ingredients

- 3 eggs
- 12 tablespoons of sugar
- 15 tablespoons of flour
- 6 tablespoons of oil
- 9 tablespoons of milk
- 2 teaspoons of baking powder
- 1 tablespoon of lemon juice
- 1 cup of seedless black cherries
- ½ a package of vanilla

Directions

1. Spread parchment paper on the bottom of a cake mould. Grease the paper with margarine and cover in flour. Preheat the oven.
2. Mix the oil, sugar and lemon juice together in a large bowl. Add in the egg yolks and whisk. Then stir in the milk.
3. Whisk the egg whites and stir into the bowl.
4. Mix together the flour, baking powder and vanilla, and sieve. Slowly stir into the bowl, mix together and pour into the cake mould.
5. Lightly press black cherries on the top and cook in an oven on medium heat for 35-40 minutes. Remove from the heat and let cool. Once tepid, remove from the mould, and remove the parchment paper. Pour hot sauce over the cake with a spoon.
6. SAUCE: Boil 5 tablespoons of sugar with 3 tablespoons of water on a low heat until the sugar dissolves. Add in 4 tablespoons of lemon juice, 4 tablespoons of melted margarine or butter and vanilla, and whisk together. Pour over tepid cake when it is hot.

Feride Çiçekoğlu
arkadaş

CARROT CAKE

Ingredients

- 4 eggs
- 1 cup of oil
- 2 ½ cups of sugar
- 3 cups of flour
- 3 cups of thinly grated carrots
- 1 cup of chopped walnuts
- ½ a grated lemon peel
- ½ a package of vanilla
- 2/3 a tablespoon of cinnamon
- 2/3 a tablespoon of baking powder
- ½ a teaspoon of salt

Directions

1. Grease a cake mould with softened margarine and cover in flour. Preheat the oven.
2. Mix flour, vanilla, baking powder and salt together and sieve.
3. Wash and grate the carrots with the smallest grate. Dice the walnuts.
4. Mix together the oil, sugar and grated lemon peels in a large bowl. Add in egg yolks and whisk.
5. Whisk egg whites and stir into the bowl.
6. Add in grated carrots and walnuts, and beat together.
7. Slowly stir the flour mixture into the bowl. Then pour into the mould.
8. Cook in an oven on medium heat for 40-45 minutes. Remove from heat and let cool. Remove the mould and place onto a serving dish.

BROWNIE

Ingredients

- 4 eggs
- 4 tablespoons of cocoa
- 4 tablespoons of milk
- 1 ½ cups of sugar
- 1 ½ cups of flour
- 1 ½ cups of diced walnuts
- 250 g of margarine (melted and re-frozen)
- 1 teaspoon of baking powder

Directions

1. Whisk eggs, sugar and cocoa together in a pot. Add in oil and beat together.
2. Add in milk, baking powder and sieved flour and mix together.
3. Lastly add in the walnuts. Pour mixture into a greased bread pan or tray 25 cm in diameter and cook in an oven for 25-30 minutes.
4. Remove from the oven, let cool and slice.

CHOCOLATE CAKE WITH LIQUEUR

Ingredients

- 4 eggs
- 2 cups of sugar
- 2 ½ cups of flour
- 250 g of margarine
- 1 cup of milk
- 2 tablespoons of cocoa
- 2 tablespoon of fruit liqueur, whisky or cognac
- 1 ½ teaspoons of baking powder
- ½ a package of vanilla

Directions

1. Grease a cake mould 25-30 cm in diameter with softened margarine and cover with flour. Preheat the oven.
2. Mix together the melted margarine, 1 ½ cups of sugar, cocoa, liqueur and vanilla. Slowly add in 1 cup of milk and stir until the sugar dissolves. Pour mixture into a bowl, sparing 1 cup for later use. Add in half a cup of sugar and 4 egg yolks to the bowl and mix together.
3. Whisk egg whites and add to the bowl.
4. Add in sieved flour and baking powder and slowly stir together. Pour into the cake mould and cook in an oven on medium heat for 25-30 minutes.
5. Remove from the oven and let cool. Then remove from the mould, put on a serving plate and slice. Pour the spared cup of sauce over the cake with a spoon.

MARMALADE CAKE

Ingredients

- 4 eggs
- 1 ½ cups of sugar
- 3 cups of flour
- 190 g of margarine
- ½ a cup of milk
- 2 teaspoons of baking powder
- 1 tablespoon of lemon juice
- ½ a grated lemon peel
- ½ a teaspoon of salt
- 3-4 tablespoons of marmalade

Directions

1. Grease a cake mould with softened margarine and cover with flour.
2. Mix softened margarine and sugar together in a bowl until creamy.
3. Add in egg yolk, grated lemon peels and lemon juice. Then add in milk and stir together.
4. Sieve flour, baking powder and salt together twice.
5. Whisk egg whites.
6. Add whisked egg whites and sieved flour into the cake mix.
7. Slowly stir together.
8. Pour cake mix into the cake mould and cook in a preheated oven on medium heat for 30-35 minutes.
9. Let cool, then remove from the mould. Cut into three pieces breadth-wise. Spread marmalade in between each piece, and layer on top of each other. Sprinkle with powdered sugar.

CAKE WITH CHEESE

Ingredients

- 3 eggs
- 1 cup of yogurt
- 1 cup of margarine and oil mixture
- 3 ½ cups of flour
- 125-150 g of white cheese
- 1 bunch of dill
- 1 ½ teaspoons of baking powder
- 2 teaspoons of salt
- 2 teaspoons of black cumin

Directions

1. Grease a tray 30-35 cm in diameter with softened margarine. Preheat the oven.
2. Mix the egg, oil and yogurt together in a pot, sparing 2 tablespoons of the mixture for the top part.
3. Add grated cheese, diced dill, baking powder and sieved flour to the pot and mix together.
4. Pour the mixture onto the tray and smooth, leaving more at the edges.
5. Spread the spared egg and yogurt mixture over the top, and sprinkle with black cumin. Cook in an oven on medium heat for 30-35 minutes.
6. Remove from the oven, place on a serving plate and slice.

TART WITH CHEESE

Ingredients

- 2 ½ cups of flour
- 125 g of softened margarine
- 4 tablespoons of yogurt
- 1 teaspoon of baking powder
- 1 teaspoon of salt

FOR FILLING:

- 1 portion of white cheese (250 g)
- 1 bunch of dill
- 2 eggs
- 1 cup of milk

Directions

1. Mix margarine, yogurt, eggs, baking powder and salt together in a pot. Add in sieved flour and knead shortly. Cover and let rest for 10-15 minutes.
2. Divide the dough into two pieces, with one piece larger than the other. Flour the larger piece and roll out until it is larger than a small tray. Grease the small tray and set the dough over it, raising the edges.
3. Mix the dill and cheese together and sprinkle it over the dough. Roll out the smaller piece of dough, form into small strips, and place over the cheese filling like a grid.
4. Whisk 2 eggs and 1 cup of milk together and pour over the top. Cook in an oven until it turns pink.

OLIVE CAKE

Ingredients

- 4 eggs
- ¾ a cup of oil
- ½ a cup of yogurt
- 1 cup of pitted chopped olives
- 2 teaspoons of thyme
- Juice from ½ a lemon
- 1 ½ cups of baking powder
- 1 teaspoon of salt
- 2 teaspoons of black cumin

Directions

1. Grease a tray 25-30 cm in diameter and cover in flour. Preheat the oven.
2. Mix eggs, oil and yogurt together in a pot. Remove 1 tablespoon of the mixture for later use.
3. Add lemon juice, thyme, chopped olives and salt to the pot and mix together.
4. Add in baking powder and sieved flour. Mix and pour into the tray.
5. Smooth over, leaving more mixture at the edges. Spread the saved tablespoon of egg and yogurt mixture over and sprinkle with black cumin.
6. Cook in an oven on medium heat for 30-35 minutes.
7. Remove from the oven. Let cool, then remove onto a serving plate once tepid and slice.

CREAM CAKE WITH CHOCOLATE

Ingredients

- 5 eggs
- $2/3$ a cup of sugar
- $1/6$ a cup of melted margarine
- 1 tablespoon of cocoa
- 1 tablespoon of lemon juice
- $1/2$ a grated lemon peel
- 1 teaspoon of baking powder

Directions

1. Grease a cake mould or tray 20 cm in diameter and cover in flour.
2. Mix flour, cocoa, and baking powder together and sieve twice.
3. Whisk melted margarine, sugar, grated lemon peels and egg yolks together in a bowl.
4. Whisk egg whites for 6-7 minutes with a mixer. Add in egg yolk mixture and flour mixture after sieving again. Sprinkle lemon juice in.
5. Gently stir and pour into the cake mould. Cook in a preheated oven on medium heat for 35-40 minutes.
6. Let cool, then divide the cake in half. Spread pastry cream (see page 368) or Crème Chantilly (see page 326) onto one piece and put the other one on it. Spread chocolate cream on the top and sides. Decorate with grated chocolate, coconut and blended hazelnut or Crème Chantilly.

PASTRY CREAM

Ingredients

- 1 egg
- 7 tablespoons of sugar
- 3 tablespoons of flour
- ½ a liter of milk
- ½ a grated lemon peel
- ½ a package of vanilla
- 50 g of margarine

Directions

1. Mix egg, sugar, flour, grated lemon peel and 1-2 tablespoons of milk together in a pot.
2. Slowly add in hot milk and boil while stirring. Once the milk thickens, remove from heat.
3. Stir while it cools. Add in margarine and vanilla and whisk.
4. If desired, make chocolate cream by adding in 1 tablespoon of sieved cocoa to the mix.

VANILLA FROSTING

Ingredients

- ⅔ a cup of sugar
- ⅓ a cup of water
- 125 g of margarine
- ½ a package of vanilla

Directions

1. Boil sugar and water together in a pot and remove from heat once the consistency thickens. Let cool.
2. Whisk margarine in a bowl.
3. Add cold syrup to the margarine by the spoonful and mix together.

CHOCOLATE FROSTING

Ingredients

- 125 g of bitter chocolate
- 1/3 a cup of sugar
- 1/3 a cup of water
- 50 g of margarine

Directions

1. Boil the sugar and water together in a pot until the consistency thickens.
2. Remove from heat and add in chocolate. Melt while stirring.
3. Add in margarine and mix. Ice the cake while the frosting is still tepid. Refrigerate to harden.

CHOCOLATE FROSTING (VARIATION)

Ingredients

- 125 g of bitter chocolate
- 50 g of margarine

Directions

1. Put chocolate and margarine into a bowl and melt by putting it over a pot with hot water. Mix once melted.
2. Let cool, and pour over cake once tepid, spreading with a knife. Refrigerate to harden.

ORANGE EGG WHITE CAKE

Ingredients

- 5 egg whites
- ⅔ a cup of sugar
- 1 cup of flour
- 100 g of hazelnuts
- ⅓ a cup of orange juice
- ½ a package of vanilla
- ½ a teaspoon of baking powder

Directions

1. Grease and flour a tray 20 cm in diameter.
2. Mix the flour, vanilla and baking powder together and sieve twice.
3. Blend in the hazelnuts.
4. Beat egg whites for 6-7 minutes in a mixer, slowly adding in sugar.
5. Add in the flour mixture and blended hazelnuts. Pour in ⅓ a cup of orange juice. Gently stir and pour into the mould.
6. Cook in an oven on medium heat for 35 minutes. Remove from heat.
7. Let cool, then remove from the mould. Slice in half horizontally. Spread cake cream on the lower piece, and put the upper piece over it.
8. Frost the top and sides with vanilla frosting or Crème Chantilly with sugar. Cover with grated coconuts.

BANANA CAKE ROLL

Ingredients

FOR THE SPONGE CAKE

- 6 eggs
- 5 tablespoons of sugar
- 8 tablespoons of flour
- ½ a package of vanilla
- 1 tablespoon of lemon juice
- 1 grated lemon peel

FOR THE CREAM

- 1 egg
- 7 tablespoons of sugar
- 3 tablespoon of flour
- ½ a liter of milk
- ½ a grated lemon peel
- Vanilla
- 50 g of margarine

FOR FILLING

- 3 bananas

FOR THE TOP

- ½ a cup of pulverized hazelnuts

Directions

1. CREAM PREPARATION: Mix 1 egg, 7 tablespoons of sugar, 3 tablespoons of grated lemon peels and 1-2 tablespoons of milk together in a pot.
2. Slowly add in hot milk and bring to a boil.
3. Once it boils and the consistency thickens, remove from heat. Let cool, stirring occasionally. Add in 50 g of margarine and ½ a package of vanilla.
4. PREPARATION OF THE SPONGE CAKE: Spread out parchment paper in a rectangular tray. Grease and flour it. Preheat the oven.
5. Separate the egg yolks into a bowl, and put the egg whites in a pot. Add 5 tablespoons of sugar, vanilla, and grated lemon peels to the egg yolks, and mix until the sugar dissolves. Whisk the egg whites. Add to the egg yolk mixture and beat together.
6. Sieve the flour and add into the pot. Gently stir and add in 1 tablespoon of lemon juice.
7. Spread the cake mix out into the tray. Put on the top shelf in the oven and cook for 10-15 minutes, removing before it gets too dry. Remove from the oven and roll from the long edge with the parchment paper to practice, and then unroll.
8. Spare 3 tablespoons of cream for the top, and spread the rest over the sponge cake. Put bananas on the edges and roll along the long edge. Spread the cream over the top and sprinkle with hazelnuts.

DRY BEAN PASTRY

Ingredients

- 3 eggs
- 2 cups of beans
- 1 cup of largely chopped walnuts
- 1 ½ cups of sugar
- ½ a package of baking powder
- 1 package of vanilla

FOR THE CREAM

- 2 eggs
- ½ a liter of milk
- 1 cup of sugar
- 3 tablespoons of flour
- 1 tablespoon of cocoa
- 40 g of margarine or butter

Directions

1. Wash and soak beans overnight. The following day add in ⅓ a tablespoon of sugar and boil. Sieve the out the water and blend together.
2. Add in egg, sugar, baking powder and vanilla and blend together for 3-4 more minutes. Add in walnuts and pour into a greased oven-proof glass tray. Cook in an oven on medium heat for 30-35 minutes.
3. PREPARATION OF THE CREAM: Mix sugar, flour, cocoa and 2 tablespoons of milk in a pot. Slowly stir in half a liter of hot milk and bring to a boil. Remove from heat, add in oil, and stir occasionally until tepid.
4. Whisk two eggs, add in cream by the spoonful and mix together.
5. Once the bean cake gets tepid, pierce it with a fork in 4-5 places. Pour tepid chocolate cream over it and spread over.
6. Let cool then refrigerate.

FRENCH PASTRY (FLORENTINE)

Ingredients

FOR DOUGH

- ½ a cup of milk
- 1 ½ tablespoons of sugar
- 40 g of margarine
- 1 egg
- 2 ½ cups of flour
- 2/3 a tablespoon of yeast
- ½ a teaspoon of salt
- 1 grated lemon peel

FOR THE TOP

- 4 tablespoons of milk
- 2 tablespoons of sugar
- 50 g of margarine
- ⅓ a tablespoon of strained honey
- 1 yolk
- ½ a cup of diced hazelnuts

FOR THE CREAM

- 2 cups of milk
- 6 tablespoons of sugar
- 25 g of margarine
- 2 ½ tablespoons of flour
- 1 egg
- ½ a package of margarine

Directions

1. FOR THE DOUGH: Dissolve yeast and 1 teaspoon of sugar in a pot with tepid milk. Wait for 10 minutes to let the yeast ferment. Add in the margarine, egg, remaining sugar, salt and lemon peels.
2. Add in sieved flour until the dough is soft, and then knead together. Cover and let sit in a warm place until the dough rises to twice the size.
3. Grease a tray 20-25 cm in diameter with softened margarine. Knead the dough again and put into the mould, leaving more dough at the edges. Spread the hazelnut mixture over the dough and cover. Let rise again in a warm place for 30-35 minutes.
4. HAZELNUT MIXTURE FOR THE TOP PART: Boil the milk and sugar together in a small pot and remove from heat. Add in the margarine, honey and hazelnuts and mix together.
5. After the dough rises, cook in an oven on medium heat for 30 -35 minutes. Remove from the oven and let cool. Then cut in half horizontally. Spread cream on the bottom half and put the upper half over it. Refrigerate for a while then serve.
6. PREPARATION OF THE CREAM: Mix eggs, sugar, flour and 1-2 tablespoons of milk together in a pot. Add in hot milk and boil while stirring. Once the mixture thickens remove from heat. Let cool, stirring occasionally. Add in vanilla and margarine and whisk for 2-3 minutes.

TIRAMISU (CHEESE PASTRY WITH CAKE)

Ingredients

- 1 round chocolate cake

FOR SAUCE

- 1 cup of water
- 2 tablespoons of instant coffee
- 2 tablespoons of sugar
- 1 tablespoon of cognac or whiskey

FOR CREAM

- 3 eggs
- 4 tablespoons of sugar
- 1 package of cheese
- 1 package of small cream

Directions

1. PREPARATION OF THE CREAM: Separate the egg yolks and egg whites. Whisk the yolks with sugar. Add the cheese and cream in.
2. Whisk the egg whites separately. Add in the yolk and cheese mixture and mix together.
3. FOR THE SAUCE: Dissolve 2 tablespoons of coffee and 2 tablespoons of sugar in 1 cup of hot water. Add in 1 tablespoon of cognac or whiskey.
4. Cut the cake in half horizontally. Wet both halves of the cake with water and coffee mixture. Spread prepared cream on the bottom half and put the other piece on top.
5. Spread the remaining cream over the top. Cover and refrigerate overnight. Sprinkle cocoa or grated dark chocolate over the cake before serving.

TIRAMISU (CHEESE PASTRY WITH BISCUITS)

Ingredients

- 450 g of Savayer Cookies (see page 415)

FOR CREAM

- 3 egg yolks
- ½ a liter of milk
- 2 tablespoons of flour
- 1 cup of sugar
- 1 package of vanilla
- 2 packages of pasteurized cheese

FOR SAUCE

- 3 tablespoons of instant coffee
- 3 tablespoons of sugar
- 1 tablespoon of cognac or whiskey
- ⅔ a cup of hot water

Directions

1. Whisk 3 egg yolks, 1 cup of sugar, 2 tablespoons of flour and some milk together in a pot. Add in half a liter of hot milk and bring to a boil while stirring. Let cool, stirring occasionally. Add in 2 packages of cheese and vanilla, and mix together.
2. Dissolve 3 tablespoons of coffee and 3 tablespoons of sugar in 1 cup of hot water by stirring. Add in 1 tablespoon of cognac or whiskey.
3. Wet the biscuits into the coffee mixture and layer onto a plate with the cheese mixture. Pour the remaining cream on top, cover and refrigerate overnight. The following day, sieve the cocoa over the dessert and serve.

CHOCOLATE CREAM PASTRY WITH SAVAYER COOKIES

Ingredients

- 200 g of Savayer Cookies (see page 415)
- 1 package of powdered Crème Chantilly
- 1 cup of cold milk

FOR CREAM

- ½ a liter of milk
- ⅓ a cup of sugar
- 1 ½ tablespoons of cocoa
- 1 egg and 2 egg yolks
- 125 g of margarine
- 1 package of vanilla

FOR THE TOP

- Some fruit candy

Directions

1. FOR THE CREAM: Mix sugar, flour, cocoa and 2-3 tablespoons of milk together in a pot. Slowly add in hot milk and bring to a boil while stirring.
2. Remove from heat and add in 1 egg, 2 egg yolks, 125 g of soft margarine and vanilla once tepid. Whisk for 5 minutes.
3. In a bowl, whisk powdered Crème Chantilly and 1 cup of cold milk for 5 minutes.
4. Pour half of the cream into a round, glass casserole dish with the cocoa and spread out. Break the biscuits to the height of the dish, and set them along the edges.
5. Divide the remaining biscuits and set half of them on top of the chocolate cream.
6. Put the prepared Crème Chantilly in the middle, and set the rest of the biscuits on top.
7. Spread the chocolate cream over the top and decorate with fruit candies.
8. Cover and refrigerate overnight. Serve cold.

CAT'S TONGUE COOKIE PASTRY

Ingredients

- 300 g of cat's tongue cookies (see page 414)
- 6 eggs
- 1 cup of powdered sugar
- 500 g of Crème Chantilly (sugar free cream)
- 2 tablespoons of instant coffee
- 1 package of vanilla

Directions

1. Separate the egg yolks into a large bowl and put the egg whites in a pot.
2. Mix the yolks, powder sugar and vanilla together.
3. Whisk the egg whites with a pinch of salt.
4. Whisk the Crème Chantilly separately.
5. Gently stir in the sugar and yolk mixture and the whisked egg whites into the Crème Chantilly.
6. Divide the mixture in half. Add ground coffee to one half and gently stir.
7. Layer the cookies and cream in a rectangular, glass tray with the coffee cream and the plain cream. If desired, decorate the top with some fruit candy.
8. Refrigerate overnight. Serve cold.

CHOCOLATE PUDDING WITH APPLES

Ingredients

- 4 eggs
- 7 tablespoons of sugar
- 1 tablespoon of cocoa
- ½ a cup of diced walnuts
- 2 small apples
- 1 ½ teaspoons of baking powder
- ½ a teaspoon of salt

FOR THE TOP

- ½ a tablespoon of sugar
- ⅙ a cup of water
- 1 tablespoon of fruit liqueur, cognac or whiskey

FOR THE SAUCE

- 1 egg
- 5 tablespoons of sugar
- 1 tablespoon of starch
- 1 tablespoon of cocoa
- 2 cups of milk
- ½ a package of vanilla

Directions

1. Grease a tray 20-25 cm in diameter with softened margarine and coat in flour. Preheat the oven.
2. Mix 7 tablespoons of flour with the cocoa, baking powder and salt and sieve together.
3. Wash the apples, remove their cores, and cut into quarters. Then peel and dice them.
4. Separate the egg yolks from the egg whites. Add 7 tablespoons of sugar to the egg yolks and mix until the sugar dissolves.
5. Whisk the egg whites. Add in the yolk and sugar mixture and whisk.
6. Add the flour mixture and chopped walnuts to the egg mixture and slowly stir in the diced apples.
7. Pour the cake mixture into the mould and cook in an oven on medium heat for 30-35 minutes. Let cool, then remove the mould and put on a serving plate. Pour a mixture of 1/6 a cup of liqueur, sugar and water over. Then pour chocolate sauce over by the spoonful.
8. PREPARATION OF THE SAUCE: Mix 1 egg, 5 tablespoons of sugar, 1 tablespoon of starch, 1 tablespoon of cocoa and 1-2 tablespoons of milk together in a pot. Add in 2 cups of hot milk and boil while stirring. Continually stir to prevent the cream from condensing. Add in vanilla.

DAISY PASTRY

Ingredients

FOR THE DOUGH

- 14 tablespoons of flour
- 150 g of margarine
- 22 tablespoons of powdered sugar
- 1 egg
- ½ a grated lemon peel
- Vanilla

FOR THE FILLING

- 1 ½ cups of ground walnuts or hazelnuts
- ½ a cup of powdered sugar
- 3 eggs
- ½ a grated lemon peel
- Vanilla

FOR THE TOP

- 10-15 almonds

FOR THE INSIDE

- 3-4 tablespoons of marmalade

Directions

1. PREPARATION OF THE DOUGH: Mix 150 g of soft margarine, 2 tablespoons of powdered sugar, 1 egg, grated lemon peels and vanilla together in a pot.
2. Sieve 14 tablespoons of flour and quickly add to make dough. Cover and let rest in a cool place for 14 minutes.
3. Roll out the dough until it is larger than the mould. Spread 3 tablespoons of marmalade over it.
4. FOR THE FILLING: Mix ground walnuts, powdered sugar, 3 eggs, grated lemon peels, and vanilla together with a spoon in a large bowl.
5. Pour the filling over the marmalade in the mould and spread out. Place almonds on top which have been peeled in hot water and divided in half like a daisy.
6. Cook in an oven on medium heat. Once cooked, remove from heat. Let cool, then place on a serving plate.

Note: *If desired, make 15-20 small daisy pastries by using a smaller mould.*

QUICK BISCUIT PASTRIES

Ingredients

- 300 g of plain biscuits
- 100 g of chocolate biscuits
- ½ a cup of largely copped walnuts

FOR THE CREAM FILLING

- 1 egg
- 1 ½ cups of sugar
- 3 tablespoons of flour
- 2 tablespoons of starch
- 1 liter of milk
- ½ a package of vanilla

FOR THE CREAM ON THE TOP

- 1 tablespoon of flour
- 1 tablespoon of starch
- 2 tablespoons of cocoa
- 3 tablespoons of sugar
- 1 ½ cups of milk
- ½ a package of vanilla

Directions

1. Crumble the biscuits with your palms and put in a bowl. Add in chopped walnuts and mix together.
2. PREPARATION OF THE CREAM FILLING: Mix the egg, sugar, flour, starch and a few tablespoons of milk together in a pot. Add in 1 liter of hot milk and slowly bring to a boil, stirring occasionally. Remove from heat and add in vanilla once it is tepid.
3. Cover a deep round bowl in aluminum foil or parchment paper, and wet the paper.
4. Add crumbled biscuits and walnut mixture into the tepid cream and stir together. Pour into the bowl and press with a spoon. Refrigerate for 6-7 hours.
5. PREPARATION OF THE CREAM FOR THE TOP: Mix 1 tablespoon of flour, 1 tablespoon of starch, 2 tablespoons of cocoa, 3 tablespoons of sugar and a few tablespoons of milk together in a pot. Add in 1 ½ cups of hot milk and bring to a boil while stirring. Remove from heat and let cool, stirring occasionally. Add in vanilla.
6. Turn refrigerated bowl upside down onto a serving plate, and remove the paper. Pour the prepared cream on top. If desired, sprinkle grated coconut or hazelnuts on top. Refrigerate again. Slice and serve chilled.

FRUIT TARTS

Ingredients

FOR THE DOUGH
- 14 tablespoons of flour
- 150 g of margarine
- 3 tablespoons of powdered sugar
- 1 egg
- ½ a grated lemon peel
- Vanilla

FOR THE CREAM
- 1 egg
- 7 tablespoons of sugar
- 3 tablespoons of flour
- ½ a liter of milk
- ½ a grated lemon peel
- Vanilla

FOR THE TOP
- Fruits according to season (strawberries, kiwi, bananas, peaches, apricots, etc.)
- 1 tablespoon of apricot marmalade
- 3 tablespoons of preapared Créme Chantilly

Directions

1. Mix 150 g of softened margarine, 3 tablespoons of powdered sugar, 1 egg, the grated lemon peel and vanilla together in a pot.
2. Add in 14 tablespoons of flour and quickly form into dough. Cover and let sit in a cool place for 15 minutes.
3. Flour the dough and roll it out until it is larger than the mould. Cook in an oven on medium heat.
4. Remove from the oven and let cool. Then place it on a plate and spread the cream on top. Set desired fruit slices over it.
5. Spread apricot marmalade over the fruits. Decorate with Crème Chantilly.
6. PREPARATION OF THE CREAM: Mix egg, sugar, flour, grated lemon peels and 1-2 tablespoons of milk together. Add in hot milk and slowly cook while stirring. Let cool, stirring occasionally to prevent the cream from condensing on top. Add in vanilla.

APPLE TART

Ingredients

- 1 cup of oil
- ½ a cup of sugar
- 4 eggs
- 1 teaspoon of baking powder
- ½ a package of vanilla
- Flour (as needed)

FOR APPLE SAUCE

- 8-10 small apples
- 1 cup of sugar
- 1 ½ teaspoons of cinnamon

Directions

1. PREPARATION OF THE APPLE SAUCE: Wash the apples then cut them into quarters. Remove the cores and grate. Cook apples in a pot with 1 cup of sugar. Let cool, then add cinnamon.
2. Mix oil, sugar, eggs, baking powder and vanilla together in a pot. Add in flour to make dough. Cover and let rest in a cool place for 10-15 minutes.
3. Divide the dough into two pieces, with one larger than the other. Flour the larger one and roll it out until it is bigger than the mould (25 cm in diameter). Set the dough into the mould, leaving it higher at the edges.
4. Pour the cold apple sauce into the mould, and spread over. Roll out the other dough and cut into strips. Set them over the mould like a grid.
5. Cook on medium heat until it turns light pink. Remove from the oven and sprinkle with powdered sugar.

APPLE PIE

Ingredients

- 125 g of margarine
- 2 cups of flour
- ½ a teaspoon of salt
- 5 slightly tart apples
- 8 tablespoons of sugar
- 1 ½ tablespoons of cinnamon

Directions

1. Grease a pot with oil and cover in flour. Add in half a teaspoon of salt and 2-3 tablespoons of flour to make dough.
2. Divide the dough into two pieces, with one being larger than the other. Cover and let rest in a cool place for 10-15 minutes.
3. Flour the larger piece of dough and roll it out to 23 cm in diameter. Set it onto an oven-safe glass tray which is 20 cm in diameter.
4. Wash the apples and cut them into quarters. Remove the cores and slice them thinly.
5. Set the apple slices back to back over the dough in the tray, and sprinkle 8 tablespoons of sugar and cinnamon on top.
6. Roll out the second piece of dough until it is 20 cm in diameter and cover it over the apples. Press the excess dough from the larger piece (hanging over the edge of the tray) over the top piece along the edges.
7. Pierce the top of the pie with a fork in a few places. Cook in an oven on medium heat until it turns light pink. Serve tepid.

COCONUT PASTRY

Ingredients

- 4 eggs
- 1 cup of sugar
- 2 cups of flour
- 200 g of margarine
- 1 cup of grated coconut
- ½ a teaspoon of baking powder
- ½ a tablespoon of lemon juice
- ½ a grated lemon peel

FOR THE FILLING AND TOPPING

- 2 packages of Crème Chantilly
- 2 cups of cold milk

Directions

1. Spread parchment paper on the bottom of 2 trays which are 20 cm in diameter. Grease the paper and edges of the trays with softened margarine. Preheat the oven.
2. Mix sugar with softened margarine until it is creamy. Add in egg yolks, grated lemon peels and lemon juice, and whisk together.
3. Whisk the egg whites separately. Add in the sugar and yolk mixture, the mixed flour and baking powder, and the grated coconut and gently stir.
4. Pour into two trays. Cook in an oven on medium heat for 30-35 minutes.
5. Once cooled, turn the trays upside down onto serving plates and remove the papers. Spread half of the Crème Chantilly onto one of the cakes and put the other cake on top. Spread the remaining cream over the sides and top of the cake. If desired, sprinkle grated coconut over the cake. Decorate with orange or cherry candies.

AMMONIA SODA PASTRY

Ingredients

- 2 eggs
- 1/3 a cup of sugar
- 1/3 a cup of melted margarine
- 1/3 a cup of milk
- 1/3 a tablespoon of ammonia soda
- Flour (as needed)

FOR THE CREAM

- 2 eggs
- 1 cup of sugar
- 2 tablespoons of flour
- 1 tablespoon of starch
- 3 ½ cups of milk
- ½ a grated lemon peel
- Vanilla
- 125 g of margarine

Directions

1. PREPARATION OF THE DOUGH: Mix eggs, sugar, margarine, milk and ammonia soda together in a pot. Add in flour until dough is formed. Cover and let rest for half an hour.
2. Divide the dough into four pieces. Roll out each piece until it is 22-25 cm in diameter and cook in an oven one at a time.
3. Spread hot cream over the dough and stack the pieces on top of each other. Coat the sides and top with hot cream and sprinkle grated coconut or ground hazelnuts on top. Keep covered in a large pot to keep it soft. Refrigerate over night.
4. PREPARATION OF CREAM: Mix sugar, flour, starch, grated lemon peels and 2 tablespoons of milk together in a pot. Slowly add in 3 ½ cups of milk and bring to a boil while stirring. Remove from heat and add in margarine and vanilla. Use while hot.

SPONGE CAKE

Ingredients

- 5 eggs
- ½ a cup of sugar
- ½ a grated lemon peel
- 1 ½ cups of flour
- 1 tablespoon of lemon juice
- ½ a package of vanilla
- ½ a teaspoon of baking powder

Directions

1. Separate the egg yolks into a bowl and put the egg whites in a pot.
2. Mix the yolks with sugar and grated lemon peels until the sugar dissolves.
3. Mix the flour, vanilla and baking powder together and sieve twice.
4. Grease a tray which is 20 cm in diameter and cover in flour.
5. Whisk egg whites with a mixer.
6. Add the yolk mixture and flour mixture to the egg whites. Add in lemon juice and gently stir.
7. Pour the cake mixture into the mould. Cook in an oven on medium heat for 35-40 minutes. Let cool, and then remove from the cake mould. If desired, top with cream.

Note: *While preparing the sponge cake, replace ½ a cup of the flour with ground hazelnuts or walnuts.*

SUALA CREAM PASTRY

Ingredients

FOR THE DOUGH

- 125 g of margarine
- 2 cups and 2 tablespoons of flour
- 4 eggs
- 2/3 a tablespoon of sugar
- ½ a teaspoon of salt

FOR THE CREAM

- 1 egg
- 1 cup of sugar
- 3 tablespoons of flour
- ½ a liter of milk
- 50 g of margarine
- ½ a grated lemon peel
- Vanilla

Directions

1. PREPARATION OF THE DOUGH: Boil 2 cups of water in a pot with the sugar, salt and 125 g of margarine. Add in 2 cups and 2 tablespoons of sieved flour and let cook.
2. Remove from heat, and mix in eggs one at a time once the dough is tepid. Put the dough into a dough bag with a funnel on the top, and squeeze dough into walnut or finger sized pieces onto a greased tray.
3. Slowly cook in an oven on medium heat so that the dough does not cave in and is crusty.
4. Once cooked, remove from heat and fill the insides with cream using an icing bag. Cover the tops with chocolate.
5. PREPARATION OF THE CREAM: Mix eggs, sugar, flour, grated lemon peels and 2 tablespoons of milk together in a pot. Add in half a liter of hot milk and bring to a boil while stirring. Remove from heat, and add in margarine and vanilla once it is tepid.
6. If desired, sprinkle powdered sugar on top, or mix together 50 grams of bitter chocolate with 50 grams of margarine and 1 tablespoon of powdered sugar in a small bowl over hot water. Sink the pastries into the mixture, turn upside down and let harden.

PRETZELS

Ingredients

- 2 ½ cups of flour
- 150 g of margarine
- 1 tablespoons of yogurt
- 2 eggs (1 yolk for the top)
- ½ a teaspoon of baking powder
- 1 teaspoon of sugar
- 1 ½ teaspoons of salt
- 2 teaspoons of black cumin

Directions

1. Mix margarine, yogurt, 1 egg, 1 egg yolk, baking powder, sugar and salt together in a pot by hand.
2. Sieve the flour, and knead to make dough. Cover and let rest for 10-15 minutes.
3. Divide the dough into pieces a little smaller than walnuts. Roll them out into rods and twist them together in pairs. Set them onto a tray. Spread yolk mixture combined with 2 teaspoons of milk over the pretzels. Sprinkle black cumin on top and cook in an oven until they turn light pink.

SESAME PRETZELS

Ingredients

- 1 teaspoon of lemon juice
- ½ a cup of water
- ½ a cup of oil
- ½ a cup of melted margarine
- 1 teaspoon of baking powder
- 2 teaspoons of salt
- 1 teaspoon of sugar
- Flour (as needed)
- 1 egg yolk (for the top)
- 2 tablespoons of sesame seeds

Directions

1. Mix the first 6 ingredients together in a pot. Then add in sieved flour until the dough is soft but not sticky.
2. Cover and let sit for 15-20 minutes. Divide the dough into pieces a little smaller than walnuts. Roll them out into rods and twist them together in pairs.
3. Set them onto a tray. Spread egg yolk over them, and sprinkle with sesame seeds. Cook in an oven on medium heat.

SALTED BREAD PRETZELS

Ingredients

- 2 ½ cups of flour
- 125 g of margarine
- 2 tablespoons of oil
- 2 tablespoons of yogurt
- ⅓ a tablespoon of yeast
- ⅙ a tablespoon of sugar
- 2 eggs (1 yolk for the top)
- 1 ½ teaspoons of salt
- 1 tablespoon of sesame seeds and black cumin mixture

Directions

1. Mix yoghurt, yeast and sugar together in a pot. Add in softened margarine, oil, 1 egg, 1 egg yolk and salt and mix by hand.
2. Sieve 2 ½ cups of flour. Add to the pot until the dough is soft but not sticky. Cover and let rise in a warm place until the dough is twice its size.
3. Divide into walnut sized pieces and from into rings. Cover each one with the yolk mixture combined with 2 teaspoons of milk. Sprinkle black cumin on top.
4. Cook in the oven on medium heat.

SWEET ANISE PRETZELS

Ingredients

- 2 ½ cups of flour
- 125 g of margarine
- 2 eggs (1 egg white for the top)
- 2 ½ tablespoons of powdered sugar
- 4 tablespoons of anise seeds
- 1 teaspoon of baking powder
- 1 teaspoon of grated lemon peels
- ½ a teaspoon of salt
- 2-3 tablespoons of sesame

Directions

1. Wash and boil 3 teaspoons of anise seeds with ⅔ a cup of water. Boil until 2 tablespoons of water is left. Sieve and save the water.
2. Sieve flour into a pot. Make a space in the middle and add in softened margarine, 1 egg, 1 yolk, powdered sugar, 2 tablespoons of anise water, 1 teaspoon of anise water, baking powder, grated lemon peels and salt, and mix together.
3. Quickly form into dough. Cover and let sit for 10-15 minutes.
4. Divide the dough into pieces slightly smaller than walnuts, and form into rings. Spread egg yolk mixture over the tops of the dough and sprinkle with anise.
5. Cook in an oven on medium heat until the dough turns pink.

CHEESE PRETZELS (FROM SHEEP'S MILK)

Ingredients

- 250 g of margarine
- 250 g of yellow cheese or strips of cheese
- 1 egg (egg white for the dough and yolk for the top)
- 1 teaspoon of baking powder
- Juice from ½ a lemon
- 1 teaspoon of sugar
- 1 ½ teaspoons of salt
- 3-3 ½ cups of flour

Directions

1. Mix lemon juice and baking powder together in a pot. Add in margarine, grated yellow cheese, egg white, sugar and salt and mix by hand. Add in sieved flour and form into dough. Cover and let sit in a warm place for 10-15 minutes.
2. Divide the dough into 4 pieces. Flour each piece and roll out until it is the size of a plate. Cut each piece into four, and each of those pieces into 3 (totaling 12 pieces). Curl the pieces, starting from the widest edge, and set them onto a tray. Cover the dough with a whisked egg yolk combined with a few teaspoons of milk. If desired, sprinkle on sesame or black cumin. Cook in an oven until it turns light pink.

KANDIL SIMIT

Ingredients

- 125 g of margarine
- 2 tablespoons of oil
- 2 tablespoons of yogurt
- ⅓ a tablespoon of mahaleb
- 1 egg (yolk for dough and white for top)
- 1 ½ teaspoons of salt
- 1 teaspoon of sugar
- 1 teaspoon of baking powder
- Flour (as needed, about 2 ½ - 3 cups)
- 50 g of sesame seeds

Directions

1. Mix margarine, oil, yogurt, mahaleb, 1 egg yolk, salt, sugar and baking powder together in a pot.
2. Add in sieved flour until the dough is soft but not sticky. Cover and let sit for 10-15 minutes.
3. Divide the dough into golf-ball sized pieces, and form into rings. Dredge the dough in egg white and cover with sesame.
4. Set onto a tray and cook in an oven on medium heat.

SABLE COOKIES WITH HAZELNUTS

Ingredients

- 2 ½ cups of flour
- 150 g of margarine
- ½ a cup of powdered sugar
- 2 eggs (1 egg and 1 yolk for the dough and 1 egg white for the top)
- ½ a teaspoon of baking powder
- ½ a package of vanilla
- ½ a grated lemon peel
- ½ a cup of diced hazelnuts

Directions

1. Sieve flour into a pot. Make a space in the middle and add in softened margarine, powdered sugar, 1 egg, 1 yolk, baking powder, grated lemon peels and vanilla. Mix until it forms into dough.
2. Flour the dough and roll out until it is 3 mm thick. Cut with cookie cutters and cover the tops with egg whites and hazelnuts.
3. Set onto a tray and cook in an oven on medium heat.
4. Remove the cookies from the oven and sprinkle a mixture of vanilla and powdered sugar on top while they are still hot.

Note: Sable dough can also be prepared as follows:

1) *Divide the dough into small pieces and roll in palms. Make holes in the centres and flatten out.*
2) *Cover the tops with egg whites and dip into diced hazelnuts. Put some marmalade in the centers and cook in the oven.*

CHEESE BALLS

Ingredients

- 125 g of margarine
- 2 tablespoons of oil
- ½ a cup of yogurt
- 1 egg (egg white for dough and egg yolk for the top)
- 2 small cubes of cheese
- 5-6 sprigs of dill
- 1 teaspoon of baking powder
- 1 teaspoon of salt
- Flour (as needed)
- 1 teaspoon of black cumin

Directions

1. Mix together softened margarine, oil, yogurt, 1 egg white, grated cheese, diced dill, baking powder and salt in a pot by hand.
2. Add in flour until the dough is soft but not sticky. Cover and let sit in a cool place for 20-30 minutes.
3. Divide the dough into walnut size pieces and roll in between palms to form ball shapes.
4. Set onto a lightly greased tray. Spread a mixture of egg yolk and a few teaspoons of milk over the dough and sprinkle black cumin on top.
5. Cook in an oven on medium heat.

KALBURABASTI

Ingredients

- ½ a cup of melted margarine
- 1 cup of milk
- 1 teaspoon of baking powder
- ¼ of a teaspoon of baking soda
- ⅓ a tablespoon of sugar
- 1 teaspoon of salt
- 1 cup of oil (for frying)

Directions

1. Mix melted margarine, milk, baking powder, baking soda, sugar and salt together in a pot.
2. Add in sieved flour and mix until the dough is soft but not sticky. Divide the dough into large walnut sized pieces and flatten with your palms. Press the thinner part of the dough and twist together.
3. Heat oil in a small pot, add in some dough and gently shake the pot. Once the dough slightly hardens, turn over with a sieved ladle. Remove onto a paper towel to absorb excess oil.
4. Serve with tea.

HAZELNUT CINNAMON COOKIES

Ingredients

- 250 g of margarine
- 1 package of cornstarch
- 1 egg
- 1 cup of powdered sugar
- 1 grated lemon peel
- ½ a package of vanilla
- 1 teaspoon of baking powder
- Flour (as needed)

Directions

1. Mix margarine, egg, grated lemon peel, vanilla and baking powder together in a pot by hand.
2. Add in powdered sugar and cornstarch. Then add in sieved flour and mix until the dough is soft but not sticky.
3. Divide the dough into small pieces and form them into small balls with your palms. Put half a hazelnut on top of each piece and cook in an oven until the hazelnut turns light pink.

SWEET COOKIES WITH STARCH

Ingredients

- 250 g of margarine
- 2 tablespoons of sugar
- ½ a cup of pulverized hazelnuts or walnuts
- 1 package of vanilla
- 1 teaspoon of baking powder
- 3 ½ cups of flour

FOR THE TOP

- 3 tablespoons of powdered sugar
- 2 teaspoons of cinnamon

Directions

1. Mix margarine, sugar, pulverized hazelnuts and baking powder together in a pot.
2. Add in sieved flour and quickly form into dough. Cover and let rest in a tepid place for 10-15 minutes.
3. Divide the dough into walnut sized pieces and slightly flatten them. Set onto a tray and cook in an oven on medium heat.
4. Remove from heat and sprinkle with a mixture of powdered sugar and cinnamon.

APRICOT COOKIES

Ingredients

- 2 ½ cups of water
- 150 g of margarine
- 1 egg
- ⅓ a cup of powdered sugar
- ½ a teaspoon of baking power
- ½ a package of vanilla
- 1 grated lemon peel

FOR THE TOP

- 3 tablespoons of marmalade
- ½ a cup of sugar
- 1 drop of yellow food coloring
- 1 drop of red food coloring

Directions

1. Sieve flour in a pot. Make a space in the middle and add in softened margarine, egg, powdered sugar, baking powder, vanilla and grated lemon peels. Quickly knead into dough.
2. Divide the dough into small pieces, roll out by hand and set onto a tray. Cook in an oven on medium heat.
3. Spread marmalade onto each piece of dough, and stick every two together.
4. In separate bowls add red and yellow food coloring to 2 tablespoons of water each.
5. Dip one part of the cookie into the red food coloring, and the other half into yellow food coloring.
6. Set the cookies onto serving plates and garnish with leaves.

COLORED COOKIES

Ingredients

- 2 ½ cups of flour
- 150 g of margarine
- ½ a cup of powdered sugar
- 1 egg
- ½ a teaspoon of baking powder
- ½ a package of vanilla
- 1 grated lemon peel
- 1 tablespoon of cocoa

Directions

1. Sieve flour in a pot. Make a space in the middle of the pot and add in softened margarine, powdered sugar, egg, baking powder, vanilla and grated lemon peel. Quickly mix together to make dough.
2. Divide the dough into two pieces, with one larger than the other. Add cocoa into the smaller piece and knead.
3. Roll each piece of dough until it is a rectangle, 3 mm thick and 12 cm wide. Put the smaller piece (with cocoa) over the larger piece and roll together along the wide edge, making a log.
4. Slice into 1 cm wide pieces and set onto tray. Cook in an oven on a medium heat, removing before the cookies turn pink.

PESMET (SWEET COOKIES)

Ingredients

- ½ a cup of whisked eggs (1 egg yolk will be smeared on top)
- ½ a cup of yogurt
- ½ a cup of sugar
- 1 ½ cups of melted margarine
- ¼ a cup of oil
- 2 teaspoons of baking powder
- 1 grated lemon peel
- 1 tablespoon of lemon juice
- Flour (as needed, about 3 ½ cups)

Directions

1. Mix egg, yogurt, sugar, margarine, oil, baking powder, grated lemon peel and lemon juice together in a pot by hand.
2. Add in enough flour to make dough. Cover and refrigerate for 1 hour.
3. Divide the dough into golf-ball sized pieces and slightly flatten with palms.
4. Set dough onto a greased tray and spread a mix of egg yolks and a few teaspoons of milk over the cookies. Cook in an oven on medium heat.

APPLE COOKIES

Ingredients

- 3 cups of flour
- 250 g of margarine
- 1 tablespoon of yogurt
- ⅓ a cup of powdered sugar
- 1 teaspoon of baking powder
- ½ a grated lemon peel
- Vanilla

FOR MARMALADE

- 3 sour apples
- ½ a cup of sugar
- ½ a cup of chopped walnuts
- ⅓ a tablespoon of cinnamon

Directions

1. PREPARATION OF THE MARMALADE: Wash and peel the apples. Grate and cook them with sugar until the apples absorb the water that they released. Let cool, then add in chopped walnuts and cinnamon. Separate according to the number of dough pieces.
2. Sieve flour in a pot. Make a space in the middle and add in softened margarine, yogurt, powdered sugar, baking powder and grated lemon peel. Quickly mix to form dough.
3. Divide the dough into golf-ball size pieces. Roll out into oval shapes until each piece is 9-10 cm in diameter. Put apple marmalade in the middle. Roll up the dough and bring the edges underneath, forming a crescent shape.
4. Set the dough onto a tray. Cook in an oven on medium heat. Remove from the oven and sprinkle with a mixture of powdered sugar and vanilla.

WALNUT MOON BUNS

Ingredients

- 3 cups of flour
- 100 g of margarine
- 2 eggs (1 for dough, 1 egg white for walnut filling, and 1 yolk for the top)
- 1/3 a cup of milk
- 3 tablespoons of powdered sugar
- 2/3 a tablespoon of yeast
- 1 grated lemon peel

FOR THE FILLING

- 1 cup of grated walnuts
- 1 egg yolk
- 3 tablespoons of bread crumbs or crumbled biscuits
- ½ a cup of sugar
- 2 tablespoons of seedless raisins
- 2 teaspoons of cinnamon
- 1 teaspoon of allspice

Directions

1. PREPARATION OF THE DOUGH: Mix tepid milk, yeast and 1 teaspoon of sugar together in a pot. Mix in margarine, 1 egg, powdered sugar, and grated lemon peels. Add in sieved flour and knead together. Cover and let rise in a warm place until it is twice its size.
2. PREPARATION OF THE FILLING: Mix together walnuts, biscuits, allspice, raisins and 1 egg white in a bowl. If necessary, add in a few drops of milk. Add in sugar. Separate according to the number of dough.
3. Divide the risen dough into golf-ball size pieces. Lightly flour each piece and roll out into oval shapes 9-10 cm in diameter. Put the walnut mixture in the middle of each piece, and twist up with the dough into a crescent shape. Set dough onto a tray and spread a mixture of egg yolk and a few teaspoons of milk over each one. Cook in an oven on medium heat.

WRAPPED BUNS WITH RAISINS AND WALNUTS

Ingredients

FOR DOUGH

- 3 cups of flour
- 2 eggs
- ⅔ a cup of milk
- ⅓ a cup of oil
- 3 tablespoons of sugar
- 1 teaspoon of salt
- 2 teaspoons of baking powder
- ½ a tablespoon of lemon juice
- ½ a grated lemon peel

FOR FILLING

- 1 cup of seedless raisins
- ½ a cup of crushed walnuts
- 2 tablespoons of sugar
- 2 teaspoons of cinnamon
- 2 tablespoons of oil

FOR THE TOP

- ½ a cup of powdered sugar
- 10 drops of lemon juice

Directions

1. PREPARATION OF THE DOUGH: Mix egg, milk, oil, sugar, salt, baking powder, grated lemon peel and lemon juice together in a pot.
2. Add in sieved flour and knead until the dough is soft. Cover and let rest in a cool place for 15-20 minutes.
3. Flour the dough and roll out to a 36 cm square shape. Brush 1 tablespoon of oil over it.
4. Spread walnuts and raisins over the dough. Sprinkle a mixture of cinnamon and sugar on top, and roll starting from one edge into a log.
5. Cut the dough into 12 pieces, each 3 cm wide. Place on a greased tray and cook in an oven on medium heat for 30-35 minutes.
6. Pour a mixture of ½ a cup of powdered sugar, 10 drops of lemon juice and 1-2 teaspoons of water over the buns in thin lines.

EASTER BUNS

Ingredients

- 4 ½ cups of flour
- 1 cup of sugar
- 2 eggs (1 yolk for the top)
- 50 g of margarine
- 1 tablespoon of yeast
- ⅔ a tablespoon of powdered mahaleb
- 1 tablespoon of largely chopped hazelnuts
- 1 teaspoon of salt

Directions

1. Dissolve yeast in tepid milk in a pot. Mix 1 egg, 1 egg white, sugar, margarine, mahaleb and salt together in a pot. Add in flour until the dough is soft but not sticky. Cover and let rise in a warm place until it is twice its size.
2. Divide the dough into 9 pieces. Roll out each piece with more dough in the middle, and thinner at the edges, until it is 20 cm long.
3. Braid each three pieces of dough together, forming 3 Easter buns. Place them on a greased tray, leaving room for each to rise more.
4. Spread a mixture of egg yolk and a few teaspoons of milk over the dough. Sprinkle diced nuts, black cumin, sesame seeds or poppy seeds over. Cook in an oven on medium heat.

MARMALADE CROISSANT

Ingredients

- 4 ½ cups of flour
- 1 cup of milk
- 1 tablespoon of yeast
- 1 tablespoon of sugar
- 3 tablespoons of oil
- 250 g of margarine
- 2 eggs
- 2 teaspoons of salt
- 3 tablespoons of marmalade

Directions

1. Dissolve yeast in tepid milk in a pot. Mix sugar, oil, 1 egg, 1 egg white and salt together. Add in sieved flour and form into dough. Cover and let rise in a warm place until it is twice its size.
2. Knead the dough again and cover in flour. Roll out in a rectangle until it is ½ a cm thick. Spread ⅓ of the softened margarine over the dough, and then fold it into 3. Refrigerate until the margarine hardens.
3. Spread with margarine and fold into 3 two more times, refrigerating in between.
4. Roll out the dough into a rectangular that is 3 mm thick and 20 cm long. Cut into 10-20 cm pieces.
5. Put some marmalade onto each rectangle. Curl the dough, roll it and set it onto a tray. Let it rise for half an hour and spread a mixture of egg yolk and a few teaspoons of milk on top. Cook in an oven.

MACAROON

Ingredients

- 3 egg whites
- 1 ½ cups of sugar
- ⅓ a tablespoon of vinegar
- ½ a package of vanilla

Directions

1. Whisk egg whites and sugar together with a blender.
2. Add in ⅓ a tablespoon of vinegar and vanilla and whisk for a few more minutes.
3. Spread parchment paper onto a tray. Drop whisked egg whites onto the tray in piles.
4. Cook in an oven on a low heat for a long time with the oven door closed until the macaroons are dry.
5. Remove from the oven. Let cool, then remove from the paper.
6. Place on a serving dish. If desired, pour chocolate sauce over.

CAT'S TONGUE COOKIES

Ingredients

- 3 eggs
- 1 cup of powdered sugar
- 1 cup and 2 tablespoons of flour
- 150 g of margarine
- ½ a grated lemon peel
- ½ a package of vanilla

Directions

1. Spread parchment paper onto a tray, grease and flour.
2. Mix soft margarine and powdered sugar together in a large bowl. Add in grated lemon peel and egg yolk, and mix everything together.
3. Whisk egg whites together. Stir in yolk mixture. Mix together the vanilla and flour, and gently stir into the eggs.
4. Fill the dough into a bag, with a pen sized funnel at the bottom. Squeeze the dough onto the greased tray into 5-6 cm long cookies.
5. Cook in an oven on medium heat. Remove from the oven and once cooled, remove the paper.

Note: *Cat Tongue Cookies can be used to make different fruit pastries and can be served with ice cream.*

SAVAYER COOKIES

Ingredients

- 6 eggs
- 1 cup of powdered sugar
- 1 cup of flour
- ½ a grated lemon peel
- ½ a package of vanilla

Directions

1. Spread parchment paper into a tray, grease and flour.
2. Separate egg yolks into a large bowl and egg whites into a pot. Mix yolks with powdered sugar and grated lemon peels. Whisk egg whites. Add egg yolk mixture to the egg whites and beat together.
3. Mix sieved flour with vanilla and slowly stir into the eggs.
4. Fill the dough into a bag with a finger sized funnel at the bottom. Squeeze the dough onto a greased tray into 6-7 cm long cookies.
5. Sieve powdered sugar on top. Cook in an oven on low heat until they are crusty.

Note: Savayer Cookies can be used to make different fruit pastries and can be served with ice cream.

IX

JAMS, MARMALADES, LIQUEURS, BEVERAGES, ICE CREAMS AND CANDIES

QUINCE JAM

Ingredients

- 1 kg of quinces
- 6 cups of sugar
- Juice from 1 lemon

Directions

1. Wash the quinces and cut into quarters. Remove the core and seeds, peel and chop as desired.
2. Boil the core, seeds and peels with 4 cups of water and save the stock.
3. Sieve the stock, and boil it with the chopped quinces, without letting the fruit get too pulpy, until they are soft.
4. Add in sugar. Slowly cook, tilting the pot occasionally. Once the mixture thickens and the color turns pink, add in lemon juice and remove from heat.
5. Let cool, and pour into jars once it is tepid.

BLACK CHERRY JAM

Ingredients

- 1 kg of black cherries
- 6 cups of sugar
- Juice of 1 lemon

Directions

1. Wash black cherries, and remove stems and pits.
2. Layer the cherries with sugar in a large pot, shaking to mix them together. Cover and let sit overnight or 5-6 hours for the mixture to get watery.
3. Boil on a low heat without adding any water, shaking occasionally.
4. Add in lemon juice once it boils. Remove from heat (if it boils too long, the color turns dark), and put into a porcelain or enameled container. Cover with gauze and let sit in the sunshine for 3-4 days until it reaches the desired thickness.

BLACK CHERRY JAM (VARIATION)

Ingredients

- 1 kg of black cherry
- 6 cups of sugar
- Juice of 1 lemon or 1 teaspoon of citric acid

Directions

1. Wash the black cherries, and remove stems and pits.
2. Put the cherries in a pot and close the lid. Boil on a high heat for 3-5 minutes.
3. Add in sugar, stir and boil for 4-5 minutes with the lid open.
4. Add in lemon juice or citric acid, boil for 1 minute and remove from heat. Put into jars once it cools.

APRICOT JAM

Ingredients

- 1 kg of apricot
- 6 cups of sugar
- Juice from 1 lemon

Directions

1. Wash apricots and remove seeds, preserving the fruit's shape.
2. Mix sugar with 3 cups of water in a pot, and bring to a boil. Add in apricots one at a time and mix by shaking the pot. Once it is boiling, remove from heat and let the apricots sit for one day in their own stock.
3. The following day, boil the jam and add in lemon juice. Pour into an enameled, glass or porcelain container and cover with gauze. Let it sit in the sunshine until it reaches the desired thickness.

DRIED APRICOT JAM

Ingredients

- ½ a kg of dried apricots
- 5 cups of sugar
- Juice from 1 lemon

Directions

1. Wash the apricots and soak them overnight. The following day, boil them with 3 cups of water until they are soft.
2. Add in sugar and cook slowly until the mixture thickens. Add in lemon juice, bring to a boil, and remove from heat.
3. Let cool, and pour into jars once it is tepid.

ORANGE JAM

Ingredients

- 4 oranges peels (should be thick)
- 6 cups of sugar
- Juice from 1 lemon

Directions

1. Wash the orange peels and remove the outmost shiny layer of the peel with the thinnest part of a grater.
2. Wash the orange peels again, and boil them for 20-25 minutes, without breaking any of the peels.
3. Sieve the water, let cool, then chop into quarters lengthwise. Slice each one into 1 cm wide pieces.
4. Layer peels in a pot with sugar, shaking to mix better. Wait for a couple of hours for the mixture to get watery.
5. Slowly boil the peels on a low heat. Once the mixture thickens, add in lemon juice and remove from heat.
6. Let cool, and pour into jars once the jam is tepid.

ORANGE JAM (WITH PEELS)

Ingredients

- 4 oranges peels (should be thick)
- 5 cups of sugar
- Juice from 1 orange
- Juice from 1 lemon

Directions

1. Slice orange peels into large pieces. Cover them with water in a pot, and slowly boil them, preventing them from getting too soft.
2. Drain the stock. Add in 3 cups of water and bring to a boil. Add in sugar and let simmer until the mixture thickens. Add in orange and lemon juice and cook for a while. Remove from heat. Pour into jars once the jam is tepid.

STRAWBERRY JAM

Ingredients

- 1 kg of strawberries
- 6 cups of sugar
- Juice from 1 lemon

Directions

1. Place strawberries into a container covered with water. Properly wash, getting rid of any sand or dirt, and sieve.
2. Remove the stems and layer into a large pot with sugar, shaking the pot to mix together. Cover and let sit for 5-6 hours or overnight.
3. Slowly bring the strawberries to a boil without adding any water, as they should let out their own water. Once the mixture thickens, add in some lemon juice and remove from heat. Pour into a glass, porcelain or enameled container and cover with gauze. Let sit in the sun until it acquires the desired thickness.

FIG JAM

Ingredients

- 50-60 small figs
- 5 cups of sugar
- Juice from 1 lemon

Directions

1. Wash and peel the figs. Slowly boil them with 5-6 cups of water, removing before they get too soft.
2. Spare 1 cup of stock and throw away the rest.
3. Set the boiled figs in a large pot and pour in sugar and the spared stock. Cover and let sit for 5-6 hours or overnight.
4. Once the sugar gets wet from the fig juice (without adding any water), slowly bring to a boil to thicken the water.
5. Add in lemon juice and tilt the pot in different directions. Boil on a low heat again, and pour into jars once it gets tepid.

Note: *While boiling the fig jam, add in 1-2 attar plant leaves for a nice scent.*

PEACH JAM

Ingredients

- 1 kg of hard peaches
- 6 cups of sugar
- 1 lemon

Directions

1. Wash and cut the peaches in half. Remove the pit, slice and peel.
2. Layer peach slices in a pot with sugar. Shake the pot to mix together. Cover and let sit for 6-7 hours or overnight.
3. Once the water has left the peaches, bring the mixture to a boil and add in the lemon juice.
4. Pour the mixture into a glass, enameled or porcelain container and cover with gauze. Let sit in the sun until it acquires the desired thickness.

Note: *If desired, replace peaches with apples and follow the same directions to make Apple Jam.*

MARMALADES

Ingredients

- 1 kg of fruits (quinces, cornelian cherries, hard plums, peaches, etc.)
- 4 cups of sugar
- 1 lemon

Directions

1. Wash the fruits. Chop quinces, cornelian cherries, hard plums or peaches, cover with two cups of water, and bring to a boil on a low heat.
2. Once boiling, remove from heat, cool, and sieve. Add in sugar and boil on a low heat until the mixture thickens.
3. Add in lemon juice, boil for a few more minutes and remove from heat. Once the marmalade gets tepid, pour into a jar.

Note: *If using soft fruits such as apricots, strawberries, soft plums, or peaches, do not boil. Sieve them after washing, add sugar and boil while stirring.*

APRICOT MARMALADE

Ingredients

- 1 kg of sweet apricots
- 4 cups of sugar
- Juice from 1 lemon

Directions

1. Wash apricots and remove the pits. Crack the pits, put them into hot water, and immediately take out. Remove the skin and beat it into a mortar.
2. Boil the apricots in a pot with sugar. Add in ground pits and boil together for a while.
3. Add in lemon juice and remove from heat. Let cool, and pour into jars once tepid.

STRAWBERRY AND BLACK CHERRY LIQUEUR

Ingredients

- 1 kg of strawberries or black cherries
- 3 cups of sugar
- 1-2 sticks of cinnamon
- 2-3 cloves
- ½ a liter of cognac

Directions

1. Wash strawberries or black cherries. Put in a jar with sugar, and layer with cinnamon bars and cloves.
2. Close the jar lid and leave in the sun for 10 days. Shake occasionally, allowing the fruit to release water.
3. Add in half a liter of cognac and wait for 3 more days.
4. Filter and put in a bottle.

ORANGE, TANGERINE, AND LEMON LIQUEUR

Ingredients

- 2 juicing oranges
- 2 tangerines
- 1 lemon
- 2 ½ cups of sugar
- ½ a liter of cognac

Directions

1. Wash oranges, tangerines and lemon, slice each one into 8 pieces and mix together into a jar.
2. Add in cognac and close the lid. Shake occasionally and let sit for 15 days.
3. Softly press the fruits and remove them from the cognac.
4. Boil 2 ½ cups of sugar with 2 ½ cups of water in a pot until it is a fairly thick syrup.
5. Remove from heat, mix in fruit stock once it cools.
6. Filter and put in bottle.

WALNUT LIQUEUR

Ingredients

- 8-10 pieces of fresh green walnuts
- ½ a liter of rum or cognac
- 1 ½ cups of sugar
- 1 stick of cinnamon
- 2 cloves

Directions

1. Peel the walnuts, divide in half and put into jars.
2. Add in rum or cognac and close the lid. Let sit in the sun for 1 ½ months, shaking occasionally.
3. Filter, then add sugar, cinnamon and cloves, and close the lid. Let sit in the sun for another week, shaking occasionally.
4. Sieve and fill into bottles.

LEMONADE

Ingredients

FOR A CUP OF LEMONADE

- 1 cup of cold water
- 1 ½ tablespoons of sugar
- ½ a grated lemon and its juice

Directions

1. Wash and grate the lemon. Mix with sugar and rub with a spoon.
2. Add in cold water and lemon juice and mix until the sugar dissolves. Sieve, refrigerate for a short while, and serve chilled.

SAHLEP

Ingredients

- 1 liter of milk
- 1 tablespoon of sahlep
- 7 tablespoons of sugar
- 1 teaspoon of ground cinnamon

Directions

1. Put cold milk in a pot and sprinkle in sahlep.
2. Cook on low heat while stirring.
3. Add in sugar. Cook for 5 more minutes and pour into cups. Sprinkle with cinnamon and serve.

SWEETENED FRUIT JUICE (LOHUSA SERBETI)

Ingredients

- 2 ½ cups of sugar
- 9-10 sticks of cinnamon
- ⅓ tablespoons of ground cloves
- 1 small piece of ginger (hazelnut sized)
- 1 piece of golgant (alpinia officinarum) (hazelnut sized)
- 1 drop of red food colouring
- ½ a cup of roasted unsalted almonds

Directions

1. Put cinnamon, cloves and golgant (alpinia officinarum) in a pot. Add in 10 cups of water, cover and slowly bring to a boil.
2. Add in 2 ½ cups of sugar and red food coloring. Remove from heat after 10 minutes. Let sit covered until cool.
3. Sieve and pour into glass bottles. Serve hot or cold, and sprinkle ground almonds over.

THICK FERMENTED GRAIN DRINK (BOZA)

Ingredients

- 3 cups of bulgur
- 2 ½ cups of sugar

FOR YEAST

- 1 teaspoon of boza or ⅔ tablespoons of yeast
- 1 package of vanilla

FOR GARNISH

- Ground cinnamon

Directions

1. Soak the bulgur overnight.
2. Boil the following day until they are pulpy, adding water if necessary.
3. Let cool, then sieve with a spoon. Pour into enameled, glass, or porcelain containers.
4. TO FERMENT: Add in ½ a cup of boza and 5 tablespoons sugar and stir. Let sit in a warm place, stirring occasionally to let ferment.
5. A SECOND WAY TO FERMENT: Dissolve 2 tablespoons of yeast with 1 cup of tepid water and mix in 5 tablespoons of sieved bulgur. Let sit in a warm place, stirring occasionally to let ferment.
6. A THIRD WAY TO FERMENT: Add in 5 tablespoons of sugar (do not add in boza or yeast), and let sit in a warm place, stirring occasionally to let ferment. (This way takes more time).
7. Once some small holes appear at the top of the boza, and a savoury scent is noticeable, add in sugar and vanilla and stir together. Refrigerate.
8. Pour into cups and sprinkle with cinnamon. If desired, serve with unsalted yellow roasted chickpeas.

Note: *If the boza is not mixed occasionally the taste becomes acrid.*

VANILLA ICE CREAM

Ingredients

- 1 liter of milk
- 1 ½ cups of sugar
- 3 egg yolks
- 1 tablespoon of corn starch
- ½ a grated lemon peel
- 1 package of vanilla

Directions

1. Beat 3 eggs yolks, sugar, starch, lemon peel and one tablespoon of milk together in a pot.
2. Add in 1 liter of milk and boil while stirring. Remove from heat.
3. Let cool, stirring occasionally. Add in vanilla and whisk for 10 minutes.
4. Put into ice moulds and freeze. Mix occasionally to prevent it from becoming too hard and icy.

Note:

1) If desired, make ice cream with fruits and egg whites.

2) If desired, once the vanilla ice cream has cooled, whisk:

a) 1 tablespoon of cocoa

b) Diced and roasted hazelnuts or pistachios

c) Small diced candies with oranges, cherries, figs etc.

ICE CREAM WITH CREAM

Ingredients

- 1 liter of milk
- 1 package of sahlep (10 g)
- 1 teaspoon of corn starch
- 1 ½ cups of sugar
- 2-3 pieces of mastic

Directions

1. Put sahlep, starch, sugar and beaten mastic in a pot. Slowly add in milk and cook while stirring.
2. Remove from heat, and let cool while stirring occasionally. Whisk for 10 minutes.
3. Put into ice moulds and freeze. Mix occasionally while freezing.

BLACK CHERRY ICE CREAM

Ingredients

- ½ a kg of black cherries
- 2 cups of sugar
- 3 egg whites
- 2 cups of water

Directions

1. Wash black cherries. Beat and sieve them. Mix the pulp with 2 cups of water and sieve again.
2. Mix egg whites with sugar. Add in sieved cherry juice and mix until the sugar dissolves.
3. Pour into ice moulds and freeze. Mix occasionally while freezing.

Note: *If desired, variate recipe by replacing cherries with strawberries, apricots or peaches, and follow the same quantities and directions.*

MELON ICE CREAM: *Dice 1 kg of melon. Add in half a cup of sugar, 3 egg whites and a juice from half a lemon, and mix with a blender. Pour into ice moulds and freeze.*

BANANA ICE CREAM: *Follow the same quantities and directions as in Melon Ice Cream, but replace the melon with banana.*

LEMON ICE CREAM: *Mix 5 grated lemon peels, 2 cups of sugar and 3 egg whites together. Add in 3 cups of water and juice from 5 lemons, and mix together. Pour into ice moulds and freeze. Mix occasionally while freezing. (If desired, replace lemons with oranges to make orange ice cream.)*

CHOCOLATE ICE-CREAM BAR

Ingredients

- 5 cups of milk
- 1 ½ cups of sugar
- 2 tablespoons of corn starch
- 2 tablespoons of flour
- 1 ½ - 2 tablespoons of cocoa
- 100 g of margarine
- ½ a package of vanilla
- 2-3 tablespoons of diced hazelnuts or walnuts

Directions

1. Mix sugar, starch, flour and cocoa together and melt in a pot with 2-3 tablespoons of sugar.
2. Add in 4 cups of milk and bring to a boil while stirring.
3. Let cool, stirring occasionally. Add in softened margarine and vanilla, and whisk for 10 minutes.
4. Add in diced hazelnuts or walnuts. Pour into wet ice moulds and freeze.
5. Serve cold by slicing.

PARFAIT

Ingredients

- 1 package of dried Créme Chantilly
- 1 cup of cold milk
- 6 egg whites
- 1 cup of sugar
- ½ a package of vanilla

Directions

1. Whisk Créme Chantilly with milk until the mixture thickens.
2. Whisk together eggs whites, sugar and vanilla.
3. Add Créme Chantilly into the eggs whites and mix together.
4. Pour into a wet ice mould and smooth over. Freeze and serve chilled by slicing.

COFFEE PARFAIT

Ingredients

- 5 eggs
- 8 tablespoons of sugar
- 2 cups of milk
- ½ a tablespoon of starch
- 1 tablespoon of instant coffee
- 1 package of dried Créme Chantilly
- ½ a package of vanilla
- 8-10 cherry candies (diced)

Directions

1. Mix 5 yolks, 4 tablespoons of sugar, starch, coffee and 2-3 tablespoons of milk together in a pot.
2. Add in 1 ½ cups of hot milk and stir. Cook briefly for 1-2 minutes and remove from heat, stirring occasionally. Add in vanilla once cooled.
3. Whisk 1 package of Crème Chantilly with half a cup of cold milk until the consistency thickens.
4. Whisk 5 egg whites with 4 tablespoons of sugar in a bowl.
5. Mix coffee mixture, crème chantilly mixture and egg white mixture together, and add in diced cherry candies.
6. Cover the inner part of a deep bowl with aluminum foil and sprinkle with water. Pour the mixture into the bowl and freeze.
7. Turn upside down onto a serving dish and remove aluminum foil before serving. Slice and serve chilled with biscuits.

ALMOND PASTE

Ingredients

- 1 cup of salt free almonds
- 1 cup of powdered sugar
- 1 egg white

Directions

1. Put almonds in hot water and let sit for a short while. Remove the skins and blend.
2. Beat in a mortar and mix with vanilla and egg whites in a bowl.
3. Roll out (with roller or with palms) into a cylinder shape 2 cm long, cut into 2 cm pieces and put onto a plate. Cover to prevent drying.

HAZELNUT FONDANT

Ingredients

- 3 cups of sugar
- 2 cups of ground hazelnuts
- 1 tablespoons of lemon juice

Directions

1. Combine 3 cups of sugar with 3 cups of water in a pot. Gently shake the pot and slowly bring to a boil.
2. Once the consistency thickens, dip into a bowl full of cold water. It should gain a soft gummy consistency, and form into drops. If it does not, add in lemon juice and remove from heat.
3. Stir slowly once it gets tepid.
4. Add in 1 ½ cups of ground hazelnuts and knead together. Form into small balls with your palms, and cover in hazelnuts. Set onto a plate and cover to prevent drying.

Note: *If desired, make fondant with milk by mixing the sugar with the same amount of milk and boiling, stirring occasionally. You must experiment to gain the appropriate consistency, as is the same for hazelnut fondant. Once the mixture gets tepid, gently stir and add in ground hazelnut or coconut and knead together. Form into small balls with your palms and cover with hazelnuts, coconuts, etc.*

EASY-TO-MAKE CANDY

Ingredients

- 250 g of crumbled cookies
- 250 g of margarine
- 1 cup of powdered sugar
- 1 tablespoon of cocoa
- 3 tablespoons of ground hazelnut
- 3 tablespoons of shaved coconut

Directions

1. Beat the cookies in a mortar.
2. Mix powdered sugar and soft margarine together in a bowl until it is creamy.
3. Sieve cocoa into the bowl. Add in ground cookies and hazelnuts, and knead together.
4. Form into small balls and cover with coconut shavings. Set into plates, cover and refrigerate.

NOUGATS

Ingredients

- 2 cups of powdered sugar
- 1 cup of unsalted pistachios
- Juice from ½ a lemon
- ¼ a teaspoon of baking soda

Directions

1. Keep pistachios in hot water for a while, peel the covers and roast lightly.
2. Put powdered sugar in a pot. Cook on low heat, add in lemon juice by the drop, and melt. Add in baking soda to make the mixture harden.
3. Pour into a lightly greased enameled tray and spread out. Sprinkle pistachios over it and cut as desired before it cools. Let cool and serve.

CARROT CANDY

Ingredients

- 1 bowl of thinly grated carrots
- 1 bowl of sugar
- ½ a cup of chopped walnuts
- 3 tablespoons of coconut shavings

Directions

1. Wash and grate carrots with the smallest grate. Heat 1 bowl of carrot shavings in a pot with 1 bowl of sugar until it attains a paste-like consistency.
2. Remove from heat and add in walnuts once it is tepid. Divide into small pieces and form into small balls with palms (or flatten on a table by pressing out to 1 ½ cm thick pieces, then cut into rectangles 2-3 cm wide by 5-6 cm long). Cover with coconut shavings and set into a box or plate. Cover to prevent drying.

ORANGE CANDY

Ingredients

- 1 bowl of pureed orange peel
- 1 bowl of sugar
- ⅓ a cup of orange juice

Directions

1. Wash the orange peels and boil with plenty of water until they soften. Sieve the stock, rinse with cold water, and blend.
2. Measure out one bowl of pureed orange peel into a pot. Add in the same amount of sugar and ⅓ a cup of orange juice. Cook on a low heat, stirring occasionally. Remove from heat once the mixture thickens.
3. Once tepid, divide into small pieces and form into small balls with your palms. Cover with sugar, and set in a box or a plate. If desired, add in diced fruit candies, and cover to prevent drying.